C000154625

Sherlock Holmes:
Adventures in the Realms of Steampunk

Sherlock Holmes:
Adventures in the Realms of Steampunk

Volume 1: Tales of a Retro Future

Edited by
Derrick Belanger

Belanger Books
2019

Sherlock Holmes: Adventures in the Realms of Steampunk
© 2019 by Belanger Books, LLC

ISBN: 9781094607009

*Print and Digital Edition © 2019 by Belanger Books, LLC
All Rights Reserved. No part of this book may be used or
reproduced in any manner whatsoever without written
permission except in case of brief quotations embodied
in critical articles or reviews.*

*This book is a work of fiction. Names, characters, businesses,
organizations, places, events, and incidents either are the
products of the author's imagination or are used fictitiously.
Any resemblance to actual persons, living or dead,
events, or locales is entirely coincidental.*

For information contact:
Belanger Books, LLC
61 Theresa Ct.
Manchester, NH 03103

derrick@belangerbooks.com
www.belangerbooks.com

Cover and Back design by Brian Belanger
www.belangerbooks.com and *www.redbubble.com/people/zhahadun*

TABLE OF CONTENTS

The Detective in the Days of Steam by Derrick Belanger.............. 3

The Silver Swan by Cara Fox.. 5

The Adventure of the Pneumatic Box by Robert Perret 42

The Adventure of the Portable Exo-Lung by GC Rosenquist 76

The Body at the Ritz by Stephen Herczeg................................... 116

The Hounds of Anuket by John Linwood Grant.......................... 150

Treasure of the Dragon by Thomas Fortenberry.......................... 194

Sherlock Holmes and the Clockwork Count by Benjamin Langley

....221

About the Contributors 257

Special Thank You Section 261

COPYRIGHT INFORMATION

All of the contributions in this collection are copyrighted by the authors listed below, except as noted. Grateful acknowledgement is given to the authors and/or their agents for the kind permission to use their work within this anthology.

"The Adventure of the Tiger's Topaz", "The Detective in the Days of Steam", and "Dr. Watson's Neglected Fragments" ©2019 by Derrick Belanger. All Rights Reserved. First publication, original to this collection. Printed by permission of the author.

"The Adventure of the Purloined Piston Valve" ©2019 by Minerva Cerridwen and L.S. Reinholt. All Rights Reserved. First publication, original to this collection. Printed by permission of the authors.

"Doctor Bear, I Presume" ©2019 by Harry DeMaio. All Rights Reserved. First publication, original to this collection. Printed by permission of the author.

"Treasure of the Dragon" ©2019 by Thomas Fortenberry. All Rights Reserved. First publication, original to this collection. Printed by permission of the author.

"The Hounds of Anuket" ©2019 by John Linwood Grant. All Rights Reserved. First publication, original to this collection. Printed by permission of the author.

"The Adventure of the Brompton Mausoleum" ©2019 by Paula Hammond. All Rights Reserved. First publication, original to this collection. Printed by permission of the author.

"The Body at the Ritz" ©2019 by Stephen Herczeg. All Rights Reserved. First publication, original to this collection. Printed by permission of the author.

"The Deductive Man" ©2019 by Paul Hiscock. All Rights Reserved. First publication, original to this collection. Printed by permission of the author.

"Sherlock Holmes and the Clockwork Count" ©2019 by Benjamin Langley. All Rights Reserved. First publication, original to this collection. Printed by permission of the author.

"Sherlock Holmes and the Moongate Sabotage" ©2019 by Derek Nason. All Rights Reserved. First publication, original to this collection. Printed by permission of the author.

"The Adventure of the Pneumatic Box" ©2019 by Robert Perret. All Rights Reserved. First publication, original to this collection. Printed by permission of the author.

"The Adventure of the Portable Exo-Lung" ©2019 by Gregg (GC) Rosenquist. All Rights Reserved. First publication, original to this collection. Printed by permission of the author.

"A Second Case of Identity" ©2019 by S. Subramanian. All Rights Reserved. First publication, original to this collection. Printed by permission of the author.

The Detective in the Days of Steam

Editor's Introduction

Imagine a slight change to our historical timeline. While mankind did switch from an agrarian to industrial way of life, the industrial revolution heated up much quicker than expected. Technological marvels such as airships, trains, battleships, and submarines came into being much earlier. They were followed by steam-powered wonders such as mechanical men, flying ships, and even crafts which could reach the deepest fathoms of the sea or travel to distant celestial orbs.

That is the world where Sherlock Holmes and his Boswell, Dr. Watson find themselves in *Sherlock Holmes: Adventures in the Realms of Steampunk*. I wrote "world" but I really should have written "worlds" for each author has their own unique take on the steam-powered Victorian and Edwardian eras of the great detective.

In some cases, the world is almost the world we know of Sherlock Holmes, a London of cobblestone streets, thick fog, and hansom cabs rattling along the streets. Yet even in these worlds, something is slightly different, airships may coat the skies or steam-powered tools may help with daily conveniences. Then there are those that go a step further imagining a Victorian version of the Internet or clunky mechanical men who live to serve their wealthy masters. Finally, we have the most astounding of the adventures where

Holmes and Watson can switch bodies, travel through time, even meet animal versions of themselves.

Yet, no matter how far each author took their vision of the steampunk world, Holmes and Watson remain essentially their same selves. They still read the *Times*, enjoy Mrs. Hudson's cooking, and see clients in their sitting room at 221B Baker Street. Holmes still solves the crimes while Dr. Watson is always impressed, always one step behind the mind of the great detective.

There is one other piece of the canon these stories retain and that is the *fun* of the adventures. There is a sense of optimism to the Sherlock Holmes tales, a sense of optimism which permeated through the writings of the Victorian era. That sense of wonder is in full view in these stories. Gone is the pessimism which runs through much of the current "hard" science-fiction of today. It is the sense of wonder, the fun of it all, that makes *Sherlock Holmes: Adventures in the Realms of Steampunk* a sheer delight. I hope you love these tales as much as I do. Now, it is time for you to turn the page and discover a Victorian London like you've never seen before.

Sincerely,

Derrick Belanger
March 2019

The Silver Swan

by Cara Fox

"An outbreak of mass hysteria in West Brompton has been attributed to the unexpected appearance of a mechanised swarm in the skies over London. According to eyewitnesses, at least two dozen of the creatures descended upon Brompton Cemetery, shortly after midday on the nineteenth of September. They were first noticed amongst the clouds by Mr. J. M. Vernon of 102, Granville Place, who was attending the funeral of his uncle. Mr. Vernon reports that the swarm moved rapidly towards the small crowd and then swept as one cohesive mass through the cemetery until the screams of the mourners attracted the attention of a passing constable. His arrival disturbed the creatures, who retreated from the graveyard and dispersed in different directions."

Delighted by the tale that was unfolding as my eyes swept across the page, I continued as soon as I caught my breath.

"Scotland Yard have yet to comment on the afternoon's disturbance, but it is reported that seven ladies fainted and at least two enterprising men discharged their pistols. Whether a successful shot was scored is unclear, but it appears that the swarm escaped capture. Their origin is unknown, as is their whereabouts. West Brompton remains on high alert and a significantly increased police presence

5

was noted in the district throughout the night." When I reached the end of the article, I clapped my hands together. "How truly singular, Holmes!"

My companion clicked his tongue as I laid the morning copy of *The Times* upon the coffee table, but his grey eyes were bright and alert as he peered over his hawk-like nose at the mismatched assembly of objects before him. His tall, gaunt frame was folded in half, for he was crouched in front of the table. For a moment I thought he had not listened to a word I said, but then he spoke.

"Come now, Watson, surely you do not imagine there is anything in that article to hold my interest?"

"I thought that there might be, yes," I said. "You do not like to stagnate, Holmes, and I confess myself intrigued by the report. It struck me as something that might be nuanced enough to attract your attention."

"Hardly." Holmes did not glance up from the test tubes that vied for space and attention upon the crowded table, his body held tense and a tremor passing across his hands. "I imagine it is nothing more sinister than an ill-judged prank by an intelligent yet undertaxed student of these modern sciences you hold in such high esteem, Watson."

"Such a sophisticated scheme could not be conceived in mere jest!"

"I must venture to disagree. One should never underestimate the capacity of a boy's unoccupied mind to resort to mischief and mayhem," he said gravely as a puff of putrid yellow smoke erupted from one of the test tubes. He rocked back to evade it and finally looked over at me. "No, a mind must be constantly stretched to its full capacity if it is not to either go to ruin or subvert itself to such troublesome experiments as those seen in West Brompton. On the scant evidence provided by the report, I am confident it is nothing more than that."

As he waved his hand through the air to dispel the noxious fumes, I crossed the room to open the window. The fresh air brought with it the unmistakable sounds of carriage wheels rolling across the cobbles. That was not unusual, for at this time of day Baker Street was a constantly thrumming hive of Londoners passing through, but the lady who descended from the carriage on the coachman's hand would surely stand out in any crowd. Tall and slender, she wore a black veil pulled back over her head, allowing a glimpse of the carefully coiffed blonde curls gathered beneath the veil. Her gown was a muted shade of dark grey trimmed with rich purple lace, and across the short distance between us, I could see that she wore a simple gold locket.

As heads turned towards her from every direction, her gaze settled upon our house. When she directed the coachman to use the knocker to attract our landlady's attention, I felt a leap of anticipation.

"Holmes?" I said, my eyes fixed on the window. "I believe we have a visitor."

No sooner did the echo of my words fade away than there came a tap on the door.

"Mr. Holmes?" It was Mrs. Hudson, our long-suffering landlady. "Are you willing to receive a lady into your rooms, sir?"

We looked at each other, and I was relieved to see that now familiar whisper of intrigue spark in his grey eyes. We shared a swift smile and he turned to sweep his travelling cloak away from the nearest chair as he called out his response.

"Certainly, Mrs. Hudson. Please show her in."

Within moments the door opened to reveal the lady. She swept into the room upon a cloud of floral perfume and breath-taking elegance, her self-assurance and confidence tangible in the way that her shoulders were drawn back, and she held herself tall despite her far from insignificant height. Holmes towered over the both of us, of course, but I estimated that she was almost a match for my height, albeit far slenderer than I. Her almond-shaped blue eyes travelled over the remarkable disarray of the cluttered parlour, but her youthful face remained unchanged as she dropped into a curtsey.

"Thank you for receiving me, gentlemen," she said.

"My condolences on the loss of your husband," Holmes returned without preamble.

The lady's eyes briefly widened. "Have we met, sir?"

"No. I have no idea who you are. However, it is evident that you are in mourning. You wear mourning attire and are evidently a lady of some standing, yet you have come to me unaccompanied. That suggests you have independent means and the freedom to choose your own actions. Thus, I deduce that you have been widowed; a little over a year ago, I must assume from your dress."

Once more I marvelled at his innate skill for deduction as the lady inclined her head. "I have made the right decision in coming here, Mr. Holmes," she said. "You are quite correct. May I introduce myself properly?"

He waved one hand through the air in lieu of a spoken answer.

"I am Lady Amelia Seymour, the Dowager Countess of Richmond."

My ears pricked up at that, for the lady's deceased husband had been a popular topic for the papers and London society for many months following his premature death. The

Earl of Richmond drowned in the Thames late at night, leaving behind his wife and infant son barely more than a year after his marriage. The scandal was eagerly devoured, but as Holmes noted, some time had elapsed since the earl's death. It did not seem to be the reason why his widow was here.

Holmes nodded briskly and moved to stand by the fireplace. "Good morning to you, madam. As you are aware, my name is Sherlock Holmes, and this gentleman is my good friend, Doctor John Watson. May I be so direct as to ask why you have come to us today?"

Lady Amelia glanced down at the open copy of *The Times*. "You have read about the events in West Brompton?"

I looked over at Holmes, but although his jaw twitched, he did not acknowledge the lift of my eyebrows. "Yes, madam," was all he said.

"Then there is your reason, sir."

I could not stay silent. "My lady, the report made no mention of your involvement. Were you at the funeral?"

"No, but it is my fault that the mourners were caught up in the horror that ensued."

Now we came to it.

"Why?" Holmes said.

The lady's pale face crumpled and she shivered despite the heat of the late summer day as she turned to face us. "I fear I was the intended target of the elegant assassins, gentlemen."

"Indeed!" I said, but neither she nor Holmes acknowledged my interjection.

"Assassins?" he said sharply. "Why do you describe them as such?"

"Because a significant detail was omitted from the newspaper report." She reached into her purse and extracted a vicious silver dart. As Holmes's breath quickened and he plucked it from her outstretched fingers, she broke the tense silence that had settled. "One of the beastly contraptions fired this in my direction."

"It did not make contact, I presume?"

"No. If it had, I suspect I would not be standing here with you now."

"Quite."

I agreed with them both on that point. The dart was a little under six inches long, and its feathered shaft tapered to a caustically sharp tip that would slice through flesh and muscle like a knife through butter. Had it made contact with the lady, it would have caused a grievous wound at the very least.

Holmes held it aloft and stared at it intently as he spoke. "Was this the only dart that was fired?"

"Yes. I was visiting the earl's grave with my son, and my husband's brother -"

"Did you travel there with the brother?"

She was evidently confused, but she answered politely nonetheless. "No. He lives nearby on Merrington Road, so we walked to the cemetery from his residence. My son was in his perambulator, and I am convinced it was only his presence which spared my life. The assassin dared not risk him becoming collateral damage in the attack, and once I was alerted by the first of the darts, I snatched my son into my arms to flee with him. I did not realise my folly until we were safely away from the cemetery, for he was undoubtedly far safer in the perambulator than in my arms, but a mother's instinct to protect her child is irrepressible."

Lady Amelia buried her face in her hands. It seemed that we ought to try to comfort her, but Holmes was fixated upon the emerging case at hand.

"Your son has inherited the earldom, I presume," he said.

"Naturally."

"I see." He turned the dart this way and that, running his fingers along it all the while even as he stared intently at the lady. "And where is your son whilst you are talking to us?"

"With my sister, sir."

"Not with his nursemaid, then. Your sister's name?"

Even in profile as she was now, I saw the lady tense. "Does it matter?"

"Probably not." His voice was a perfect model of calm, steadfast and unwavering. "Yet I would know nonetheless, my lady. If you want my assistance, I must insist that you answer my questions frankly and fully, no matter how irrelevant they may seem to you."

I knew that Holmes never asked a question without good reason. Lady Amelia seemed loathe to surrender the information, though the question seemed innocuous to me. As the silence stretched out until it became deeply uncomfortable, hanging over the parlour like the thick London smog outside, she finally smiled tightly and gave him what he sought.

"I would prefer to keep her out of this, but if you insist. Her name is Rosalind Rooper."

"Miss, or -?"

"Mrs. Her husband is Granville Rooper."

"The inventor?"

"Yes. Father employed him to help with the business when he was alive."

Holmes cocked his head. "You are close to your sister, I must presume, if you would prefer to leave your son in her care whilst you come to me."

"Yes, naturally."

"Naturally? No, it is not always so with families. I have seen many divided, with oft fatal consequences. Evidently not your family."

Lady Amelia barely moved as she jerked her head from side to side.

Holmes watched closely, letting the hand holding the dart fall to his side for now. "Do they know that you are here?"

"Yes. In fact, it was Granville who indirectly recommended that I come to you for what I seek."

"And what is it that you seek from me, madam?"

She drew a shallow breath and pulled her veil lower over her face, but before she did so, I was certain I saw tears swell in the corners of her eyes. "Two things, Mr. Holmes," she said. "Protection from my would-be assassins, and answers as to who sent them."

"Yet both of those could be provided by Scotland Yard," he said. "Why have you come to me for protection and not them, Lady Amelia?"

"Because you are the best, sir," she said directly. "Granville once mentioned that he had cause to do business with a Mr. Jabez Wilson, who recommended your talents most wholeheartedly. Whatever intrigue has woven its web around me, I am convinced that you are the man to discover it and hand the criminal over to the police for them to deal with as they see fit."

I could not help but smile at the recollection of Mr. Wilson and the Red-Headed League. Holmes, however, did not seem to be similarly amused. A tiny frown creased his face, and instead of responding to the compliment as he often did, he came towards me and positioned himself so that she could not see his face.

"One moment whilst I assemble my thoughts, if you please," he said.

"Of course, Mr. Holmes."

As the lady turned away again, he bowed his head towards mine confidingly. "So, what think you, Watson?" he said. "Is this a case where I may be able to render my assistance?"

I only barely resisted the compulsion to remind him that I had said precisely that upon reading the article in the newspaper. "Certainly," I said instead. "Why, Holmes, the application of your keen mind to the problem seems to be a necessity, and you can hardly decline the lady when she is so distressed by the matter. I cannot help but wonder, who could want to do harm to a creature such as she?"

"Who indeed, my dear Watson? That is the conundrum we face."

Despite the lady's misery and fear, Holmes's delight was clear to see. Gone were the restless agitation and jittery nerves of an hour before. I knew he intended to take the case even before he strode across the parlour, picking a path through the discarded papers and stoppered glass bottles to reach Lady Amelia.

"I should very much like to come to your residence and ensure it is secure, my lady," he said.

She lifted her veil once more. "Then you will help me, sir?"

"Certainly, if you are willing to pay my consultancy fee."

"Of course."

"Superb. Then when may I call to assess your residence?"

"I am hosting tonight, Mr. Holmes. You and Mr. Watson would be welcome to attend. If you mingle with the crowd, your presence should not appear in any way remarkable."

"That sounds acceptable. Then in that case, Lady Amelia, I shall bid you farewell. No doubt you are eager to return to your son after the traumatic events of yesterday. May I summon you a carriage for your journey?"

"There is no need, sir. My coachman is waiting for me outside."

"Then allow my assistant to accompany you to the street."

I stepped forward and offered the lady my arm, and she gratefully accepted. Before we left, Lady Amelia handed Holmes her embossed calling card with her address written on it, then proffered her earnest thanks for his service by means of farewell.

As we descended the staircase and I held open the front door for her to pass through, I smiled reassuringly. "You need not fear, my lady," I said quietly. "I have never known Holmes fail to find a culprit in all the time I have been acquainted with him."

She glanced back at me but did not answer. In silence she departed, and I lingered only long enough to watch her coachman assist her safely into the waiting brougham. My task complete, I returned to the parlour where Holmes was once again examining the dart. As he turned it between his long fingers again and a small frown creased his face, there came another knock on the door.

"Would you mind, Watson?" he said without looking away from the dart.

"Of course."

I leapt to my feet again to answer the summons and opened the door to reveal Mrs. Hudson, breathless with excitement as she darted into the parlour where the scent of the lady's perfume still lingered, almost absurdly incongruous amongst the scattered remnants of Holmes's discarded experiments and distractions.

Our landlady was bearing a pot of coffee and three cups. She looked around in vain for somewhere to set the tray down, so I reached out to relieve her of the burden as her face fell when she looked past me into the parlour.

"Has the Dowager Countess departed already, Mr. Watson?" she said.

I could barely stifle a small smile. "I am afraid so. Her business with Holmes is concluded for now."

"I had hoped she might stay long enough to take coffee with you, at least. But oh, to think that a lady such as she called into my house!"

Neither Holmes nor I were particularly interested in the goings-on of London society, but it struck me then that Mrs. Hudson seemed to have at least a passing knowledge of the Dowager Countess. She might be able to cast some more light on the lady's circumstances.

"Holmes," said I, "perhaps we should ask Mrs. Hudson to take coffee with us instead, if she can spare the time."

"What?" Distracted, he spared me barely more than half a glance as I breathed in deeply to allow the heady, rich aroma of the coffee to fill my lungs. "Oh. Yes, of course. A splendid idea, Watson."

Mrs. Hudson smiled widely as she moved into the space so recently vacated by Lady Amelia. "Thank you, Mr. Watson," she said. "I trust that the lady is not in any danger?"

"I cannot share the details of her confidence," I said. "However, you may rest assured that Holmes is devoting his time to her concerns."

"I am glad to hear that, Mr. Holmes!" she said as she turned towards him. "She is a fine lady indeed, particularly when one considers the humble origins from whence she came."

"Origins? I am afraid I do not know what you mean," Holmes echoed, but he was not looking at her. His attention seemed to be wholly consumed by the dart he still held.

"Why, Lady Amelia's family, of course."

"Her family?" As I set the coffee tray down carefully on the floor, his tongue darted out across the side of the viciously sharp tip of the dart, then retreated back into his mouth as he muttered under his breath. Whatever he found there seemed to please him, for he exhaled and flashed us the briefest of smiles. "Forgive me, Mrs. Hudson. Where were we?"

She clucked her tongue and wagged one finger in his direction. "Do you truly not recall, Mr. Holmes?"

"You know I care little for society's machinations, Mrs. Hudson."

"Yes, but I thought you might have remembered. I distinctly recall us discussing it at the time!"

Unabashed, Holmes smiled again. "I simply do not have the capacity or inclination to recall such menial pieces of trivia, I am afraid. Pray, do refresh my mind if it pleases you to do so."

"Lady Amelia's name is known throughout the city," said Mrs. Hudson as she settled into the nearest armchair to catch her breath. "She and her sister rose to the height of society on the tide of new money that came with the technological revolution. They were quite the darlings of the ton, and it came as no surprise when the Earl of Richmond asked Cyrus Sephton for his youngest daughter's hand less than a year after her debut."

"Sephton?" He whirled towards her, alert once more. "The inventor and pioneer of early steam technology?"

"One and the same, Mr. Holmes. Lady Amelia was his second daughter, God rest his soul."

He muttered and lifted the dart towards the window to cast another appraising glance over its sleek, polished lines. "Mrs. Hudson, do you know what became of the family business after Sephton's death?" he said.

She looked at him blankly.

"No, of course not," Holmes said without waiting. "That, then, must be our second line of investigation."

I cocked my head. "Second? Then what is the first?"

"We must seek an interview with the husband's brother."

"Shall I compose a letter for you, Holmes?"

"A letter? No!" Positively ablaze with renewed energy, he bounded across the parlour, staying only long enough to nod cheerfully to Mrs. Hudson. "We shall take a chance on the lord being home to callers this morning. Come along, Watson."

With one last wistful look at the steaming coffee pot, I followed him from the room.

*****

I glanced longingly towards the airships that soared unchecked high above London's spires, but as was his habit, Holmes had insisted we travel on the ground. Our destination was the home of Lord Marcus Seymour, a mere two hundred yards from Brompton Cemetery. Holmes's long, loping strides were hard to keep pace with, but I hastened in his wake, stumbling over the cobbles as heavily laden carriages rolled past and constant chatter buzzed all around us.

17

His mind was evidently just as busy, for he had not stopped running through the case since we left Baker Street. "A swan is a graceful creature, a being that all but epitomises elegance," he said now, his eyes darting ceaselessly from side to side all the while. "Would it be a man's first choice for an assassin?"

"I -"

"I think not," Holmes said without waiting for me to opine. "In my experience, a man with murder on his mind seeks the most direct route. No, my instinct is that our inventor and would-be assassin is someone who appreciates the finer details, with a sublime sense of culture and the beauty that can be found in modern life."

"Perhaps he sought to fascinate and enthrall Lady Amelia, to transfix her with the beauty of the beast before it fired," I offered.

His nose wrinkled. "Again, though, we return to style over substance. This is an inefficient means of assassination, Watson, as proved by the fact that the lady survived to seek our help. Not only that, but I could find no trace of poison on the shaft on the dart."

"Surely an assassin would want to ensure that the deed was done by any means necessary," I said. "The logical path would be to poison the darts to ensure that any contact would be fatal."

"Indeed. Yet I was confident that it was not so," he said. "Lady Amelia was wearing gloves when she passed it to me, but I saw fingerprints running along the full length of both the shaft and the pointed tip. It had been well handled, which indicated to me that poison was not a component of the attempted assassination. My suspicion is that our culprit, therefore, is far more comfortable with new technology than the older, more reliable methods of such a scheme."

"You seem to be developing a thorough sketch of our target, Holmes!"

He smiled. "Yes, but they remain faceless for now. Come along, Watson, and we shall see if the brother fits the mould."

He said nothing further until we reached our destination, a handsome townhouse in the heart of West Brompton. A coin pressed into the palm of a passing robin procured the number of the lord's residence, and Holmes wasted no time in springing up the narrow steps two at a time to lift the knocker.

His billowing travelling cloak fell still as the wind abruptly died away, and I moved to stand behind him as the butler opened the door from within.

The butler's keen, penetrating eyes swept across us, not relaxing even when they took in our neat tweed suits and smartly polished boots.

"Good morning, sir," Holmes said courteously. "Is Lord Marcus at home? We are not expected, I am afraid, but it is of utmost importance that we speak with him today."

"Your names and business with the lord, please?"

"I am Sherlock Holmes and this is my friend, Doctor John Watson. Our business is a delicate family matter, sir."

The butler's face creased in a faint grimace. "Then I must ask that you wait here whilst I consult with Lord Marcus, Mr. Holmes."

"But of course."

Holmes tipped me the smallest of winks as we waited in silence on the doorstep for no more than a minute before the butler returned and held the door open wide.

"Lord Marcus says that you may come through, sirs."

We followed him into a narrow hallway that stretched the full length of the house. A young maid bowed her head as she passed by us and left through the open front door. Holmes's eyes followed her outside, then swivelled neatly towards the study ahead where Lord Marcus seemed flustered as he took the high-backed leather chair behind his desk, busying himself with sweeping away a stack of papers as the butler showed us both into seats opposite the lord. As he scurried to stash them inside the open drawer, one fell to the carpeted floor and he cursed as he swiftly kicked it beneath the desk before finally looking up at the two of us.

He was younger than I had anticipated, barely more than a boy. He seemed closer in age to Lady Amelia than his deceased brother, whom I recalled from the reports had been in his late thirties when he died. Lord Marcus, though, I would estimate to be a mere twenty years old or so, but despite his unlined face and evident youth, he held himself as if he had the weight of the world on his shoulders.

Holmes wasted no time. "Good day to you, sir," he said crisply. "Permit me to be direct. I come to you from an interview with your sister by marriage, the Dowager Countess."

The lord sighed. "And what is your association with her?"

"I have been engaged by the lady to investigate the circumstances of the attack."

"I am deeply relieved that somebody is doing so. How is Amelia today, Mr. Holmes?"

The intimacy of his use of her given name struck me immediately. I watched him closely as Holmes pressed onwards. "She is badly shaken, as I am sure you appreciate," he said. "It is my hope that you can help me understand who might hold a grudge against her, so that I can ensure they are caught before they can strike again."

"Believe me, I want nothing more. I am entirely at your service, though I confess I am struggling to understand what knowledge I can offer you."

"You were at the scene of the crime, Lord Marcus, and you are the brother of her husband. I imagine there is much that you can tell me, if you are willing." Holmes threaded his long fingers together and set them on top of the desk. "We will start, with your permission, by talking about the earl, for it was Lady Amelia's marriage to him that brought her fame. Was it your brother's first marriage, my lord?"

Lord Marcus swallowed hard and pushed back in his chair. "Yes," he eventually said. "He married somewhat later in life than our family expected, but he admired Amelia and was determined to make her his wife."

"Admired?" Holmes said sharply. "Forgive me, but your words seem a little cold for the basis of a marriage. Were they happy together?"

"Jolyon loved her in his own way, Mr. Holmes, but no, I would not call theirs a happy marriage," he said cautiously. "My brother could be a difficult man to live with, and I will not deny that he had his faults."

"Yet their marriage was strong enough to produce an heir."

"Yes, and I was glad for Amelia's sake that it was so, particularly with the tragedy that followed so soon after Tristram's birth."

"Indeed." Holmes leaned forward. "Yet it strikes me that had Lady Amelia not given birth to a son a few months before the earl's death, you would have inherited the title and estate instead."

"I have not given it much thought, for it matters not to me. Tristram is the earl and that is the end of the matter. I would not have it any other way."

"You must have been afraid for him and his mother when the swans struck yesterday."

"Afraid?" Lord Marcus's hoarse laughter was entirely lacking in mirth. "Sir, I was terrified for them both. I have not been able to stop myself from reliving the events over and over since we left, and I wish Amelia had permitted me to stay with them last night to ensure their continued safety."

"Did you offer?"

"Naturally, and without hesitation. I love my nephew dearly, Mr. Holmes."

Holmes slowly nodded. "Then you are close to them, I must presume."

"Not as close as I would like. I have not seen anywhere near as much of my nephew as I want to over the past few months, so when Amelia asked me to accompany them to the cemetery, I instantly agreed. She does not often request my company these days," he said with another low sigh.

"Was it that way when your brother was alive?"

"No. No, we were so close that I saw her as my sister as much as Jolyon was my brother."

"I see." Holmes paused and I knew he was silently filing away everything that Lord Marcus had said thus far before he spoke again. "My lord, I need to see your brother's will."

Lord Marcus paled. "I cannot see its relevance to this matter, Mr. Holmes."

"No doubt, but I believe it could assist me greatly."

Silence fell, unbroken until Holmes stretched out one hand to gesture towards the closed drawers on the other side of the desk.

"I wonder, sir, if one of those papers you were so keen to conceal contained a copy of the will?"

The lord smiled tightly. "Do you?"

Holmes did not flinch. "You surely and rightly consider yourself the custodian of your brother's privacy. Yet perhaps, just perhaps, there is something more to hide."

"If there was - and I am not saying that there is - then you must respect that it should remain between my brother and me."

"But the will is a matter of public record, sir. One way or another I will discern its contents, you realise."

"That may be so. However, if you are so determined to waste your time reading it, you will have to find another source."

The dismissal within his words was curt and clear. Holmes inclined his head as he rose to his feet, and I did likewise.

"Thank you for your time, Lord Marcus," he said calmly. "I think I have enough to be going on with."

The younger man exhaled and relaxed in his chair for the first time since we had arrived. "Then I shall bid you good day, sirs. I have a busy day ahead of me and much lost time to make up for after yesterday's events."

"Certainly," Holmes said as they shook hands, but when we reached the open door, he turned back. "I saw an invitation from Lady Amelia on your desk before you cleared it away, Lord Marcus. I presume, therefore, that we will see you tonight."

The lord stilled, his jaw twitching irritably before he forced a fresh smile onto his face. "You have a keen eye, Mr.

Holmes, to go with your inquiring mind. Yes, I will be there. As will you, apparently."

"Indeed. Enjoy your day, Lord Marcus."

Holmes and I exchanged a swift glance as the butler showed us out, but I knew better than to voice my impressions of the lord until we were alone. However, as the door closed behind us and we stepped out onto the sunny London street, we heard our names being hollered in the distance.

My head turned to see Inspector Tobias Gregson, an associate of Holmes's from Scotland Yard, striding towards us with urgency in his step and a faint sheen of sweat upon his brow.

"Ah, inspector," Holmes greeted him. "Are you here to interview the young lord?"

The inspector came to an abrupt halt. When his eyes alighted upon Lord Marcus's door, he frowned and shook his head. "Lord Marcus Seymour? No," he said. "No, I am here following up on the incident in Brompton Cemetery yesterday."

"As are we," Holmes said. "I can only presume, therefore, that you do not know the intended target of the creatures, Inspector Gregson."

He flushed dully, his jaw clenched and his hands trembling as he brushed a speck of dust from his neatly-pressed uniform. "Target? I am afraid I do not know what you mean."

"Then you should know that these creatures were no jest or prank, inspector. On the contrary, they are the vehicle of a would-be murderer."

"Good heavens, Holmes!" The inspector whipped his notebook and pencil out of a pocket. "That is a bold statement indeed. What are your grounds for making it?"

"The fact that the intended victim has engaged me to investigate and provided me with the physical evidence of the attempted attack."

"Their name?" Gregson said, his pencil hovering eagerly over the paper.

"The Dowager Countess of Richmond, sister by marriage of Lord Marcus. Fear not, though, inspector. I am confident I shall have the culprit for you soon. You merely need to look out for my summons and I shall gladly hand them into your custody."

The inspector gaped, then sighed as he pocketed the pencil and notebook once more. "Ensure that you do, Holmes."

Gregson straightened his hat and bustled away as Holmes laughed quietly.

"Watson, return home to rest before our appointment at Lady Amelia's gathering," he said to me. "I shall join you shortly. If I am right, we shall have to be at our sharpest tonight."

*****

Holmes and I were punctual as ever, arriving at Lady Amelia's sprawling, brightly-lit manor before the guests arrived. We spoke to her briefly, assuring her of our intention to blend into the background as observers of the gathering and her home, and now we were walking around the boundaries of the manor so Holmes could sketch an accurate picture of it in his mind.

As we completed our second circuit, he drew me aside. "Watson, you brought your Webley tonight, I presume. I should like to take charge of it, if I may, for I suspect I will have need of it before the night is through."

I handed it over without hesitation and he concealed the revolver moments before a maid passed us by, her arms laden with freshly pressed cloths for the dinner table. I smiled courteously, but when she blanched and stumbled quickly through the nearest open door, a memory sparked in my mind and I seized at Holmes's arm.

"Holmes, that woman -"

"Was at Lord Marcus's home today. Yes." He was staring at the door through which she had disappeared, but made no move to pursue her.

"Then the maid is surely in league with the young lord," I said in hushed tones. "She has been passing information about her mistress to him, assisting with this terrible scheme. He is the culprit!"

"That seems plausible," Holmes said, but his tone was absent and his attention was already elsewhere. With that faraway look that I knew meant he was assembling the pieces of the puzzle inside his head, he continued down towards the grand entrance hall until we passed through the open door to where Lady Amelia was greeting her guests.

A woman I did not know stood at her side, but the familial resemblance was undeniable. They had the same blonde curls and elegant Grecian features, but Lady Amelia's sister - for that was surely who it was - was shorter, less statuesque, and her eyes were brown as opposed to the lady's expressive blue.

As Lord Marcus approached, Mrs. Rooper rose onto the tips of her toes to whisper intimately into the lady's ear. Lady Amelia visibly shivered and bowed her head, her smile fading away as she held out her hand for the lord to take.

I could not hear the words that passed between them, but the taut lines on the lord's brow and his grimace spoke volumes when he let her hand fall from his lips and turned away. For a moment I thought he wanted to say something, but instead he sighed and followed the flow of people towards the largest of the parlour rooms, with its French doors thrown open to lead into the pretty, carefully arranged garden at the rear of the manor.

I expected Holmes to lead us in his wake, but instead he took a slow step towards the sisters, his finger against his lips to silence me as he strained to hear their words, for a low but fierce argument seemed to have broken out between them.

"You should not have invited him, Amelia," the elder sister said.

"Rosalind, he is my son's uncle, and Jolyon's brother!"

"Precisely!" The other woman threw up her gloved hands in frustration. "Remember what we said about him, sister, and where his interests truly lie."

She received no answer to those words. Instead, Lady Amelia pulled away from her sister's side and followed in Lord Marcus' wake. Mrs. Rooper stared after them, her face impassive, then turned to retreat as Holmes clicked his tongue and steered me into the midst of the gathering.

As the sounds of the small orchestra and lively conversation swallowed us up, something that had been troubling me since this morning finally clicked into place.

"Holmes," said I, "it strikes me that our would-be assassin must have been present at the cemetery to know when to fire the dart upon the lady, and to stop when she snatched her son into her arms."

"Ah, I wondered when that thought would occur to you," he said.

"Then you agree?"

"Of course."

Alarmed by how relaxed he seemed, I waved away a lurking waiter. "But then that leads us to only one suspect!"

"Does it?"

Now I doubted my conviction, though I did not understand why Holmes was content to sit back and allow Lord Marcus to continue roaming unchecked through the lady's home when all the evidence pointed towards him. My gaze switched between him and Lady Amelia, who had now left her sister's side to move through the gathering with practiced ease. Despite the distance that separated us, she seemed tense to me, her face pale and her smile flickering whenever she thought herself unwatched. It came as no surprise when she made her way towards the doors for a breath of air, but no sooner did she reach them than her piercing scream rent the jovial atmosphere in two.

Holmes was the first to react. He leapt through the shell-shocked crowd and withdrew my trusted Webley revolver as he reached Lady Amelia's side, and the moment that I gathered my wits I rushed towards the two of them, seizing hold of the lady to shield her behind me as the flight of swans soared across the silvery moon, then dived down towards us.

Now I understood why they had provoked such hysteria when they appeared at the cemetery. Their terrible majesty took my breath away. To see such beauty wrapped up in the form of cold, lifeless assassins was a juxtaposition that perfectly encapsulated this brave new world in which we found ourselves. I confess that I found myself frozen in horror, transfixed by the sheer incredibility of what I saw before me.

Lady Amelia was similarly affected, but she, of course, knew that she was their target. She looked at the swans and then back at the revolver as a loud sob erupted from the back of her throat, her terror arousing a fierce instinct in me to protect her. I could not understand how anyone could want to do her harm, but the proof that somebody did was mere feet away from us.

As the foremost bird opened its beak wide in preparation to attack, Holmes struck. He raised his right arm, closed one eye and fired once, twice, three times.

His aim was true.

The foremost swan plummeted to the ground, crashing to a halt no more than twenty feet in front of us as Holmes glanced over his shoulder at the screaming throng. He paused for a few moments, then lowered the revolver when he turned back to see the remaining swans turn and retreat into the night sky.

As gentlemen rushed towards us to come to Lady Amelia's aid - Lord Marcus at their head, I noticed, not without a small throb of unease - Holmes muttered under his breath and strode towards the fallen swan, inspecting it for no more than ten seconds before he returned. I saw him snatch a scrap of paper and a pen from his pocket, then scribble something I could not see before concealing it inside his fist as together we approached the lady.

"I do apologise if I alarmed you with the revolver, madam," Holmes said with a crisp bow, but the spark in his eyes belied the apology. "The threat is past, and I am confident enough to assert that it will not strike again tonight. Therefore, I shall depart with the swan and see what I can make of it - if you do not object, of course."

She held one gloved hand to her brow as one of her many admirers produced a glass of water and an arm to help her into the nearest chair. "Of course, I do not object, Mr. Holmes. Good heavens, how can I ever repay you?"

"By staying safe until I have secured the culprit. To that end, now that you are safely in the bosom of your friends and family, I shall depart with my prize." He leaned in closer and clasped the lady's hand firmly. I was certain that his mouth still moved, but I could not hear his words until he straightened up again.

"Thank you for your hospitality, madam," Holmes said. "I wish you well until we meet again."

*****

Safely back in our lodgings at Baker Street, Holmes and I devoted ourselves to the forensic examination of the fallen swan. It was truly remarkable. Even the wound pierced in its breast by Holmes's bullet only somehow afforded it a sense of stolen vitality that should not be possible for a mechanical mimicry to attain. I half-expected its graceful neck to rise to my touch and those vast wings to spread and soar like quicksilver once more.

As I watched from my favoured chair, Holmes's long fingers flew across the exposed belly of the beast, then plunged inside to rapidly pull apart hundreds of cogs and gears. Fascinated, I watched him work. I knew that what might seem random to onlookers was in fact conducted with perfect precision.

That first cursory examination completed, he replaced the metal plates and covered the swan with a woollen blanket before he sprung up again and began to examine each part he had removed in more detail.

"Did you see her face?" Holmes darted restlessly around the parlour, snatching up half a dozen different gleaming components before tossing them aside once more, muttering under his breath all the while.

I blinked rapidly. "Whose?"

"The sister's, of course."

"Lady Amelia's sister?"

"Yes!"

"Holmes, I was not looking at her, for my attention was solely with Lady Amelia!" I said incredulously. "I imagine that Mrs. Rooper was terrified -"

"No."

"No?"

"Oh, no." Holmes flashed me the swiftest of smiles. "That is what she wanted everyone to think. She was not afraid, Watson. She was furious when I shot the swan down, and even more so when I proposed that I would take it away with me. That tells me there is something to be found inside it which will confirm that I am on the right track."

"What track?"

I might as well have saved my breath.

"And here it is!" He held one of the tiny gears aloft with triumph blazing in his grey eyes. "This particular style of gear has not been used for over a decade. It has been replaced by a superior model; they are not even in production now. But when they were, they were made by Sephton Industries."

"Sephton?" I marvelled once more at his capacity to recall the smallest detail. "That was Lady Amelia's maiden name."

"And her father's business. Yes."

"Then..." I hesitated as my mind scurried along in his wake. "Then you do not suspect the lord?"

"Lord Marcus? No! Certainly not."

Evidently content with what he had discovered, Holmes set the gear down on the mantelpiece and picked up his old briar pipe instead, leaning back against the wall as gentle whirls of blue smoke rose to wind around his head and obscure those keen, aquiline features I knew so well. I wanted to question him, to search his brilliant mind, but instead I sat there in silence and waited until there came a knock on the door.

I opened the door to see two of the lads that Holmes fondly called his Baker Street Irregulars. The eldest of the two, Wiggins, saluted smartly.

"Reporting as ordered, Mr. Holmes, sir," he said.

"Both of you at once? How punctilious." Holmes beamed widely and set his pipe down. "So, what have you to say? Wiggins first. What can you tell me?"

"As you thought, sir. I asked around and it ain't good. Seems the workers weren't paid last month, and the folks are always arguing about money."

"Good." He whispered in Wiggins' ear and slipped him a coin before he straightened up, patting him on the head in clear dismissal before he beckoned the second boy forward. "And what do you have for me, Chapman?"

The child handed over a tightly-furled scroll and grinned toothily. "Just what you asked for, sir."

Holmes unfurled the scroll and his keen eyes began to shine as they swept across the words it contained.

"An illegitimate child and a generous allowance for the brother too," he muttered. "Money to be paid in perpetuity to both. And the executor? Yes, of course. The motive is thus clear."

He reached into his pocket for another coin, then sent Chapman away too with his brow creased deep in thought. It came as no surprise when he cut across the parlour to stand in front of me and spoke without preamble.

"Recall, if you will, the gentleman whom Lady Amelia said recommended me to Mr. Rooper," he said.

"Why, Mr. Jabez Wilson, of course."

"Indeed. And do you remember Wilson's profession, Watson?"

I gazed at his face, aflame with anticipation. "A pawnbroker, Holmes. Granville Rooper had cause to seek out Jabez Wilson's services."

"Precisely my conclusion. There should be no shame in doing so, of course, but it was my first insight to the state of the Sephton empire. With that knowledge, I sent Wiggins to ask around, and what he reported back to me just now confirmed that I was right."

"About what?"

His steadfast smile widened. "My suspicions were strengthened by Lady Amelia's sister's outrage when I brought down the swan. Her fury was due to the sheer amount of money it cost to assemble them. No doubt she hoped that Mr. Rooper would be able to discreetly sell each one when this messy affair was concluded to her satisfaction. Yes, her motives are as transparent as glass to me, Watson."

"Then pray, Holmes, do illuminate we lesser mortals!"

Yet Holmes remained implacable as ever. "Soon, Watson," he said, taking his seat and allowing his eyes to close. "Soon. We await two players to conclude this act; one whom young Wiggins has gone to summon for me, and the other who will doubtless arrive within the hour to discover if her honey has snared its fly."

I suspected I knew now the direction in which his thoughts had turned, but I must confess that I did not comprehend how he had reached that conclusion. However, I knew him well enough to be certain that he would not explain himself until he was ready. There was naught I could do but impatiently wait, my eyes scanning the street all the while in search of the two people Holmes awaited.

Eventually the peace of night was broken by a flicker of movement across the street, and when I squinted into the illumination of the gaslights, I saw two people hastening towards our lodgings, one of whom I instantly recognised.

"It is Lady Amelia," I said.

Holmes sat bolt upright. "Good. As I requested. And is she alone?"

I peered into the night. "No, Holmes. Her sister is with her."

He rubbed his hands together and leapt back to his feet as we heard Mrs. Hudson open the door downstairs, their voices muffled until Holmes wrenched our door open to summon them inside.

"Lady Amelia," he said with that impassive smile he wore so well. "I have been expecting you - and your sister too. How very pleasant! Please, do come in."

Ashen-faced, the lady did as he asked, followed two paces behind by her elder sister. As they walked past me, Holmes leaned in close.

"Watson, guard the door," he said, his low words for me and me alone.

I knew better than to doubt or question him. Without hesitation I moved to stand in front of it as he began to prowl the confines of the parlour.

"Thank you for coming as I requested, my lady, for I appreciate the lateness of the hour," he said. "It was good of your sister to offer to accompany you."

He was evidently right in that passing comment, for neither lady corrected him. I remained silent, for I was aware he considered us to be at the denouement of the entire plot. It was clear from his little mannerisms I knew so well after our time together; the slight flare of his nostrils, the dilation of his pupils, the way he clasped his hands and moved restlessly around the room. I would never match his powers of observation, but I was coming to be a good enough study when it came to Holmes himself.

Lady Amelia turned to address him. "You said that you thought you would have the answers by the end of tonight, Mr. Holmes."

"Indeed I did - and I shall. Before I give you my conclusion, I have two last questions for you, my lady. Tell me this first. Who else accompanied you and Lord Marcus to Brompton Cemetery?"

"As I said when we first met, my son was with us -"

"And your sister."

"Yes," she said. "Rosalind too, of course."

Mrs. Rooper glanced towards the door and drew a sharp breath when she saw me standing in front of it. My eyes narrowed, but before I could draw Holmes's attention to that fact, he spoke again and I forgot all else.

"You should know that your would-be assassin accompanied you that day, Lady Amelia, and was with you again tonight," he said.

Stricken, Lady Amelia clutched at her sister's arm. "Then it truly was Marcus? Rosalind, you were right!"

I watched in astonishment as Holmes swiftly shook his head and advanced towards them, his hand drifting almost nonchalantly towards the Webley he still carried. "No," he said. "You must recall that Lord Marcus came only on your invitation. My lady, who proposed that he should accompany you?"

All the colour drained from the lady's face and she swayed dangerously where she stood. Fearing that she was about to swoon, I leapt forward from my post at the door until Holmes's shout arrested me where I stood.

"Watson, no!"

Lady Amelia cut between her sister and the door, even though she was visibly trembling. "Rosalind, I do not understand," she said.

"Mrs. Rooper, I promise that there is no escape," Holmes said grimly. "The very least you owe your sister is the truth. Must I force it from you, or will you do this one last thing for her?"

"Rosalind, please." Lady Amelia's eyes shone with tears that clung tremulously to her long lashes, but she composed herself and drew her shoulders back with a strength of spirit that did her great credit. "You are my sister and I love you dearly. If what Mr. Holmes suggests is true, even a little of it, then for the sake of all we have shared, you must explain why you would do this to me!"

The two sisters stared at each other until Mrs. Rooper's face slowly changed, all warmth and tenderness nothing but a memory as her top lip curled back.

"Money," she said simply. "You have it, and we do not."

"We?"

"Granville and me. Amelia, you know as well as I do what it is to be poor. I could not survive the horror of being cast back into such abject poverty!"

Holmes cocked his head. "You had a difficult childhood, I believe."

"Difficult?" Mrs. Rooper's laughter was cold and entirely mirthless. "We were penniless and reliant upon charity until our father's inventions finally found traction with those who had the power to make them noticed."

Amelia was staring at her elder sister as if seeing her for the first time. "Yes, we were, but we endured it together and our lives are far different now -"

"For you, perhaps!" Mrs. Rooper turned towards Holmes, impassive though he was towards her. "She has everything, Mr. Holmes, everything I always craved - the manor, money, security. The family business is all that Granville and I can rely upon. Amelia has Jolyon's estate, yet that is not enough for her! She refused time and time again to relinquish her stake in Sephton Industries when I asked."

"Because she needs the money just as much as you, even if her pride prevents her from admitting it," Holmes said.

Lady Amelia turned her wide-eyed stare towards him and touched her throat. "How... how on earth can you know that, sir?"

"Because I have reviewed the earl's will, my lady. I know that the estate is bound to pay a handsome allowance to both Lord Marcus and to the illegitimate son that Jolyon sired by your maid - and I know too that the estate is worth far less than anyone would imagine. I suspect that the earl badly misrepresented himself to you and your father, Lady Amelia."

She swallowed hard and inclined her head as her shoulders slumped. "That would be a fair assessment, sir. I did not discover the height of his deception until shortly before his death. But Rosalind, still I do not understand. What has all this to do with the attacks on me? I could have died, and Tristram would have been left an orphan!"

"No, Amelia! I never intended you to get hurt. I only wanted you, and everyone else, to believe that the swans posed a genuine threat to your life."

Unwilling comprehension dawned on the lady's face. "And you wanted everyone to think that Marcus was behind it."

"Yes." Mrs. Rooper shivered and clutched her shawl tighter around her chest. "I intended to frame Marcus so that he would lose his claim on Jolyon's estate, and then the allowance he always ensured was paid to that damned maid and her bastard would no longer be issued either. I thought that once that was done, you would let me and Granville take over the entirety of Father's business."

Holmes towered over the two women, his grey eyes filled with icy disapproval. "That would never have happened," he said. "Your sister needs the money from the business for her son, Mrs. Rooper, to prevent him from sinking into the poverty that you too are desperate to avoid."

Lady Amelia bowed her head as she opened the gold locket around her neck. What I thought contained a miniature of the earl and a lock of his hair, instead held a pale blond baby curl and the image of a cherubic child; her son.

"Everything I do, it is all for him," she said without looking at us, only her silent sister. "I could not bear the risk of returning to such abject poverty. For my son's sake, I had to ensure that I retained my rightful stake in Sephton Industries, hoping desperately that it would soon see a return to its former good fortune."

"Under the poor financial management of the Roopers, I am afraid that seems unlikely," Holmes said gravely. "I can recommend some fine people to you, though, who, all being well, can help you salvage a future for it going forward."

Clearly dazed, Lady Amelia shook her head and moved closer to Holmes, away from her sister's side. "I... Yes... Thank you, Mr. Holmes. But how on earth did you realise Rosalind's culpability in all this? Even I was convinced that Marcus must be at fault."

Holmes smiled. "Watson, will you put your steady surgical hand to good use and reopen the belly of the beast?"

I did as he asked, and when I removed the last of the metal plates he gestured towards the lifeless internal workings of the swan.

"You will see that the gears turning each component part are outdated versions of those that were manufactured by Sephton Industries," he said. "That was my first hint that Lord Marcus could not have been responsible. From there, the path to the true culprit was clear to see with all the facts laid out before me."

Lady Amelia swallowed hard as she looked up at him. "And that culprit is my beloved sister."

"I am afraid so. Take a seat, my lady," he said with consummate kindness. "You have had a terrible shock, but you need fear no longer."

I helped the lady into one of the high-backed armchairs, and as I offered a blanket to tuck over her lap, there came a knock at the door.

"Ah, and here comes the last player in our little scene," Holmes said. When he opened the door, he seemed wholly unsurprised to see Inspector Gregson standing there.

"Your boy said you needed to see me urgently, Holmes," the inspector said directly.

"Indeed I do, inspector. My thanks for coming so promptly."

The inspector peered past Holmes to see Lady Amelia in her chair, with me standing next to her and the fallen swan at my feet. "Good heavens, has there been another attack?" he said.

"There will be no more attacks, for I have your culprit, Inspector Gregson," Holmes said calmly. "Rosalind Rooper is willing to provide you with a full and frank confession at the station."

Mrs. Rooper blanched, but she made no move to deny those words. Gregson gaped as he looked between her and her stricken sister, then shook his head to clear it as he advanced towards her.

"Then my lady, I must ask that you accompany me back there without delay," he said.

She clearly knew that the game was up. Without as much as a solitary word of parting for her sister, she bowed her head and allowed the inspector to steer her out of the room.

Her departure was the catalyst to bring the night - and the case - to its close. I was dispatched to fetch Lord Marcus, who came to his sister's side without hesitation, enunciating his thanks to Holmes over and over again before he accompanied Lady Amelia home. I felt certain that she was in safe hands with him, and that the damage done to their friendship by Mrs. Rooper's poisonous words would soon be repaired.

When they left, Holmes and I were alone once more. As he sat in his chair with his pipe in one hand and the revealing gear in the other, toying with it between his long fingers, I broke the comfortable silence that had settled over us.

"London will feast upon this sensation for years, Holmes."

"I imagine so." His distaste was tangible. "It is deeply unfortunate for Lady Amelia to suffer two tragedies in close succession, and no doubt her sister's betrayal will be known throughout the city as soon as day breaks."

"Yes, the papers will surely carry the news of her arrest. Society will be shocked that such a scheme could come from someone as admired and lovely as Rosalind Rooper, though."

"Beauty of form does not preclude a person from the capacity to commit terrible crimes, Watson."

Watching him amidst the gentle puffs of smoke that made him seem almost detached from those of us who did not possess his astounding wit, I quietly mused on the bitter truth of his words.

The Adventure of the Pneumatic Box

by Robert Perret

T he waxed canvas hood covering my face had become more than a trifle close as the Ministry carriage clattered on. My breath made the interior hot and humid, causing me to perspire which only worsened matters. My head would be positively damp by the time this charade of secrecy had concluded. There were scant few places Holmes's brother, Mycroft, was likely to have us taken, his own experience of the world intentionally limited to a handful of locales; White Hall, the Palace, his own quarters, and of course the Diogenes Club, where Mycroft sat as a minor potentate. As the carriage mounted an incline and began looping round and round it was obvious we were at the dirigible moorings. No doubt the Ministry's private mooring or its location would not be kept a secret.

"Steady on, Watson," Holmes said, seated immediately to my right. "We're but two rotations from the platform."

I realized that I had begun gasping for air within my tiny cloth prison.

"Most unsightly," Mycroft groused. He sat across from us, and no doubt was not obliged to have a heavy bag over his head. "Like a fish that has fallen from its bowl."

As the carriage stopped rough hands pulled me from my seat, corralling me along the creaking planks of the platform. We were four stories above the channel, I knew. At least the wind whipping through my light woollen suit gave some relief from my physical misery. Along the hands prodded me, pushing me up a gangplank. I was decisively sat down when we had gained the deck. Holmes's lithe steps across the wood were nearly imperceptible, while Mycroft made a series of dull thuds which seemed to rock the whole vessel.

"Can we finally remove these blasted things?" I asked, moving my hands upward. My wrists were quickly caught and forced back down to my sides.

"Not just yet, Dr. Watson," Mycroft replied.

The soldiers' boots moved towards the bow. I could tell from the way we began to be tossed about in the air currents that they were releasing the moorings as they went. We were soon adrift and moving away from the sounds of London, out over the violent crashing of the sea.

"That should be sufficient," Holmes said.

"It seems I won't hear the end of it until you feel the sea breeze in your hair," Mycroft sighed. "Fine."

My hands darted up and clawed at the knot hanging by my clavicle. After what seemed like an eternity of fumbling, I yanked the hood off and was met with an overwhelming burst of sunlight. As my eyes adjusted, I saw figures form all about me, like ghosts taking corporeal form. They were sailors, clearly, but not Ministry men. They were wan and haggard, all salt-encrusted beards and over worn trousers. Yet what struck me most was that each wore a metal collar of interlocking plates, almost like scales.

"Ah, the Croyden out of Belfast," Holmes said through steepled fingers.

"Do you know all of the airship crews by sight?" I asked.

"That would not be an impossible feat," Holmes said. "Even today there are hardly more than a hundred such craft frequenting London. Yet in this case, I surmise this is the vessel which has fallen three days behind on its route."

"'Tis true, you're as sharp as they say, Mr. Holmes," said one of the sailors.

"I take it you are the captain?" Homes asked.

"Fanofir's my name," the man held out a calloused hand to Holmes, who shook it firmly and without hesitation.

"Thank you for allowing us to board," Holmes said.

"It wasn't exactly my choice," Fanofir said, shooting a sour look at Mycroft.

"I see," said Holmes. "And I sympathize. Why are we imposing ourselves upon the good captain, Mycroft?"

"Best to let Fanofir here tell it," Mycroft said.

"We've been tasked with a delivery," Fanofir said. "But the other Mr. Holmes won't allow us to make it."

"Whyever not?" Holmes asked his brother.

Mycroft nodded to two of the sailors, who reluctantly went below deck and returned with a metal box carried gingerly between them. It was square, but all 12 edges appeared to be lined with glass ampules, each containing a fluid. From where I sat, I could see pitch black, a golden amber, and a dusky merlot colour all represented. Diagonally from each corner to its opposite ran what appeared to be a spring, suggesting that a disruption to any part of the box would have repercussions upon each of the ampules.

"A bomb?" I asked.

"If we knew that for a certainty, I would not have gone through the inconvenience of traveling to Baker Street and back."

I struggled to refrain from commenting upon the relative inconveniences of our journey here.

"Either way, why not simply toss it into the North Sea and be done with it?" Holmes asked. "These gentlemen can settle up with their client, who gave them such a suspect piece of cargo that the Ministry would have no choice but to intervene."

The sailors each tugged at their metal collar.

"There's a bit more to it," Fanofir said. "We are being strangled. Slowly, but inevitably it seems."

"The collars are squeezing your necks?" I asked, moving to inspect the closest man.

"Tighter and tighter, every hour," Fanofir said.

I leaned in to listen, and there was a discernible ticking sound to the collar.

"Much tighter and we'll be trading our balloons for wings," Fanofir said.

"Much tighter and my head will pop off," wheezed the man I was examining.

"Can't we cut through the collars?" I asked. "A petrol powered alternating saw, certainly. Might be a few knicks but I'll stand ready to patch these men up."

"As a last resort only," Mycroft said. "We have a diamond-tipped saw at the ready."

"Why wait?"

"The engineer of these diabolical devices is clearly concerned about tampering," Holmes said, gesturing to the box. "What if cutting into the collar causes it to immediately contract? OR release some noxious vapor?"

One of the sailors clutched at his throat and moaned.

"Steady on, Smithy," Fanofir said.

The Croyden was approaching another dirigible, which seemed to be loitering at a lower altitude. Mycroft's soldiers shot a line across into the opposing deck like they were harpooning a whale. The crew of the other ship pulled the line taught and secured it. Mycroft ponderously stepped into a harness which was then clipped to the line.

"I hope you will have resolved this before supper," Mycroft said. "Chef does a rather nice braised shank. It would be a shame if I were to miss it." One of the soldiers slid down first, then Mycroft gave a jaunty wave to us before following, and finally, the remaining soldier slid down. Lest there be any confusion in the matter, Mycroft cut the line on the far side, leaving the rope dangling uselessly over the ocean.

"It seems we have our work cut out for us," Holmes said.

I sighed. "I don't suppose we might at least have a cup of tea while we wait to explode."

"The finest from the subcontinent, sir," Fanofir said, nodding to one of his men. "From my own supply." The sailor shuffled into the Captain's cabin and I turned to see Holmes already at work.

"Fascinating," Holmes said. "These aren't isolated chambers as I first suspected. Look, when I turn the box each liquid stays in the same relative position."

It was true, as the box was slowly turned over each liquid kept its place by traveling through an apparently interconnected system that was obscured within the box.

"There's a neat trick of specific gravity," Holmes said. "Our man has art in his blood."

"Who are you meant to deliver it to?" I asked.

"Her Royal Highness, of course," Fanofir said.

"However, did your client convince you to wear the collars?" I asked,

"We were somehow made to be unconscious," Fanofir said. In response to my sceptical look, he continued. "It wasn't a spiked barrel of grog, Dr. Watson. Contrary to the popular images, we are not bawdy pirates of the sky. These airships are basically bombs with propellers attached. We are dead sober when on duty. As for myself, I haven't had a drop of liquor since I was a boy."

"Could it have been introduced in your food?" Holmes asked.

"Not likely, it seems we were all afflicted at the same time, and we don't all take meals together. We work in shifts."

"There are only six of you here. I take it you usually have a larger crew?"

"The six of us own shares in this enterprise," Fanofir said. "We never have trouble hiring the crew we need in port. Saves on helium to not carry more than we need on any given voyage."

"It seems as if your assailant was familiar with your operation," I said.

"Hundreds of sailors have served aboard the Croyden over the years," Fanofir said.

"And the names of those with a dispensation to operate an airship are a matter of public record," Holmes said.

"I suppose," I muttered.

The sailors each clasped at their throats and grunted.

"It seems another hour has ticked by, Mr. Holmes," Fanofir gasped. "Is it a bomb or not?"

"I've never seen anything like it," Holmes said. "Which means no one has. However, given the way your entire crew was subdued simultaneously I have to assume a master chemist is involved. I suspect this is something more insidious than a common explosive."

"Poison gas, perhaps?" Fanofir asked.

"Or an agent that would render the royal family infertile. Or a solvent that would eat away the Palace walls. Or simply another knock-out drug that would leave the Palace open to plunder."

"I don't care about any of that," one of the sailors said. "I just want the blasted collar off. Let's put the saw to use and see what happens."

"Steady on, we aren't to the point of desperation quite yet," Holmes cautioned. "How much time do we have left?"

"Less than six hours," Fanofir said.

"According to what source?" Holmes asked.

"When we awoke there was a clock on the deck, running backward. When we lifted it a mechanical voice spoke to us."

"Did the voice seem to be speaking in the moment or was it a recording?" Holmes asked.

"It was a phonautogram," Smithy said decisively.

"Did you recognize the voice?" Holmes asked.

"None of us," Fanofir replied.

"Anything about it?" Holmes asked. "The accent? A striking turn of phrase?"

"The manner of speech was strange," Fanofir said. "The inflections and cadence were a jumble as if the words were spoken out of order."

"Male or female?" Holmes asked.

"Male, surely," Fanofir said. "What woman would do this?"

"Nonetheless, was the voice male or female?"

"Male, I'm certain," Fanofir said.

"I don't want to contradict the captain," one of the sailors began.

"Go ahead, Smithy, this is a matter of our lives, after all," Fanofir said.

"It's just, my sister works at the Arcade, so I've spent more than a few hours lurking around in the back rooms after hours and whatnot. They've got those spectroscopes, you know? And sometimes they play a phonautogram along with them, but the whole thing is finicky. If anything damages the glass tube it ends up sounding like a hiccup when it is played back, but other times you get these unsettling half-sounds."

"This reproduction sounded like that?" Holmes asked.

"A bit, sir," Smithy said.

"And you think it was a woman's voice?" Holmes asked.

"I think it is possible," Smithy said. "To be honest, my head was still pretty foggy."

"Do you have a net aboard this ship?" Holmes asked.

"A net?"

"For fishing? Or moving cargo?" Holmes asked.

"Certainly, but what for?" Fanofir asked.

"Rig it up so it can be lowered into the sea," Holmes said. "I am going to signal to Mycroft that we require saltwater for an experiment."

"What experiment is that?" Smithy asked.

"Can we sneak the box off of this ship right under the Ministry's noses?" Holmes replied. "Watson, you will climb into the net with the box and ride down to the water. Once there you will swim with it back to shore."

"Come now, Holmes, we are more than a mile out, and I wasn't a strong swimmer even in my heyday. Besides, surely Mycroft will notice."

"The Captain and I will be making a distraction up here as you manage the trick," Holmes said.

"I can provide you with a floatation bib," Fanofir said. "And a waterproof compass. You can just lay back and kick your way to dry land."

"This is a preposterous idea," I objected.

"These men are dying," Holmes said. "Perhaps all of London is in danger."

"Why don't you manage the feat, then? You are the superior athlete."

"My brother needs to be focused on me, up here, putting on a theatrical performance for his benefit. This is a shell game, and Mycroft is never going to keep his eye on you."

The brave sailors around me were already in great distress from the collars restricting their throats.

"I hope you know what you are doing, Holmes," I sighed.

In just a few scant minutes I found myself dangling over the crashing waves curled up around the fantastical box in a rancid net that had spent years wicking up the rotten odours of the sea. The Croyden appeared to swing back and forth above me, and as I watched, there was a great flash and then smoke began billowing from the ship. Had I not known that Holmes was intentionally creating a spectacle to distract his brother I would have been most concerned. As it was, I felt my pulse rush with a wave of momentary panic. Then the net found the ocean and began to close around me. I had been meant to subtly roll myself into the water. Instead I madly clawed my way across the sinking net while being battered by the rolling waves. Once over the edge and free in the water I held fast to the box and waited until the flotation suit had settled. Just as Fanofir had promised I was now gently

50

bobbing on my back, my head supported by an inflated bladder. Using the compass, I pointed my back at London and began kicking. Smithy began winching up the net, now laden with brine, and I felt truly alone in a way I had not experienced since I lay bleeding on the hardscrabble of Afghanistan.

As with most mortal terrors, when the initial rush of animal panic subsided, I found myself bored. Kick, kick, kick, sky, sky, sky, for who knows how much longer. Naturally, the pneumatic box occupied my thoughts. Was it generating heat, I wondered, or were my hands merely numb? Could I hear a ticking sound or was it my imagination? Was the pulsing I felt coming from the box or my own heartbeats? My first sign that my odyssey was coming to a close was a rather rude comment shouted from the riggings jutting out at the horizon. Dangling among the ropes and nets trailing down from the piers, like malnourished monkeys in a rather depressing zoo, were the disenfranchised of London. At first, their whoops and whistles were merely annoying as I continued pushing against the waves, but then I realized that some of them were pacing me, following from above. I imagined a rather rough welcome when we, at last, met on shore. My first thought was to swim up the channel until I found a police jetty, but of course I could not risk the police seizing the pneumatic box and prying it open. Worse, I was completely exhausted and needed an immediate resolution. Watching the human scavengers above me gave me an idea. To avoid being nipped apart by jackals I must leap into the lion's den. Or rather, the broken hull of an iron-hulled freighter that was known colloquially as Davy Jones' Locker. The ship's original sobriquet had long been lost to the public's memory.

I had never been near the place; no respectable person had. The vessel had been run aground by pirates nearly twenty years ago and they hadn't ceded the ship since. A dozen flags of black and red were hung from the stern. A simple rope bridge ran from the prow to the docks, designed to be intentionally easy to sever in case the police ever took it into their heads to assault this fortress of iniquity. To date, that had not occurred. From within, a raucous debauchery could be heard morning and night. There were few corners of London where Holmes had not trodden, but I believe that this is one of them. As I changed my course to head there even my would-be assailants seemed astonished. A few called out warnings before breaking off and returning to their regular haunts. For a moment I thought I might make my way to the shore unmolested without entering the locker, but the most predatory of the underdock lurkers still watched my progress, if now from some distance.

Just as I bumped against the Locker's rust-eaten hull I found myself hooked and hoisted, being drawn up inside the terrifying structure. It was pitch black, but I heard cruel cackling and guffawing all about me.

"Hello?" I said. "Who's there?"

This was met with raucous laughter. The pneumatic box was ripped from my grasp.

"Well, well, what do we have here?" came a voice from the darkness.

"Please, wait!" I said. "It might be a bomb!" As the voices muttered to each other I briefly reflected that if one wanted to do some good for Queen and country, allowing a bomb to explode inside the Locker would not be entirely without merit.

"You are swimming around in your natty togs with a device that might be a bomb?" the voice asked. "How have we never met before?"

Before I could answer another voice called out, "It's Doctor Watson, it is. Sherlock Holmes's cabin boy."

"Now see here," I began.

"Are you certain?" the first voice asked the second.

"Most certain," the second voice said. "Every villain who sets foot in London knows of the man."

A score of others began to call out their own grievances with my friend. As I dangled there at the end of some kind of winch, I began to suspect that the underdock scavengers would have been preferable. At least my eyes were adapting. The hold of the ship had been converted to a place not much worse than some of the West End pubs I had seen on occasion. Indeed, I rather suspected at least some of the furniture had been pilfered from the finest liners to cruise the channel. At the far end of the chamber sat a kind of throne, and upon that throne the owner of the first voice, a feral mass of ropey muscle and briny hair. He turned the pneumatic box over in his hands.

"I've never seen anything like it," he said. "And that means no one has."

"Am I addressing Mr. Davy Jones?" I asked.

The room fell into hysterics.

"Davy Jones is a god, Doctor Watson," the man said. "Old and cruel. I am but a humble man."

Again, the room laughed.

"They call me Red James, Blood Scourge of the Waves."

"Pleased to make your acquaintance, Mr. James," I said.

"Red James, and you won't be pleased for long." He pressed on a lever and a whooshing sound began below me. Looking down I could only see that something flashed across the opening every few seconds.

"Piano wire," Red James explained. "Lengths attached to a kind of pivoting gyroscopic hoop."

"Like being lashed from all directions at once," the man to his right offered.

"The flesh will be inexorably flayed from your bones," Red James laughed. "My only regret is that it is so mercifully quick."

"Wait," cried the other voice from earlier. "I claim the right of satisfaction."

"We aren't at sea," Red James rebutted. "The pirate code does not apply here."

A shot echoed in the room, knocking Red James' barnacled crown from his head.

A man stood with smoke trailing up from his pistol. I wouldn't have recognized him as a sailor on dry land. While greasy and tattered, his clothes read more Highgate than high seas. Perhaps he had been press-ganged, I conjectured. In any event, his gun commanded respect, at least for a moment. Then the shocked disbelief of the crowd broke like a wave and the criminals burst into chaos. Such a brazen attack upon their cruel master served as a catalyst for every avaristic instinct these vile wretches held. I was jostled when a pair of grappling men fell into the portal beneath me and were quickly torn to a red paste. I hardly noticed when I was pulled to safety by my belt and freed from the hook.

"This way, Doctor Watson," the man who had fired the shot said. "Now that these brigands have seen Red James humbled, they will be in a frenzy until order is restored with bloodshed. No one is safe here."

As if to punctuate the man's remarks a boy lunged at me with a rusty fish knife, missing me only because he tripped upon a body already laying on the bloody floor. I nodded and followed my erstwhile saviour around the pit, where he provided cover while I again took possession of the pneumatic box. He threw open a nondescript hatch in a darkened recess of the chamber, and we stepped out into the fresh air.

"You have the advantage, sir," I said, leaning back against the wall and trying not to think about the drop into the ocean below.

"Daniel Newson," the man said, while deftly threading a knife through the lever mechanism of the hatch. Even as he pulled against the handle to ensure it was sound, the door rattled. "That won't hold them for long." He gestured to the rope bridge that connected the Locker to land.

"I can't," escaped my mouth before I realized it.

"It is that, or back in the sea, or wait for Red James to take you," Newson said. "I think you'll manage. Grab hold to the lines on both sides and keep your eyes on your feet. The ropes will hold."

Remembering the icy water churning below, I found myself unable to move forward. The door behind us began to give.

"As you will, Doctor Watson," Newson said, stepping easily out onto the bridge. He had no need of the guide lines. He'd made it three or four steps before I called out for him to stop. He lithely pivoted and made his way back.

"The box," I said. "I can't manage it."

"I will take it," Newson said.

Reflexively I turned away. The hatch was groaning now. Any moment the brigands would force their way through. "You will return it to me at the other end, upon your honour?"

Newson grinned. "My honour isn't worth much in the way of collateral, but I promise you man-to-man I will return the box. Hurry, the door is giving."

I was sure I was being played for a fool somehow, but short of taking one final plunge into the waters from which I had so recently escaped I saw no alternative. I relinquished the pneumatic box, and Newson made his way lightly across the gap, having no doubt spent much of his life upon the rigging of ships. For my part, I gripped the waist-high guidelines for dear life and picked my way across the swaying rope bridge, my eyes never leaving my feet. From the commotion, I assumed the door was open. Newson was firing shots back at the wretches coming through. Just as the pier was in sight Newson shouted for me to hold on and then the bridge dropped away behind me, leaving me dangling perpendicular to my former attitude. Newson reached down and lifted me by the collar, like a kitten being carried by its scruff.

"Quickly," he said, once he had set me down.

Looking back, I saw Red James himself drawing a bead on me. The shot only flew false because he was jostled in the melee that had spread onto the Locker's deck.

I forced myself to stumble after Newson until we had reached the end of the pier. He pushed the pneumatic box into my chest and put my arm snugly around it.

"As promised," he said. "Fly quickly and true, Doctor Watson."

With that, he disappeared into the throngs that so colourfully inhabited the London docks.

"Get back here!" I cried to no avail. My mysterious saviour was gone, leaving me with the pneumatic box and a rather uncertain task at hand. My suit ruined, myself worn thin and grey, I garnered little attention as I slumped against a kerb and recuperated. After regaining some vigour, I attempted in vain to hail a cab. No reputable driver would stop for me in my current condition. So it was that I found myself leaving a trail of sodden footprints all the way to Baker Street. Of course, it was hardly a surprise to find Holmes in his mouse-colored housecoat, absently watching the smoke from his clay pipe drift up and dance across the ceiling. "At last, Watson," he said. "Men's lives are at stake."

I let the pneumatic box fall in his lap with more force than was strictly necessary. "Need I really ask for an explanation?"

"The faithful fire brigade," Holmes replied. "As you can imagine, a fire aboard an airship is not taken lightly. It seems my little pyrotechnics show was observed by an air patrol as well as by my brother. Even the Machiavellian Mycroft Holmes was no match for a sparkplug of a fire brigade captain who ordered that all gas be vented from the Croyden immediately. Of course, Fanofir, his crew, and I were all taken into custody first. The airship was in the water and being towed back to land before Mycroft could even get on board to argue the point. Of course, I am well known at Scotland Yard so it was a simple matter to make my excuses there. The Ministry took charge of Fanofir and his crew again, and Mycroft was delightfully perturbed to discover that you had absconded with the pneumatic box. He made it quite clear that he would not rest until you were known as the greatest traitor in the history of England should the box prove deadly."

"Yet he will be the greatest hero should we succeed in disarming the thing, I presume," I said.

"Of course," Holmes said. "My brother is nothing if not a kind of bureaucratic Atlas, always the master of leverage."

"Well, I hereby wash my hands of it," I said. "I have done more than my share."

"Now, now, Watson, a hot meal and a stiff drink and you'll be set to rights again," Holmes called after me as I retired to my room. A short while later Mrs. Hudson knocked, and when I refused to answer, called through that she was leaving my dinner by the door. When she had gone, I surreptitiously took the snifter and left the rest.

The next morning after my ablutions, I was much restored. In the parlour, Holmes was tinkering with the infernal package. I had resolved to ignore the matter altogether, but I could not rid my mind of an image of my beloved Baker Street as a smoking crater. "Is that really wise, Holmes?"

"It is a prop, Watson," Holmes said. "It has to be. I've gone back through every reference, chemical and alchemical, mechanical and theoretical, and there is no means by which this device can explode. The various fluids already intermix, the metal matrix of the box completely telegraphs kinetic shocks along its frame, while utterly insulating whatever may be contained within. Simple stagecraft."

"I would hardly call those strangulating collars stagecraft. Perhaps it would be best to pry it apart somewhere other than a residential block of London?"

"Tut, tut, Watson," Holmes said. "No lives have been lost yet." Nonetheless, he set down the prybar with which he had been prodding the box. I sighed with relief before he began sparking an acetylene torch.

"Holmes, I really must insist," I began, when a knock came at the door.

A few moments later Mrs. Hudson came bowing and scraping in. "Lady Wynthorne to see you, Mr. Holmes," she said. A grand woman entered the room forthwith. Her stiff dress the colour of an icy mountain lake, betrayed no movement as she came to the centre of the room, giving her an almost ethereal impression.

"I am here to speak with Mr. Sherlock Holmes," she declared. "I understand you have come into possession of an unusual package. You will surrender it to me."

"My dear Countess," Holmes replied. "I would, of course, be delighted to be of service, but I am afraid I am not familiar with the object to which you refer."

To my surprise, the pneumatic box was nowhere to be seen. That was a neat trick, even for Holmes.

"Don't play the fool, Mr. Holmes," Wynthorne said. "My family is well placed in all the highest reaches of the kingdom. I know that the Ministry was called upon to intercept this package, and I know that you pilfered it out from under your brother's nose."

"Lady, I can assure you that if I had any parcel addressed to your Honour, I would deliver it forthwith."

"It may not be labeled with my name, but..." she stopped short. "Never mind. If you will not cooperate, then I call upon you to remember that I attempted to resolve this in a civilized fashion." She passed a haughty glance around our sanctum before turning on her heel.

"Now that is interesting," Holmes said with a relish most men would reserve for a rare vintage of wine or an exotic tobacco.

"She was certainly abrupt," I said, plucking a corner of toast from the rack. "I don't imagine she hears no very often. She seemed to be at a loss as to how to respond."

"I also imagine it is a rarity for her to conduct such business on her own behalf, or indeed travel unescorted." Holmes was watching her progress out of the window. "A hired carriage, not even her own. That, however, is not what interests me most."

"Indeed?" I replied, more interested in steeping my Earl Grey and enjoying the lingering scent of perfume the lady had left lingering in our rather stale domicile.

"Let us consult the Babbage about one Lionel Wynthorne."

By us, of course, he meant me. I crossed to the old lumber-room which now contained Holmes's differential machine. Holmes was not one to chase the latest fancy but he had been one of the first private citizens to purchase one of these infernal mechanical brains. In odd moments, he tinkered with the gears and pistons of the thing and I rather suspect Mr. Babbage would be hard pressed to recognize it. Yet when it came time for the mundane tasks of entering and retrieving the data it held that task was always left to me. Using a kind of typewriter modified to punch holes in a prescribed card stock, I composed a query. Taking the resultant perforated card, I fed it into a receiving slot and turned a crank much as if the whole device were a whimsical player piano. Once the inquiry had been input successfully, I pushed at a foot pedal to send the mechanisms spinning and whirling. After a few moments, the ticker tape at the far end rendered its declaration. A brief biography of Lionel Wynthore was typed out across a spooling length of paper, which Holmes ripped from the serrated dispenser before handing to me.

"*The scion of the Wynthorne family, Lionel possesses a precocious intellect, graduating summa cum laude from Cambridge at seventeen years of age, writing upon modern engineering. Defying expectations he then toured the continent for several years, apprenticing to various artists of an avant-garde bent before disappearing in the Orient, leaving behind only an eccentric collection of work valued more for its association with the Wynthorne line than for its own artistic merit. Notably, the family has made little obvious effort to find their wayward heir.* From there it lists his known relations and so forth, including his sister, whom we just met."

Holmes began wrapping the box in plain brown paper. "I suspect Lady Wynthone recognized her brother's handiwork. Let us see if an art expert will as well."

"Your entry on the man suggests he is but a dilettante. Is there such a thing as an expert upon his work?"

"I happen to know that the National Gallery holds three pieces. Admittedly a small collection, but we haven't time to travel nor the leeway to travel to the Louvre or the Hermitage."

"All because of his family connections?" I groused.

"Take heart, Watson. His works molder in some darkened storeroom while the old masters retain pride of place."

"Still, think of all the inspired art that languishes in obscurity, with not even a storeroom to preserve it."

"Come, Watson, it is not even yours to rewrite the ways of the world. We can but solve the little puzzles laid before us."

Holmes quickly worked his way through the hierarchy of the Gallery, from docent to sub-curator and so on until we found ourselves sitting before Mr. William Pembroke, whose spartan office and bespoke suit suggested something more in the line of actuary than art historian.

"Gentlemen, it is rare that I entertain visitors," Pembroke said, shaking hands warmly. "Someone has to keep an eye on the books while more noble aspects of the Gallery's mission are carried out," he continued as if he had read my mind.

"So, you primarily have an administrative role," I asked.

"I'm afraid so," he said.

"But you do some of the curation?" Holmes asked. "We were referred to you as the expert upon Lionel Wynthorne."

"Expert may be a bit of a flourish, but yes, I did purchase the Wynthornes. More as a kind of investment than upon their own merit. Don't get me wrong, as art they are accomplished, but they lack that spark of the muse. At least, ours do. I sincerely hope that Lord Wynthorne is still out there somewhere, having discovered some fresh inspiration, producing sublime works that eclipse our holdings."

"What if I told you that this was a new Wynthorne?" Holmes said, gesturing to the package. "Would you be able to authenticate it?"

"I suppose that I am an authority in this rather narrow field, but I can already tell you that package would be the smallest work he is known to have produced."

"He worked on large pieces exclusively?" Holmes asked.

"As I say, his artistic inspiration was lacking, and he often compensated with scale. What would be mundane at a foot becomes awe-inspiring at two meters."

"It would be useful to me to know of the authenticity of this object in either eventuality," Holmes said.

I could see the flush of curiosity upon Pembroke's face. "Nothing would be harmed by a quick look. This would be a superficial evaluation only. If it seems warranted, I would be happy to investigate further. May I?"

"Please," Holmes chose a seat to recline in as if he had not a care in the world. I followed his lead.

Pembroke delicately peeled back the wrapping paper and was immediately intrigued. "To be honest, gentlemen, I was prepared to tell you that you had been snookered, but there is an undeniable aura of Lionel Wynthorne to this piece." Donning white gloves, he gingerly picked the pneumatic box up and turned it over, and then over again. "I'm going to reveal a little secret to you gentlemen," he said. "I hope I can trust your discretion."

"Of course," Holmes said. "You may rest assured."

"Excuse me for a moment," Pembroke said and exited the office.

"It seems we did well to bring the box here," I said.

"We shall see," Holmes replied.

Pembroke returned with a satchel under his arm, not unlike my own medicine bag. He set it upon his desk and carefully lifted out a device that looked a bit like a tuning fork, but with wire wound round it and some kind of metal sphere snug between the two prongs. He next produced a small electric generator, powered by a hand crank. He connected the two devices and began turning the handle on the generator, creating the characteristic snapping and buzzing of a static charge. After a minute or so he moved to touch the fork to the box.

"Wait!" I cried, still thinking of the thing as a bomb.

"I apologize for my friend," Holmes said. "Pray, continue."

"I must say, it is a most remarkable day to examine an unknown Wynthorne, and in the aid of Mr. Sherlock Holmes no less."

"You do have the eye of an appraiser," Holmes said.

"I am embarrassed I did not see it earlier," Pembroke said. "I have read all of your stories, Dr. Watson. I have collected the various editions, in fact. And so, I have seen your likenesses a hundred times over. But there was something in that moment just then that left no doubt in my mind. Perhaps I might trouble the two of you to sign my monographs. There are so few of your autographs on the market."

"I have only inscribed copies I have personally gifted," I said.

"And I have signed none at all," Holmes replied.

"I would be most appreciative," Pembroke said. "If it is not an inconvenience. Please do not consider it an obligation. This interview is honour enough." With that, he placed the fork against the box and the sides fell away. "Wynthorne was a better engineer than an artist. He developed an electromagnetic seal that can only be broken under very precise conditions. This alone is grounds to declare this object an authentic Lionel Wynthorne. A scant few even know of this technique, and I doubt even you could replicate it, Mr. Holmes."

"How do you come to know of it, then?" I asked.

"We were residents at Trinity Hall contemporaneously," Pembroke said. "Even then, Lord Wynthorne was pursuing art alongside engineering. A man in his position has no lack of admirers, but I believe he found me to be a man of genuine taste and discernment. I will even flatter myself that I contributed to the development of his aesthetic sensibilities."

"I am curious about the matrix of fluids in particular," Holmes said.

64

"As am I," Pembroke replied. "I rather expect that came from the engineering side of the house. I've certainly never seen its like. As for Dr. Watson's fear that this may be some kind of explosive, I am unreserved in offering my opinion that it is not. Lord Wynthorne simply is not the sort who would go in for that."

"May I?" Holmes asked, leaning forward to inspect the inner workings of the box. "Most peculiar. My first impression would be that this is some kind of battery, and yet there appears to be a small motor built into it, and this protrusion over here remains a mystery."

Suspended at the centre of the box was a brass cylinder, but rather than being completely smooth there was a raised slot on one side, a bit like an improbably symmetrical seashell.

"What do you suppose this toggle does?" Pembroke asked, flicking the knob as he spoke.

"Wait!" Holmes commanded but too late.

The fluids in the glass tubing now drained downwards and upwards into the brass chamber. After a moment of hesitation, the tiny motor at the top whirred to life and the device started making a grinding sound. To their credit, neither Holmes nor Pembroke flinched. A moment later we heard the flat, affectless voice the sailors had described, coming from within the cylinder. Smithy had been correct in thinking it belonged to a woman. In fact, it was the Countess herself, the strange reproduction amplifying her naturally reserved demeanour. At the end of her brief and shocking statement a plate of silver emerged from the slot.

"What strange happening is this?" I wondered.

"A moment, Dr. Watson," Pembroke said, gingerly setting the plate down. As we watched an image resolved on the surface. A daguerreotype of a man lounging against a windowsill while in the foreground a woman leans forward in her chair and gestured emphatically at him.

"That is Lady Wynthorne!" I gasped.

"And the gentleman," Holmes said, gesturing to me with a steadying hand. "Do you recognize him, Mr. Pembroke?"

"I do not, Mr. Holmes."

"It is not Lord Wynthorne?"

"Most certainly not."

"I hope that you understand that what we have witnessed here must be kept in the strictest confidence," Holmes said.

"But of course," Pembroke said.

"Very good. I shall give you my signature after all, upon a receipt for the unlocking mechanism. I am afraid it is a matter of life and death, but I give you my personal assurances it will be restored to you."

"And this device?"

"I expect it will end up in a Ministry vault somewhere. Tragic, really. I believe Lord Wynthorne has eclipsed the world on multiple fronts with this miraculous device."

Holmes drafted the document while I gathered up the strange realia the interview had produced. Taking pity on the poor curator I signed half a dozen of his books before Holmes ushered me out the door.

"The man in that picture was Captain Fanofir," I whispered to Holmes as we made our way to the street. "How is a man of his stature wound up in this business with the Countess?"

"My knowledge of fashion is a trifle rusty, but from the manner of dress and the lady's coiffure I'd place that image as taken roughly ten years ago, about the time that Lord Wynthorne disappeared."

"You don't think they really made good on their threats?"

"I think Captain Fanofir has a lot to answer for before we release his collar."

Unfortunately, when we arrived at the Ministry's secret hospital, we found the sailors had all been sedated.

"They were writhing in agony," Mycroft said. "Even I couldn't ignore their suffering."

It was ghastly to look upon their blue faces, but I dutifully went around releasing the collars by touching the electrified wand to each mechanism. All save Fanofir, whom Holmes barred me from approaching. Instead, he injected the man with a syringe pulled from a case in his own pocket.

Fanofir sprung upright and began gasping and clawing at his neck.

"Listen to me," Holmes said, grasping the man's forehead in an unmovable grip. "Watson has the means to release you in a moment, and if it were up to me this collar would stay on until I had the truth from you. However, if you asphyxiate the thread is lost. I want your word that you will tell me the whole truth."

Fanofir nodded emphatically, tears streaming from his bulging eyes. Reluctantly, Holmes stepped back, and I brought the wand forward to release the sailor. Like his fellows, he gasped and wheezed until the air had returned to his lungs.

"Explain the scene in this picture, please," Holmes held forth the damning daguerreotype.

"Where did you get this?" Fanofir demanded.

"It was contained within the pneumatic box you were charged with delivering," Holmes said.

"Only that?" Fanofir asked.

"No," Holmes replied. "Further evidence was provided."

"Evidence of what?" Fanofir asked.

Holmes merely arched an eyebrow.

"All this proves is that I once met the Countess Wynthorne," Fanofir said. "That's no crime."

"Her brother apparently does not agree," Holmes said. "Indeed, we have good reason to believe that all of this is his handiwork."

"No one has heard from Lionel in years," Fanofir scoffed.

"You are on such a familiar basis with the Count?" I asked.

"Even more familiar with the Countess, I imagine," replied Holmes.

"I take it you have proof, brother?" Mycroft said.

"The device contained within the box is among other things a kind of phonograph. The liquids mixed to create an electrical charge that drove its motor, as well as developing the image on this silver plate. See if your Ministry laboratory can get it to play again. If not, Watson and I, along with a reliable third witness, can attest to the contents."

"Which amounted to what?"

"Captain Fanofir and the Countess were recorded conspiring to murder her brother."

"Impossible!" Fanofir said.

"This seems a needlessly elaborate way to provide this evidence," Mycroft said.

"It's not evidence, it's a bundle of lies Lionel has created to frame me!" Fanofir said.

"The Count does seem to be an eccentric," Holmes said. "And I believe the baroque manner in which the message was delivered is his signature. Proof positive that he still lives and is the one delivering the blow to his would-be murderers. We've had the mechanism authenticated by an expert in Lord Wynthorne's artistic works. More so, his sister recognized it as such merely from second-hand accounts."

"Characteristic whimsy is unlikely to hold up in a trial," Mycroft said.

"The reproduction is conclusive," Holmes said.

"If it can ever be played again," Mycroft answered. "Had you not absconded with the box we could have opened it here, documented the whole thing beyond a whisper of doubt. Without that reproduction, I don't think there is a case to be made. I certainly can take no action in regard to the Countess as things stand."

"How long can you keep Captain Fanofir in custody?" Holmes asked.

"Not a moment longer!" Fanofir declared. "You've not produced a bit of evidence of any wrongdoing on my part. I'm the victim of a bizarre conspiracy and I mean to take my leave." He struggled to his feet and moved towards the door.

Mycroft caught him gently by the arm. "I'm afraid he is correct. The best I can do is hold him for medical observation for a day or so."

"You'll do no such thing!" Fanofir cried.

Mycroft pushed the weakened man back down upon the hospital bed with little effort. "A day."

We found a Ministry cab waiting to take us back to Baker Street when we stepped outside.

"Do you think Mycroft will get the reproduction to play again?" I asked.

"Lord Wynthorne went through far too much effort to simply cast his one grain of evidence out into the wind. He had to know the package would be intercepted long before it reached Her Majesty. The right ears need to hear it, or it is worthless. A man who spent a decade plotting an elaborate revenge scheme would see it through. There is an absent player at the table. Why don't we see him?"

"Daniel Newson!" I declared as we came to a stop in front of 221B.

"Who is that?" Holmes asked.

"The man in the tattered peacoat at the corner," I said. "He rescued me from Davy Jones' Locker. Actually, upon reflection, I think he may have rescued the pneumatic box. The fact that I was its courier was incidental."

"He is certainly keeping an eye on Baker Street. Let's make for the empty house across the way and double back on him."

Keeping ourselves on the far side of the carriage with our brims pulled low, Holmes and I quickly made our way across the street, through the alley, around and back again, finding ourselves quietly approaching Newson's back. When we were a few steps away he spun around towards us, gave out a startled shout, and made to bolt.

"Wait, please, Lord Wynthorne," Holmes said. "If you disappear, your sister and her companion will escape justice."

"What business of yours was this?" Wynthorne demanded.

"Such a suspicious package was never going to be delivered to Her Majesty," I said.

"The Ministry would sooner have let the sailors die," Holmes said.

"It would have only been justice," Wynthorne said. "They conspired against me."

"We heard the reproduction, and saw the picture," I said.

"That does me little good."

"My brother is highly placed within the Ministry," Holmes said. "He believes me implicitly, even when he grouses to the contrary."

"Yet the message has been spent," Wynthone said. "I am undone."

"Why were you watching Baker Street then?" I asked.

"Is that where we are? I have reluctantly taken justice into my own hands," Wynthorne said. "Now that I have revealed myself, my sister will finish what she began. She protects herself at all costs. It is the Wynthorne way."

"You sister is inside that building?" Holmes asked, indicating our abode.

"She entered a short time ago. I have been steeling myself for the confrontation."

I saw now that Lord Wynthorne had a white-knuckled grip upon his pistol. Holmes placed a steadying hand upon the man's arm.

"Come now, we shall be your comrades, but only if you agree to settle the matter with words," Holmes said.

"She deserves worse than words," Wynthorne said.

"Then let her appear before the assizes and face public humiliation," Holmes said.

A smile flashed across Wynthorne's face for a moment. "Fine, Mr. Holmes, my weapon shall stay in my pocket so long as we are prevailing."

Together we crossed the street. Upon opening the door, Mrs. Hudson cast a sour look at Lord Wynthorne and cast a staying hand.

"Mr. Holmes, your... guest will have to return later," she said. "The Countess has returned! She is awaiting you upstairs."

"My guest is the Lady's brother, and it is his long overdue appointment that we keep."

Holmes pushed by while Mrs. Hudson stood agog. Entering our quarters, we discovered the lady perched upon Holmes's wingback chair.

"I take it you have searched the premises?" Holmes asked, leaning casually against the mantel.

"As well as an amateur might be expected to," The Countess replied. "I must say, you lead a rather Bohemian life, Mr. Holmes. Rather a disappointment to your forebears I should think."

"Better watch yourself, Mr. Holmes," Lord Wynthorne said. "My sister addresses her disappointments with a fatal finality."

"Lionel, dear brother, how nice to see you again after all of these years." The ice in her gaze belied the warmth of her tone.

"I rather doubt that," Lord Wynthorne said.

"It seems Captain Fanofir has failed both of us," she said.

"Fanofir has failed all of us," came a voice from behind us. Smithy stood in the doorway with a pistol in each hand. "We were making a decent living plying the briny waves from Dublin. Privateers, we were, with the papers to prove it, nice and legal. Then Her Royal Majesty allows for private airship licenses and Fanofir gets grand ambitions. He sells our ship out from under our feet and gets the license. That does us a jolly lot of good with no airship to pilot, so we find ourselves working for wages after all in the employ of the Wynthorne family. This rankles us to no end, but Fanofir has a plan. He'll marry into the family and make himself master of the Wynthorne airship. Of course, her Ladyship here wasn't the starry-eyed innocent Fanofir had counted upon."

"Ha!" the Countess said.

"She soon had Fanofir running in circles like a trained pup, which meant we were all running in circles, with no ship and no riches to show for it. We put an ultimatum to Fanofir and he supposedly puts it to the Countess. Give us the airship or return our shares in the license, plus interest. He returns from meeting with the Lady to tell us that the airship is ours if we dispatch of the Lady's brother. We don't like it much but Fanofir has already agreed to it and so we steal into the Wynthorne estate only to discover the boy has already disappeared. Suspicion in his disappearance was cast upon us nonetheless and we were lucky to leave without shackles on our ankles. We went back to Ireland and cut a deal that saw us owning the Croyden after eight years' service to a shipping concern. We'd lived a few swell years after that until the day we woke up with Wynthorne collars around our necks again. I won't make that mistake again."

He guns drifted towards the Lord and Lady.

"Wait!" Holmes said. "We have evidence in hand that will see Fanofir and the Countess in gaol for the rest of their days."

Smithy cocked his pistols. "No more deals."

A shot rang out and a blossom of red spread upon Smithy's lapel. He gaped at Holmes in confusion for a moment before dropping to the floor. The rest of us turned to the Countess, who held a smoking nickel snub nose. It was pointed at Holmes.

"I've learned the perils of unfinished business over the years," she said.

"That's quite enough," I said, my Webley ready to bark.

The Countess moved her aim to me, and Holmes deftly stepped in and wrenched her arm around, forcing her weapon to drop to the ground. He had her in cuffs before I even observed from where he had produced them.

"Why, sister?" Lord Wynthorne asked. "I have never known your reasons for wanting me dead."

"It was nothing personal, dear brother," she said. "As long as you lived, the Wynthorne line passed through you, and I was doomed to be a simple piece of chattel traded away into marital servitude. Men like Fanofir should never even have dreamed of touching me, but some loathsome man not much better than him would have eventually laid claim to my affections. As the sole Wynthorne heir, I was mistress of my own destiny."

"So, you maneuvered Fanofir into agreeing to murder Lord Wynthorne."

"Thanks to the great Sherlock Holmes you have no proof of any of this," she sneered.

"To the contrary," Holmes said, "I may not have the inventive genius of your brother, but I have contrived a reproduction device or two of my own." He pressed a hidden switch on the mantle and a compartment opened, revealing a series of wax cylinders. The first three had been inscribed and Holmes plucked the third one out, placing it into the phonograph at the Countess' elbow. When he sent the motor turning, we heard the Countesses confession played back in her distinct voice. She lunged at the machine, but Holmes caught her by the shoulders.

The reproduction that Holmes had made and the image that Lord Wynthorne had provided were decisive at trial. Lady Wynthorne was sentenced to spend the rest of her life in the Tower, while Fanofir ended up in Blackgate. Mycroft was evasive as to whether the Ministry had ever managed to get the pneumatic box to work again, noting simply that the evidence it provided was superfluous to the needs of justice.

With Red James' bounty upon his head, Lord Wynthorne had not been seen to leave the family manor since his sister was sentenced. Yet, every once in a while, William Pembroke would invite Holmes and me to visit him in the inner sanctum of the museum, and the three of us would admire some new work the curator had acquired before they went on display. The name Lionel Wynthorne was never mentioned, but for those with an eye to appreciate the Count's eccentric work, the intricate mechanical sculptures rendered any other signature unnecessary.

The Adventure of the Portable Exo-Lung

by GC Rosenquist

CHAPTER ONE

P resently, the reader will forgive the necessary hesitancy in my writing and releasing this true account for public consumption after the passing of so many years. The reason for this hesitancy is that the events related were so out of the ordinary, so harshly unbelievable in nature at the time that I dare not test the reader's good sense and gullibility until the culture was finally acclimated to the miracles of modern technology.

The years after the professional relationship I shared with Sherlock Holmes ended was a time of incredible technological advancement; the popularity and affordability of the telephone receiver made immediate communication to all parts of the world possible, the electric lightbulb was beginning to light all the world, the steam-powered horseless carriage was slowly replacing the horse as our main mode of transportation, and man had taken to the air in both a silent torpedo-shaped balloon called a zeppelin and a noisy mechanical contraption called the aero plane. It was the birth of the modern world we know today, one that was always in forward motion at the same time I seemed to be slowing down due to the dregs of early middle age.

76

In the spring of 1910, I was taking holiday in Torquay, staying with a dear cousin who owned a cottage on the coast there. As I breakfasted every morning, I found myself perusing my cousin's copy of the London Times and was surprised to see that Holmes was back in London and working with Scotland Yard again. There had been a slew of kidnappings, the most recent one being the daughter of the Earl of Inniswitch. It had been some years since I'd last seen Holmes, and the picture they ran on the front page proved to me that he hadn't aged a day in all that time. He looked as fit and virile as ever, his aquiline features still bold and intact. It was pleasant to see him again and many memories of the adventures we shared in our youth rushed through my mind. A deep feeling of nostalgia swept over me, and I vowed to visit him when I returned to London.

I knew Mycroft, Holmes's always practical older brother, made every effort to keep our old flat at 221B Baker Street in perfect preservation for times when it was absolutely necessary to call his brother in from his retirement home for an important case that couldn't be solved without his specialized services.

So, when I finally arrived at 221B Baker Street on a pleasant but overcast day, I found a veritable beehive of activity. A large, empty, expensive-looking steam-powered Brougham was parked outside surrounded by smaller Scotland Yard hansoms. Three constables stood guard around Mrs. Hudson's entrance, all wearing frowns under their moustaches. This most recent kidnapping had indeed struck an open nerve of everyone in the city.

It all seemed very intimidating, and I hesitated a moment, wondering if it would be prudent to go in and see my friend at another, less intense time. But, missing him dearly, I decided otherwise and, with a click in my step, I approached the heavily guarded entrance. A young constable noticed me, held out an open palm against my chest and ordered me to halt. The other two closed ranks around him.

"Sorry, sir," said he. "Official police business. No one enters."

"But I'm a close friend of Sherlock Holmes-"

"I don't care if you're the King of Prussia, sir. I have my orders."

"But I'm Doctor John Watson," said I. "Perhaps you've heard of me and my previous adventures with Holmes?"

The young constable shook his head. "No, sir. Doesn't ring a bell. Sorry, sir." The other two seemed just as ignorant of my history.

At a loss for words, I stepped back. Could it have been possible that the many memorable adventures of Sherlock Holmes and his loyal assistant had already been forgotten by the populace at large? Should I have continued to publish fresh adventures, of which I still had plenty in archive?

Suddenly, the business end of a mechanical broom burst from the open entrance of 221B Baker Street, repeatedly crashing down on the head of the young constable.

"You let him in, constable!" cried an elderly female voice. Out stepped Mrs. Hudson holding the gear-driven broomstick in her hands. Her hair was generously tinselled with long strands of silver, her face etched with deeper lines than I remembered. Unlike Holmes, age had not treated her well. She brought the broomstick back up over her shoulders and threatened to strike the other constables also.

"But, ma'am, I have my orders!" protested the constable.

"To blazes with your orders, lad!" Mrs. Hudson countered, shaking the self-sweeping broom as if it were a club. "Doctor John Watson has *carte blanche* here and always will! Now step aside – all of you!"

The constable sighed, flashed me a defeated glance then dropped his hands to his side, curtly waving me in.

Impressed with that grand lady's surprising spunk, I smiled and embraced the small woman as I entered her dwelling.

"It's so good to see you again, Doctor," said she, giving me a quick kiss on the cheek.

"It's been too long, Mrs. Hudson," said I. "And I am sorry about that."

"Think nothing of it, Doctor. I see you and Sherlock in my memories every day."

"That's very kind of you," said I. "Is he upstairs?"

She smiled. "And he will be grateful to see you walk through that door."

I embraced Mrs. Hudson again then turned and went up the seventeen steps, toward the place where so many of our famous adventures began.

CHAPTER TWO

"Halloa! My dear Watson!" Holmes ejaculated as I entered the parlour. He was standing between Lestrade and a tall, well-suited man in front of a table that was covered by a large map. He removed himself forthwith and took my hand eagerly in his. "You have come at a most opportune time! Have you an opening in your schedule?"

"I am at your service completely, Holmes," I said happily.

"Splendid!" said he. "We may yet have need of your skills before this case is closed. Come, meet my client and then I will update you."

I hastily greeted Lestrade with a handshake as Holmes brought me over to the table. The other gentleman was the Earl of Inniswitch. He was a commanding presence who possessed large hands and a dignified face scratched with deep lines of worry around his blue eyes and on his forehead. His hair was thin and blond, but looked grey depending on how the light caught it. Thick reddish sideburns bordered his face and a well-groomed moustache of the same colour was tucked squarely under a long, thin, pointed nose. A pair of gold-rimmed pince-nez clung securely to the bridge of his nose. He greeted me warmly, but obviously his mind was on getting his daughter back safely.

I noticed three white business cards lying upon the map of London that covered the table; each one had a mysterious symbol upon it. The first card was marked with a single black horizontal line. The second was marked with two black horizontal lines, one on top of the other. The third was marked with an "X". When I inquired about these cards, Holmes answered: "I don't know what the meaning of the symbols are yet. The first card was sent to Mycroft in an envelope containing a stack of classified government papers that the government had to purchase back in a bold display of blackmail."

"How much was the ransom?" I asked.

"Twenty thousand pounds," Lestrade answered, a slight whiff of embarrassment in his voice.

This amount startled me. "I-I can't believe Mycroft allowed that."

Holmes nodded. "Quite. That informs you how important and sensitive the papers were, my friend. I did everything I could to solve the mystery before the deadline, but whoever is masterminding this crime spree is of impressive intelligence. The next two cards are related to the first two kidnappings which also resulted in twenty-thousand pound payoffs to get the victims back safely."

"You weren't able to secure their release?"

"We secured their releases, but unfortunately the ransom drop off locations have been cleverly staged so as to allow the perpetrator to make off with the money before we realized it was too late. But I have since come up with a possible solution to the problem." Holmes pointed to a spot on the map. "Here is where the wife of retired naval captain James Russell formerly of the *HMS Trident* was picked up by constables after her ransom had been paid – Bedford Square. Upon Investigation into Captain Russell's lineage, I have uncovered that Bedford Square was built by the Dukes of Bedford back in the late eighteenth century. The Dukes of Bedford are comprised of the Russell family.

"It's the same story with the second kidnapping victim. The poor six-year-old son of Sir Henry Hall, Danny, was discovered by constables wandering around the empty land where Shakespeare's Globe Theatre once stood, after his ransom was paid. Hall's lineage suggests he's an ancestor of one of Shakespeare's daughters. So, as you can plainly see, there's an obvious connection between the people and the places where they were found."

"You're saying that if we could discover anyone of importance in my ancestry, you would be able to figure out the release point, get there before the kidnapper and catch him?" the Earl of Inniswitch asked.

"Precisely, My Lord," said Holmes. "Have you knowledge of any such privileged lineage?"

"I am directly related to George IV, the uncle of Queen Victoria."

"Ha!" Holmes clapped his hands and leaned over the map, tracing his finger along long, winding streets and over dense London neighbourhoods. "Watson!" he called. "Quickly! Hand me the glass!"

I hurried over to Holmes's desk, took up the magnifying glass and handed it to him. He hung the glass over a certain spot on the map and grinned. "Ah, yes! Perfect! Here... Victoria Station. Always full of people coming off and going to the underground rail. The victim release can be hidden among all that chaos and noise without it ever being suspected as one. This is where your daughter will be freed, my lord."

"Excellent work, Mr. Holmes," Lestrade said. He glanced at the pendulum clock hanging on the wall. "The ransom is due at the drop-off point in under an hour. The Earl and I will go and complete the transaction immediately to start the process."

"Good. Watson and I will take your constables, and we'll stake out the grounds of Victoria Station," said Holmes. "Meet us there as soon as you can."

As Lestrade and the Earl of Inniswitch sped off in the expensive Brougham, Holmes and I joined the caravan of constable vehicles that rushed to Victoria Station.

When we arrived, there was a constant stream of people going in and out of the station. At times the human traffic was so thick it seemed like one gigantic organism. Holmes ordered the constables to take up places near the entrances and exits of the Underground but to try with great effort to stay out of sight. Holmes and I purchased a Times from a paper boy and pretended to wander around the approach concourse reading our papers, trying to blend ourselves among the crowd while we kept a vigilant eye as best as we could on the always moving mass of humanity.

I made my way along the edge of Wilton Road, watching the endless line of cabs and coaches stop, deposit or accept passengers, then move on. The air was thick with the din of people's voices and laughter and the slamming of a coach's door, the creaking of a cab's wheels and all sorts of other extraneous noises. At times, I could see Holmes's slim head poking up from across the crowd on the other side of the concourse. His eyes were narrowed and alive with concentration as he scanned his surroundings left and right. Then, his gaze fell upon me and his eyes went wide and round, his face became contorted and flushed with excitement. It took me just a moment to realize he wasn't looking at me, but behind me.

I spun around and was face-to-face with a big man; his face was reddened, his eyes were bulged out and angry. His head was completely devoid of hair, his chin was flat and sharp like the edge of a brick, his mouth was thin and clenched together so tightly it was barely visible. He was leaning out through the open door of a black coach, pushing something out on to the pavement. I glanced down and saw the limp body of a small girl with dark, curly hair and a white handkerchief tied over her nose roll out and land on my feet. Her wrists and ankles were secured by a knotted rope. The weight and surprise of the girl's body knocked me backwards. As I lay there on the pavement among scrambling feet and screaming women, I called out for Holmes.

The man heard me and the anger on his face quickly changed to concern. His eyes danced around the chaos in the crowd then he caught sight of something and his expression changed to outright fear. He cursed in a strange language, reeled backwards and slammed the door of the coach closed. Before I could get up and give chase, he was somehow already in the driver's seat at the front of the coach, impatiently whipping his mounts. The coach lurched forward, stopped, then with another violent flick of the whip, the mounts squealed and pulled the coach forward.

That was when I saw Holmes come out of nowhere, jump up on to the driver's box and accost the bald man.

CHAPTER THREE

I scrambled to my knees and watched as the constables that accompanied us to Victoria Station gave chase after Holmes and his antagonist. I was left alone with the Earl's unconscious daughter. The distinctive, sweet odour of ether rose up from the girl and knowing that prolonged exposure to this chemical can halt breathing, I quickly pulled the handkerchief off of her and dropped it next to where I knelt. Then I cut her binds with my pocket knife. As I pocketed the blade, I leaned over to check her breathing, found it too shallow for my comfort, so I pulled my own handkerchief from the breast pocket of my coat and began waving it over her nose to circulate fresh air back into her lungs.

The crowd that had dispersed only moments before, was now encroaching upon my rescue effort. I warned them to stay back, give the girl some space. There was a sudden excitement behind me, and I heard the familiar voice of Lestrade ordering people to let them through. In a flash, Lestrade and the Earl of Inniswitch were on their knees beside me. The Earl was crying out his daughter's name, his once dignified face a sloppy mess of tears.

"What's wrong with her, doctor?" he cried. "Is she dead? Have they murdered my sweet Rosalie?"

"Not yet, my Lord," I replied, still waving the handkerchief over her nose. Her face was pale and listless. "She's been ethered and it was a heavy dose. She needs to fill her lungs with fresh air immediately."

After a few more seconds of effort and concerned that she hadn't responded yet, I dropped the handkerchief and began slapping her cheeks, to instil some form of external stimulation. "Each of you, in haste, take her hand and slap it thoroughly! Quickly!" I ordered.

Lestrade and the Earl each took up one of her hands as I began waving the handkerchief again.

"Come back to me, Rosalie!" the Earl begged, patting her hand roughly.

I leaned over and listened for breathing. It was much stronger. Her chest rose and fell discernibly. "It's working!" I said and began gently slapping her cheeks again. I noticed that the colour was coming back to her face. As if to confirm this good news, she coughed once and blinked her eyes.

The Earl wailed out in joy, leaned over and took her up in his arms. She returned the embrace and began crying. It was a most beautiful thing to me. The curious crowd cheered as the touching scene continued.

I felt a hard slap on my back. "Well done, Doctor Watson," Lestrade said. "You'll receive a knighthood for this."

I shook my head and stood up. "The girl did all the work, Inspector. Her life is reward enough for me."

"Your humility is very touching, my friend," said another voice, one I recognized as Sherlock Holmes. I turned around and saw him stepping through the crowd towards me, surrounded by constables. One apparently had lost his cap during his chase with the kidnapper. Holmes, except for a minor bruise to his chin and ruffled hair, seemed otherwise unharmed.

"I'm relieved to see you, Holmes," I said. "Have you put the chains on the perpetrator?"

"It was a grand and mythical battle, my dear Watson, but circumstances proved to be in his favour this time," Holmes replied, then he reached into his inside breast pocket and pulled out a sealed envelope. "But I did come away with this." He handed the envelope to Lestrade.

"The ransom!" Lestrade exclaimed. He passed the envelope on to the Earl. "This time we're ahead of the game."

"Only temporarily, Lestrade," Holmes countered. He stepped up to the girl. "Rosalie, did your kidnapper happen to give you something? In your pocket, perhaps?"

The girl released her embrace of her father, nodded, reached into a hidden pocket in her skirt and pulled out a small white business card.

"Ah, yes. Thank you, young lady," Holmes said and took the card from her. He glanced at the Earl. "It would probably be prudent to take her to hospital, make a complete survey of her injuries – if any."

The Earl agreed and, with an escort of two constables, whisked his daughter away to his waiting Brougham.

Holmes held up the card so that I could see the fourth symbol. It was two horizontal lines, one on top of the other, with a diagonal line drawn across them from right to left. Like the other cards, the symbol made no sense to me. Was it some form of ancient writing only known to an elite few? Was it a new language invented by a linguistic genius?

Holmes seemed as in the dark as I. He pocketed the card and watched as Lestrade was suddenly given an official missive by a Scotland Yard messenger. Lestrade frowned and handed the missive to Holmes.

After a moment, Holmes folded the missive and handed it back to Lestrade.

"Come along, Watson," he said. "It seems our day has only just begun. We are needed at the British Museum. A priceless Van Gogh has been stolen, and in its place hangs a single card with a symbol on it."

CHAPTER FOUR

The director of the British Museum met us outside on top of the massive flight of steps in front of the main entrance. He was a nervous, slim little man wearing a light tweed coat, dark brown slacks and tan suede Tucsson shoes. His face was a gaggle of deep wrinkles out which sprouted a bulbous, reddish nose. His eye brows were like a pair of white flames frozen in time, his grey eyes were glassy and sunk deep inside pits of layered flesh. His hair was long, straight and white and combed straight back behind a pair of large, oval shaped ears. He shook our hands, introduced himself as Henry Epps, director of the museum, then led us between a pair of marble columns and into the building.

It was half past ten in the morning, and the museum was empty of gallery viewers. Our hurried footsteps echoed off the walls and smooth marbled floors like muffled firecrackers, and at times it was difficult to keep up with Director Epps as Lestrade, Holmes and I followed him through an endless maze of halls, galleries and staircases.

"A custodian discovered the theft this morning an hour before we opened our doors. Of course, we closed the museum for the day in light of the crime," Epps explained. "It's our contention that the painting was stolen not long after the museum closed last night and smuggled out the private entrance at the back of the building."

"Highly accurate, Director Epps. Have you questioned the on-duty night guard?" Holmes asked.

Epps let out a nervous cough. "We… we haven't been able to locate him. He's been working for the museum for a month. No one here really knew him well. We think he was the thief."

"Fascinating," Holmes said. "Were there any other guards present last night?"

"We employ a night guard in every wing," Epps answered. "But none of them heard or saw anything."

"We'll need a description of this missing guard and a name," Lestrade suggested.

"The name is irrelevant, Lestrade. It will be a false name," Holmes said. "Tell me, Director Epps, was this particular guard a large man with a bald head?"

Epps stopped in his tracks. "Why, yes. How did you know?"

Holmes smirked knowingly, rubbing his bruised chin. "Let's just say Doctor Watson and I are recently well acquainted with him."

Epps began walking again, turned down a short hallway and then into a large gallery with a huge skylight in the ceiling. Paintings lined all four walls; each was bordered on the floor with a chain and stand to keep people from getting too close. Epps led us to the far wall where a section of the wall was blank, a small white card hung where a painting should have been.

"I saw the card and knew it would be of great interest to the Yard. I ordered that no one touch it," Epps said.

"Sound thinking, Director Epps," Holmes said. He motioned towards the card with a hand. "May I?"

"Of course, Mr. Holmes."

Holmes stepped inside the chain and carefully inspected the card closely. "It's attached to the wall by means of a white thumbtack." He took the card down and handed it to me. The symbol on this fifth card was a single black wavy line, as mysterious and confounding as the other four symbols. Holmes took the card from me then pocketed it with the card the Earl's daughter gave him earlier, then he looked up at the blank wall.

"What particular painting did our bald friend pinch, Director Epps?" Holmes asked.

Epps nervously pulled at his collar. "It was Van Gogh's *Sunflowers*. Painted in Paris in 1887, three years before he committed suicide."

"How much is it worth?"

Epps pulled at his collar again, but this time stretched his neck and took a long, deep, painful breath. "Over two million pounds, Mr. Holmes."

"Quite a hit on your insurance, I would say."

"We would prefer the painting returned, Mr. Holmes."

"Naturally, Director Epps. To that end, I would suggest that Scotland Yard's theft division round up all their sources in the black market, especially in France where it would be much easier to sell off without attention and take the matter on themselves."

"You mean that you won't personally go after the painting, Mr. Holmes?"

"There's nothing I can do that the Yard couldn't do better or faster, Director Epps. No, my mind is set on a much bigger picture, its energy would be much better spent on that."

It was then that a young constable came running into the gallery. He came to a breathless stop in front of Lestrade. "Inspector!" he gasped. "Barclay and Company Bank has just been robbed! They made off with a hundred thousand pounds!"

"Bloody hell! Our bald friend has been busy today," I said.

Lestrade glanced at Holmes in disbelief. "Apparently your big picture just became bigger, Mr. Holmes."

"As I suspected, Inspector," Holmes countered. "Watson and I shall accompany you!"

CHAPTER FIVE

A tour of the Barclay and Company Bank vault was a lesson in bold efficiency and extraordinary planning. A giant hole had been pick-axed through the floor and most of the deposit boxes on the shelves, filled with bank notes, foreign currency and gold coins, were gone. None of the empty shelves held a sixth card with a symbol on it.

Lestrade, Holmes and I stood around the edge of the jagged, debris-covered hole and peered deep into the darkness below. A tunnel had been dug out underneath the bank and in the dim yellow electric light coming from a fixture hanging in the ceiling, I could just make out the shining glimmer of a pair of rails.

"A miner railcar system," Holmes said, massaging his chin. "Imaginative thinking and engineering. All the robbers had to do was place the car underneath the hole, drop the deposit boxes down into the waiting railcar and take it away. The actual robbery would only have taken a few minutes. Brilliant."

"But it must have taken weeks to dig that tunnel out," Lestrade suggested.

"That depends on where the tunnel originates from, Lestrade," Holmes countered. "Since it appears that we are being made to follow a bouncing ball, I suggest we find out where it goes."

I kicked a piece of debris into the hole, it hit bottom very quickly. "It doesn't seem too deep," I said. "I think we can climb down easily."

Lestrade pulled his police flash from its snap on his belt and flicked it on. "Follow me, gentlemen," he said, then jumped down into the hole. When he stood up, Holmes and I saw that the top of his head was only a few inches from the hole's opening. "We'll have to bend over while we travel, but only slightly."

Holmes went in next, then I. At the bottom I saw the discarded, well-worn, pick-axe the robbers used and a single deposit box that missed the railcar as it was thrown down. Lestrade trained the beam of his flash forward but it wasn't strong enough to illuminate the entire tunnel, only the nearby dirt and rock walls. We positioned ourselves on the wooden slots between the rails and began walking through the tunnel, Lestrade leading the way. Every few steps we came across a hastily made wooden support rib that shored up the walls and ceiling of the tunnel, the presence of these support beams eased my fears of a massive, tunnel-wide cave-in.

Finally, we saw a hint of white light ahead of us and as we drew nearer it became increasingly evident that it was the other end of the tunnel. The speed in which we travelled increased with the knowledge that the mystery of where the tunnel led was about to be revealed to us. We came out into what appeared to be an abandoned warehouse, completely devoid of any furniture or machinery. The rails ended with the empty railcar. The marks of the wheels of a four-wheeler were shadowed on the cement pavement. They appeared to move towards the wide, metal overhead door that was closed but obviously unlocked as the chain and lock were splayed on the pavement. In one corner of the warehouse was a pile of dirt that was piled almost as high as the ceiling, a dirty shovel lay against the bottom of the pile.

"Very clever," Holmes mused. "All the privacy you'd need to commit such a lucrative crime."

"But where are we?" Lestrade asked.

"In the abandoned mill works across York Street, in back of the bank," Holmes answered. "The robbers loaded their loot into a four-wheeler here, disguised the four-wheeler as a dirt carrier using the very debris they took out of that tunnel, took off through that door and disappeared into the city."

"Holmes!" Lestrade exclaimed as he reached into the empty railcar. He pulled his hand back and in his fingers was a small white card with a symbol on it. Holmes took it and shared it with me. Symbol number six was a circle with a diagonal line through it.

"Any instinct on what this one means, Holmes?" I asked.

"None at all, my friend," Holmes replied through a frustrated grimace. "And my inability to solve the meaning of these symbols proves that my decision to retire all those years ago was justified. I fear I can no longer perform my job at a level that a conundrum like this demands."

"Holmes, you are too hard on yourself," I comforted.

"Am I, Watson? If you fail to even make the easiest diagnosis upon an illness because your skills have waned, do you not do more harm than heal? Is that an acceptable position in your line of work?"

"It is completely different than what you do, Holmes," I said. "The problem here is that you don't have enough data to crack the case. It has nothing to do with the waning of your skills."

Holmes stood there solemnly, his chin resting on his chest, deep in thought. Finally, he took a deep breath and lifted his head, his intense glare upon me. "Perhaps you're right, old friend," he said. "I think, perhaps, it will be wise if I returned to Baker Street and put the problem to a pipe. Do you agree?"

"Wholeheartedly, Holmes," I said.

CHAPTER SIX

Holmes and I arrived at 221B Baker Street courtesy of a Scotland Yard escort not long after our investigation of the Barclay and Company Bank robbery. Once up in Holmes's flat, he took his clay pipe off his desk, filled the bowl with tobacco from the toe of that famous Persian slipper, also found on his desk, then he lit the bowl, sat in his armchair by the fireplace and crossed his legs. Immediately, his face turned to stone and he closed his eyes.

Knowing, after years of experience, that it was of utmost importance that I didn't disturb his thought processes as he smoked, I poured myself a small brandy and sat quietly on the couch behind him. In the past, I'd seen my friend solve many crimes, complete with all the details and timelines accurately deduced, using this very same method of meditation. I expected no less a result today.

Silent streams of white smoke rose up into the air and soon the entire room was filled with the pungent scent of that black shag tobacco, the only sound coming from the occasional hiss of Holmes's deep pulls from the pipe. After a quarter hour of this, my belly started making noises of its own and the faint pangs of hunger became increasingly apparent. It was now late afternoon and I'd realized that I hadn't eaten since earlier in the morning. I wondered if Mrs. Hudson would be open to the thought of a rare meal out.

She was.

She had a craving for a well-made Chinese meal, so we took an air cab to the *Golden Dragon* on Devonshire Street. It was a personal favourite of mine because they had the best egg rolls in all of London. Mrs. Hudson was so pleased to be waited on for a change. She ordered pepper steak with beef fried rice and a glass of white wine. I ordered sesame chicken and stayed with oolong tea. We took the time to catch up with each other and to renew our friendship. When we finally finished our meal, we left the restaurant and saw that dusk had fallen. It surprised us because we hadn't realized how fast time had passed. A true testament to how lovely the evening had been.

Upon entering Holmes's flat again, I found he was still sitting in his armchair, legs still crossed, smoke still rising from the bowl of his pipe. I wondered how many pipes into his process he was. I sat myself down on the couch again and relaxed pleasurably, my belly full and my mood much lightened. Before long, I began to drowse off only to be starkly wakened some time later by an impatient Holmes.

"Watson!" he shouted. "I think I've made a breakthrough."

"Jolly good, Holmes," I said groggily, rubbing the sleep from my eyes.

"Let's run through the gamut of crimes in this recent spree," Holmes began. "We have blackmail, kidnapping, art theft, and bank robbery."

"That sounds accurate, Holmes."

"What crime is glaringly omitted?"

I thought about it a moment, still fuzzy from my nap. "I-I would say murder, Holmes. No one has been permanently harmed."

"Precisely, my friend! And why would that be?"

I had no answer for that question.

"It's because in each case the crimes are designed to create income, nothing more," Holmes said. "Someone has built a very powerful and discreet criminal organization and the only way to fund it is through blackmail, kidnapping, art theft, and bank robbery. Murder has no purpose here."

I stood up. "But what about those damned symbols? What is their purpose?" I asked.

Holmes led me to the table where all six symbols had been laid out neatly in two rows of three.

"The mastermind of this criminal organization is trying to tell me something," Holmes mused.

"But what could it be?"

"Perhaps he's trying to tell me who he is, or where he is, or what his next crime is going to be. As you said earlier, my friend, the data is incomplete. Unfortunately, there's no way I can, with the evidence already gathered, be able to predict exactly when and where the next crime is going to be committed," Holmes said. "But the fact is that with each crime he commits, the more evidence he leaves behind, and the chances of catching him are increased."

"What do we do next?" I asked.

"We wait for Lestrade to arrive with news of the next crime," Holmes replied.

"You are sure that will happen?"

"Of course, Watson," Holmes answered. "It's been four hours since the bank robbery. Our mastermind is overdue, I should think."

A violent knocking upon the door interrupted our conversation. I'd seen this happen so many times before that it didn't surprise me to see Lestrade rush through the door with a constable.

"University College, Mr. Holmes," Lestrade said. "Someone tried to burn down the mathematics department."

"It appears our mastermind has progressed to arson, my dear Watson," Holmes said.

"Luckily, it being so late, no one was in the classroom when the fire broke out, so no one was injured, Mr. Holmes," Lestrade added.

"As expected, Inspector," Holmes said.

"But I fail to see how our mastermind expects to create income with this sort of crime," said I.

Holmes glanced at me. "That's because this is a personal invitation aimed at me, Watson. We must leave immediately. I suspect we are finally at the end game."

When we arrived at University College, the Headmaster, a silver haired and bearded ancient man half a head taller than Holmes led us to the college mathematical department. In the middle of the room was a pile of partially burned desks and chairs. The odour of burnt wood permeated my nostrils but strangely, there was no smoke or ambient heat coming from the pile. Someone had physically collected the desks and chairs there, poured a flammable liquid upon them then lit it like a funeral pyre.

"Amazingly," the Headmaster said. "The fire burned itself out before it could spread. I was just retiring for the night when I saw the blaze through the window in the door. I called for a constable and the fire department immediately."

Holmes briefly inspected the makeshift pyre, stepping around it with his hands behind his back. "There wasn't enough fuel added to the wood to sustain a continued blaze. It appears its purpose was to burn long enough to get attention. Tell me, Headmaster, where are the fire fighters?"

"Once they saw that it was self-contained and made sure it wouldn't reignite, they tended to a more serious matter somewhere else in the city."

Holmes continued his intense inspection of the pyre then glanced towards the far wall, where the math professor's desk used to sit. "Watson!" he exploded. "I think I have solved the mystery of the symbols!"

CHAPTER SEVEN

Against the far wall was a giant hanging tapestry, probably as old as the institution in which it hung. It was titled *Mathematical Symbols* and below the title were dozens of symbols. As if to prove his point, Holmes handed me the six cards for me to compare.

I fluttered through the cards and was gobsmacked. Sure enough, there they were; the symbol on card number one, the single horizontal line, stood for *minus*. Symbol number two, the "X", meant *multiplied by*. Symbol three, the two horizontal lines, one on top of the other, meant *is equal to*. Symbol four, the two horizontal lines with the diagonal line crossed through them, meant *is not equal to*. Symbol five, the single squiggly line, meant *is similar to*. And the sixth symbol, the circle with the diagonal line through it, meant *empty set*.

I wasn't sure what they meant as a grouping and thought that maybe, if perhaps there was a seventh symbol card hidden in the room somewhere, I could solve their collective meaning. I pocketed the cards and began searching the window sills and the walls. In my searching, I noticed Holmes speaking with Lestrade and the Headmaster near the door. I couldn't hear what they were talking about, but I did see Lestrade and the Headmaster nod then hurriedly leave the room.

"What in blazes are you doing, Watson?" Holmes asked as he approached.

"I'm searching for a seventh symbol card," I replied.

"I applaud your enthusiasm, my friend," Holmes said through a half laugh. "But I'm afraid you're chasing a ghost.

No card will be found in here. Our most recent clue will be found on the tapestry. Look at the *pi* symbol."

Halfway down the tapestry, the *pi* symbol was sandwiched between the *Theta* and the *for all* symbol, but the *pi* symbol was circled in red ink. It couldn't have been more obvious, yet I'd missed it completely.

I was familiar with *pi* and that its sum of 3.14159 was used to find the circumference and area of a circle and was confused how this related to our current predicament. I let Holmes know of my concern.

"Ah, yes," said he. "We must forget the practical use of the sum and tell me instead what the symbol resembles."

I concentrated on the symbol for a moment and said the first thing that came to mind: "A door?"

"Correct, my friend. Our mastermind is letting us know that there is a secret entrance behind this tapestry. Let us continue to follow the bouncing ball," Holmes said and rushed over to the tapestry. It hung on a long swinging arm between two stone pillars that were as tall as the ceiling. Holmes grabbed the tapestry and pulled it back, revealing a blank ancient stone and mortar wall.

I refrained from mentioning to Holmes that the wall seemed to be lacking a door, and instead, watched as he ran his fingers along the hard, rough cricks and crevices and uneven surface of the wall. He went from left to right then back again. He stopped suddenly, next to the left pillar, ran his fingers up then down then he froze in place. The fingers on his right hand were pressed against a small grey rectangular stone in which the top end was subtly higher than the bottom end.

"Have you found something?" I asked.

In answer, Holmes pressed the top end of the stone and it snapped down while the bottom end snapped up.

Immediately, there was a low hum and the floor underneath my feet vibrated. Then the entire wall slowly moved away from me, opening as a door would open, revealing a stone-walled corridor that angled down by way of well-worn stone steps. A series of yellow electric lights clung to the ceiling of the corridor, inviting us into its well-lit maw.

"Are you with me, Watson?" Holmes asked as he stole a piece of chalk from a nearby chalkboard.

"I could never let you tackle this alone, Holmes," said I.

"I appreciate the sentiment, old friend," Holmes said. "But I must warn you, what awaits us at the end of this corridor is supremely dangerous. If I haven't thought this through properly, it could mean the end of our lives."

"I've put my life in your hands before, Holmes," said I. "And I've never regretted it. I shall do it again."

Holmes gave me a reassuring pat on the arm, hurried down the steps and into the corridor. I followed him down. The ground vibrated again, I turned around and watched as the stone door swung round and sealed itself with a dull thud. No sign of the door could be discerned; it resembled a regular stone wall.

Holmes approached the door and pointed out the mechanical boxes, springs, and hinges upon which the door was connected to. "Impressive," he said. "An electrical generator and engine powered by a stack of powerful chemical batteries. A great improvement over what we have now. I can imagine this technology used a thousand different ways in the near future."

"The product of a genius," I mused in awe.

"Unquestionably, Watson... an evil genius," Holmes said, then drew a giant "X" on the wall where the door was. Holmes's body seemed filled with energy; his excitement, as we traversed the corridor, was especially displayed through the quick, smooth and youthful movements of his limbs. Every twenty or so steps, he stopped and marked the walls with an arrow pointing in the direction in which we were traveling. I thought it a prudent policy that would lead us safely back out of the winding maze.

We came to an intersection of two openings, each turned in a different direction, one to the left, the other to the right. Above each opening a mathematical sign was carved into the living stone. The opening on the left was marked by a "<" symbol. The opening on the right was marked by a ">" symbol.

"Which opening should we choose?" I asked.

"You don't remember what that tapestry taught us about the symbols, Watson?"

I shook my head. "There were too many for me to remember, I'm afraid."

"We follow the *is greater than* symbol, the opening on the right."

More downward steps as the corridor veered to the right, straightened then veered to the left. We were going deeper and deeper into the earth, the scent of dirt and must grew overpowering with every step we took.

"These latest tunnels are recent constructions," Holmes said aloud. "They are made to look ancient. I feel we are ever so close to the spider hiding in its web."

We marched on, down and down. There was no other time in my life that I yearned more to have my service revolver in my hand, but I hadn't expected to join Holmes on a case when I'd decided to visit him.

Finally, the corridor ended, and we came to a pair of stone doors on opposite, facing walls. The door on the left wall was marked by a sideways figure eight symbol. The door on the right wall was marked by an upside down "A" symbol. I looked to Holmes for guidance, watching as he worked the meaning of the symbols out in his mind while standing silently in the middle of the corridor. Repeatedly, he turned his face from one door to the other, rubbing his chin, until finally he moved towards the door on the left wall and marked it with an "X".

"Be prepared, Watson," he said. "For what is behind this door is an evil encapsulated in such hate and revenge that you've seen nothing like it before."

I took a deep breath as Holmes reached out, found the secret switch in the wall and activated it. The stone door hissed, moaned and screeched as it scratched along the stone in the floor. In the darkness of the cavernous room, beyond the screaming door, came the most spine tingling, nerve rattling sound I've ever heard.

CHAPTER EIGHT

Once Holmes and I stepped into the darkness and the door closed and locked behind us, that horrible sound grew louder. As I write this, it gives me chills to recall and describe the grizzly peculiarities of it. Its repeating cacophony echoed in the darkness, coming from somewhere in the unknown distance in front of us. It began with a disturbing high-pitched whine then fell into a low, electrical hum which led into a metallic click followed immediately by a thump and an extended hiss. It ended with a quick, raspy cough and a second thump. Over and over this nightmarish clatter cycled in the near distance.

It was all made more unsettling in the fact that I had no idea where we were. The depth and strength of the echoes called to my mind a massive underground cavern and my imagination ran away with itself, creating mile high stalagmites ready to topple over and thousands of bats whispering around in great, sweeping black clouds. It was all so overwhelming to me that I felt my legs going soft.

"Holmes…" I murmured.

"Steady, my friend," Holmes urged, easily picking up the fear in my voice.

In the meantime, that repeating, inhuman, machine-like breathing seemed to grow louder in the darkness. Then it was as if we were standing directly under the sun. That eternally deep darkness was suddenly an all-encompassing bright white light so intense that I had to cover my eyes with my arms to combat blindness. When my eyes finally adjusted, the details of our surroundings were revealed.

Holmes and I were standing upon a small square stone outcropping, large enough for the two of us to stand. In the wall behind us, on both sides of the door, were a series of brightly lit sconces that were connected to lines of thick metal conduit that disappeared up the wall and into the shadows of what appeared to be a subterranean chamber so large, the light from the sconces couldn't reach its furthest spaces. Beyond our meagre outcropping was a chasm, again, so deep I couldn't see the bottom. Across from us, perhaps twenty feet away, I could barely make out another outcropping facing ours. Whatever was making that terrible mechanical breathing was coming from the shadows that cloaked that outcropping.

Holmes squinted intensely in that direction, then he flashed a grin, as if he could see through the darkness.

The unmistakable sound of footsteps drew nearer, and I saw movement in the darkness on the other outcropping. Then the movement stopped, but the breathing continued.

"Holmes," said a weak, fragile, ancient voice that sounded more like the long, slow hiss of a snake. There was a remnant of satisfaction, or was it pleasure, colouring the attitude of the speaker.

"Come closer!" Holmes ordered. "So that my friend can see who we are captive of."

Out of the shadows came a tall bald man pushing another man in a three-wheeled wheelchair. I recognized the bald man immediately, he was the man who'd kidnapped the Earl of Inniswitch's daughter, but the man who sat in the wheelchair I didn't recognize.

He was a small, ancient man with a rather large, misshapen, hairless head. He sat hunched forward in his seat with his arms screwed up in a semi-praying mantis pose, his gnarled left hand was on a steering rod that was attached to the front wheel of his chair and his right hand struggled to keep a pistol balanced and pointed at Holmes. His useless legs were covered by a steel grey blanket but underneath I could discern that they were merely nothing but skin and bone. He seemed more insectoid than human but what was even more alarming to me was the peculiar characteristics of his chair.

Attached to the back of the chair was a jumble of mechanical contraptions, among them metallic compressors, engine generators, stacks of chemical batteries, valves, wires and cables. All this technology was apparently used to power a metallic shell that enveloped the man's torso, inside the shell was some kind of rubber bladder that inflated and deflated, squeezing the torso, helping the man breathe and jerking his entire body violently as it cycled. These were the origins of the haunting breathing and electrical hums that filled the stale air of the chamber. I'd never seen such a machine and it, quite honestly, filled me with horror. It seemed to me an abomination of everything that was good about life and death, as unnatural as men flying in their noisy aero planes.

"My-my God, Holmes-," I stammered.

"Quite, my friend," Holmes said. "There's your genius in the flesh."

"Holmes," the man hissed again, between inflations. "It has been seventeen years. Much too long."

"On the contrary, Professor," Holmes said. "I don't think it's been long enough."

"Professor?" I asked, fearing the reply I would receive from Holmes.

"Yes, Watson," Holmes said. "Reacquaint yourself with the famous, and apparently immortal, Professor Moriarty!"

CHAPTER NINE

"Good Lord!" I exclaimed breathlessly. "It can't be!" The abominable creature sitting in that ghastly chair stirred, his narrowed gaze fell upon me.

"It's true, Watson," Holmes retorted. "Now you understand the meaning of those mathematical symbol cards that were left behind at every crime scene, it was our greatest foe telling us that it was he, Professor of Mathematics, James Moriarty, returned from the dead and bent on revenge. I suspected who we were dealing with when Lestrade told us that there was a fire in the mathematical department at University College. As soon as I saw the tapestry, my suspicions were confirmed."

I stared back at Moriarty in disbelief and derision.

"Doctor Watson," he hissed. "Do you recognize my assistant?"

"Only from this morning," I answered.

A strained, gurgling laugh came from Moriarty, the pistol trembled in his hand. "Look closer, Doctor. His name is Luca. He was the Swiss youth messenger I sent to remove you. From the scene of my final contest. With Holmes. Luca was waiting for me. At the bottom of the Reichenbach Falls. Pulled me out of the water. And to the safety of my waiting carriage. While Colonel Moran tried to finish. What I couldn't do upon the mountainside. To kill Holmes."

"And he was just as successful as you were, Professor," Holmes said smugly. "Three years later I tricked the Colonel and sealed his own fate."

Moriarty's pale, inhuman, misshapen head reddened. "Yes. A good man. Loyal to me. Still rotting away in prison.

You shall pay for that also. But know that soon. Soon. I shall free The Colonel. My old friend."

I remembered well the Swiss youth who had given me that deceptive missive all those years ago. It was hard for me to reconcile the huge hulk of a man standing behind Moriarty with that fresh faced, skinny, blonde haired boy until I looked at Luca's intense blue eyes. They were the same.

"I've always suspected you'd survived the falls, Professor," Holmes said. "As your body was never recovered from the scene. And I've always wondered what had become of you."

"Luca and the Colonel whisked me away. And as you spent the next three years. Traveling the world. Dismantling my criminal empire. The finest doctors in Europe. Were trying to heal my broken body." He coughed, then continued. "My spine, crushed like a dried bug under a shoe. I lay in bed. Helpless. Immobile from the chest down. And with every year that passed. My body deteriorated until. The function of my lungs ceased. I had to be inserted. Into the grip. Of an unreliable. Steam-powered iron lung contraption. Day after day. Year after year. I lay on my back. My body wasting away. But my mind was sharp and facile as ever. My thoughts never strayed from you, Holmes. My anger. My hatred. My need for justice-"

"You mean revenge, Professor," Holmes corrected.

"-kept me alive. And I planned your demise down to the smallest detail. But in my helpless state. I could not set my plan into motion. My anger and hatred for you grew. Then, a Croatian scientist. Invented this portable exo-lung. Allowing me a reasonably normal life. And the ability to finally taste my revenge. But at great financial cost. Hence, the need to create income-"

"Not for a growing criminal empire," Holmes interrupted. "But to maintain your current living conditions. All to satisfy this obsessive need for revenge upon me."

"Exactly, Holmes."

"Ha! I'm flattered, Professor."

Moriarty groaned angrily and steadied his pistol.

"But this place," Holmes continued, motioning into the air with both hands. It seemed to me that Holmes was stalling for time, trying to keep the monster in the exo-lung talking. "How did you secure it?"

"One of my old haunts, Holmes. One of many hidden all across England. Here, your bones shall rot for eternity."

I was tired of Moriarty's continued threats, and my temper suddenly got the best of me. "You talk about Holmes being your motivation for living," I shouted. "What will become of you after he's dead? What will your motivation for living be then?"

The beast laughed again. "With your friend gone. The accumulation of new wealth. And the rebuilding. Of my criminal empire will suffice, good doctor. Unlike you and the great Sherlock Holmes, I will go on living."

"Living?" I repeated. "You call what you are, alive?"

"You disappoint me, Doctor," Moriarty said. "As a man of medicine, I was sure it would be you that would appreciate the miracles of modern technology."

"What I see sitting in that chair is not a miracle to me, Professor," said I. "It's something in between, something evil and unnatural. An abomination!"

Moriarty sighed. "You fail to see the new truth. Of our current world."

"And what new truth is that?"

"We are old men. In a new world of technological wonders, Doctor. I have accepted this truth. And will continue to embrace. What this new world has to offer."

"You talk as if you expect to live forever, Professor," Holmes said.

"You see proof of that. Before you, Holmes."

"I'm afraid you will be disappointed, Professor," Holmes countered. "Like human bodies, machines get old, they break down, they fail. Everything is finite – everything has an end."

"Perhaps, Holmes," Moriarty said, raising the pistol. "But today, only you. And the good doctor. Will have an end."

I thought this was it. This was the final end of the great Sherlock Holmes. But I was proud to go with him into the abyss of death, the two of us soldiers against all the evil doers in the world. We had done much good in our lives and I feared not for my soul in the afterlife. So, I closed my eyes and accepted my fate.

As the gunshot cracked through the air, I felt a hand grab my arm then I was pulled to the right and backwards, pushed violently against a wall. That's when the world exploded.

CHAPTER TEN

The powerful rush of a soundwave blew into me, but Holmes was holding me tight, covering me from the brunt of the debris. I managed to turn my head and see the door in which we had entered this hell had been blown out and was filled with smoke. I heard voices shouting beyond the door, outside in the corridor. Another blast rumbled from somewhere across the chasm, this one seemed stronger than the first, it shook the outcropping on which Holmes and I stood, and I feared it would crumble and fall away.

When the blast subsided, Holmes released me and we turned around. Strange thuds and cracks came from above, in the darkness. Moments later, I saw a cloud of boulders and debris falling out from the darkness. The boulders were the size of cannonballs and carriages and made deathly swishing sounds as they passed by, falling into the chasm. But the onslaught didn't subside, it continued, growing heavier with each passing second. Across the chasm I watched as the outcropping on which Moriarty and his assistant stood was pummelled relentlessly.

"The ceiling is giving way!" Holmes shouted. "We must get out of here!"

I nodded and followed him towards the door where the helpful hands of Scotland Yard constables reached out to grab our hands. The last thing I saw before escaping the chaos, was Luca releasing his grip on Moriarty's wheelchair and running away to safety. Moriarty sat in his chair, unable to propel himself out of danger. Instead, he dropped the pistol as the outcropping exploded around him and raised his fist at us. Then a giant boulder struck him, destroying the rest of the outcropping.

Moriarty was finally gone.

*****

While we stood in the corridor, Lestrade swiped the dust and debris from Holmes's shoulders. The members of Scotland Yard's demolition crew were busy surveying the immediate area, making sure there wasn't a chance of a cave in where we stood.

"You cut that a little too close, Lestrade," Holmes said.

"I apologize, Mr. Holmes," Lestrade said sincerely. "We got lost on our way down."

"But I left you arrows on the walls, directing you to where we were."

"Right, we saw them. We just took a wrong turn somewhere."

"Well, I for one am glad you finally found us," I said, sweeping off my own shoulders.

"Did you capture Luca?" Holmes asked.

"Yes, Mr. Holmes," Lestrade answered. "My men caught him coming out the door on the other side. Took three of us to secure him."

"Then all seems to be accounted for," said Holmes. "What do you say we get a spot of brandy, Watson? I believe we deserve it."

"I couldn't agree with you more, my friend," said I.

As Holmes and I journeyed back through the corridor, I realized that he, again, had been one step ahead of his adversary. Even though there had been a singular earlier moment of self-doubt, in the end, he performed as he always had. And I recalled the warning he gave me before we embarked on this latest adventure, and the answer I gave him; that I trusted him with my life.

Events, again, justified my answer. But perhaps a second visit to my cousin in Torquay, was in order.

The Body at the Ritz

by Stephen Herczeg

Life in the late nineteenth century was an active time in the annals of human history, especially in London. Man's intelligence had always set us apart from the greater animal population, but with James Watt's improvements on Thomas Newcomen's original designs for the steam engine having been put in place half a century ago, man's ingenuity had only been slightly outstripped by his imagination.

I sat on the balcony, with my breakfast coffee and looked out across the wide region that is greater London and smiled at the commotion at play as the populace went about their daily lives.

Horseless carriages, belching puffs of steam along with wisps of black coal smoke, trundled along the byways below. Dirigibles, large and small, ferried goods and people through the airways thick with clouds. Great zeppelins ploughed their way through the upper atmosphere connecting countries like never before and opening up new horizons and bringing new peoples into the modern world.

Wars were almost a thing of the past as technological improvements eradicated the ever present need to gain resources or land from neighbours.

Sadly, though, one element was always present within any society and led to the need for men such as myself and my erstwhile companion, Mr. Sherlock Holmes.

Crime.

Be it theft. Be it murder. Or any of the multitude of variations that the human mind can muster. There will always be a need for a constabulary to investigate and solve the crimes of men, and when the officials are at the end of their tethers, they call upon outside help such as only we can lend.

I finished my coffee and withdrew back inside.

There I found Holmes in an accustomed position. He sat in an easy chair, resplendent in a silk smoking jacket, a pipe in mouth, poring over the daily paper.

He looked up as I entered and smiled.

"A lovely, quiet day, eh Watson?"

I placed my cup on the tea tray nearby as I answered.

"Yes, yes, it is Holmes. A wonderful time to be alive."

He grinned.

"A bit dull though. I've had nothing to perplex my brain for a good week."

I hadn't realised this and became wary. When Holmes was unoccupied his mind slipped into a state of ennui and could have dire consequences as he sought out other means to temper his boredom.

"Don't worry Watson, I'm not going to embark on any drug fuelled fervour any time soon. I was just remarking that there seems to be a paucity of crime at the moment. Well, crime that requires my attention anyway," he said.

I sighed with relief but made a mental note to monitor my friend's movements in case of any obvious deviations from the norm that would indicate some chemical abuse.

"I was thinking of going to the Diogenes later for luncheon. Mycroft mentioned that he would be there today. It might be good to catch up with him. You never know he may let slip some little snippet of information that leads to an entertaining case," he said.

I agreed and packed up the tea tray and cups to take down to Mrs. Hudson, more for something to do than anything else, though I do like to help our landlady out when the opportunity arises.

As I reached the doorway a *shoomp* noise echoed up the stairway. Holmes looked up and grinned again. I knew the noise to mean the arrival of something in the sealed vacuum tube messaging system.

Moments later, the sound of footsteps on the stairs greeted us and the door opened to reveal Mrs. Hudson holding a rolled-up parchment. She handed the note to me and took away the tea-tray.

"Thank you, Doctor, but you needn't have minded, I'm quite able to clear the dishes away," she said with a grin as she bustled off.

I blanched at the slight rebuke, then looked down at the note. It was addressed to Holmes, so I gave it straight to him and waited, curiosity writ large on my face.

Holmes read quietly to himself, then looked up and smiled.

"The game is afoot," he said.

*****

On our ascent to the rooftop, Holmes stopped by and handed a note of reply to Mrs. Hudson.

"See this is delivered immediately, and thank you," he said to her.

I was still mystified as to the nature of the original message and intrigued about what faced us.

Once outside, I triggered the cab request lever and immediately a hidden mechanism fired up, filled a small balloon with compressed hydrogen then released it on a long line. The balloon ascended above 221B Baker Street and floated into the sky lanes to be spied by the floating network of view finders operated by the Greater London Cab company.

Within a few minutes we noticed a black dirigible deviate from the throng of others of its kind passing overhead and move in our direction.

I triggered the reverse switch on the mechanism and the balloon retracted to avoid entanglement with the vehicle as it approached.

I finally asked Holmes what the note was about.

He replied, "Lestrade has found a body."

"Nothing unusual in that," I said.

"True, but this one was found in a small alleyway off of Piccadilly."

"Again, nothing unusual."

Holmes smiled.

"Outside of the Ritz," he said.

"Oh," I said, "we've been called on the insistence of Sir Rupert, then?"

Holmes nodded and looked up as the dirigible finished its descent. Its landing claw reached out and grasped the edge of the roof platform letting out a mechanical *clank*.

We bade the pilot a good day and boarded. Whilst Holmes gave him our destination, I sat in one of the front seats so as to distribute the weight evenly. Holmes joined me, and we heard the motors whirr and felt the aircraft begin to rise. With a slight bump, as the claw detached, we were away.

The pilot ascended to join the other airships and craft flying along in the sky lanes and headed south towards St. James's Park. I craned to my right and took much pleasure in viewing the landscape below.

Within moments we were crossing Marylebone and drifting within sight of the lush greenery of Hyde Park. Soon, the architecture changed from the simple Georgian and Victorian terraces of Marylebone to towering neo-Gothic structures clad with shiny bronze scales and plates.

This style of building had only come into play in the last ten years or so and was more a reflection of the tastes of the nouveau riche than for any structural or functional purposes.

The pilot turned the airship and began his approach to the landing platform at the top of the Ritz Hotel.

I viewed the building with a slight amount of awe. The current owner, Sir Rupert Linklatter, had taken the once elegant five story Georgian hotel and added another five stories all clad in brightly shining brass plating with several glass elevators that traversed the exterior overlooking Piccadilly. At night, the hotel was lit up like a beacon with electric lights playing across the façade, reflecting off the myriad bronze plates and shining back across the roadway below and buildings opposite. It was quite a spectacle, one that I had watched on a few occasions but had never been overly enamoured with.

Sir Rupert had made his fortune from coal mining in the Newcastle region, controlling much of the fuel that drove the new industrial age and reaping the benefits. The Ritz was his domain in London. It provided both a high cost hotel to the rich and famous and a luxurious inner-London sanctum for Sir Rupert and his family.

As could be expected, Sir Rupert's status attracted a high level of protection from those in the upper echelons of the political power base. Holmes had enamoured himself to Sir Rupert a few years back when he helped to discover the true nature of the disappearance of the Countess Bruckheimer from within her suite at the Ritz. Holmes managed to solve the case quietly and quickly without drawing any adverse attention upon the Ritz and Sir Rupert. Henceforth, on orders from those in power, the local constabulary often played second fiddle to Holmes when any crimes were discovered in the general area of the Ritz.

The pilot brought us in to dock at the landing platform built out from the roof of the Ritz. I paid the man and followed Holmes from the craft. A well-dressed couple in their sixties entered the airship and were away before we had even crossed the roof to the Hotel's entrance, such was the pace of modern life.

As we approached the main doors, I saw Holmes nod towards the footman and receive a knowing look in return. I assumed this was one of Holmes's informants and wondered if he would prove useful to us later.

The footman opened the doors for us to reveal a tall, lanky man dressed in a dinner suit, waiting inside. He bowed and introduced himself as Allaister Croan, Sir Rupert's assistant. He shook our hands and led us through the hotel at a cracking pace. I struggled to keep up, but Holmes, being almost as tall, had no trouble.

"Sir Rupert expresses his gratitude, in advance, of you solving this little dilemma," Croan said.

"But, the body was found outside, surely that bears no problem for the Hotel," I said.

Croan stopped and turned to face me. His face took on a very serious tone.

"Sir Rupert has a very exclusive clientele. The mere presence of the constabulary fills him with dread and he would appreciate all avenues being taken to keep the details of this matter private and away from the day to day operations of the hotel," he said.

To punctuate his sentence further and to stress the importance to Sir Rupert, he continued with, "And the Prime Minister is evidently aware as well."

He turned and moved on. Holmes dropped back to walk beside me. I could see a familiar grin on his face. Holmes has never been one for power players. To him, a crime is a crime, whether it involves a Prince or a pauper.

As we walked, my eyes strayed to the lush pile of the carpet we traversed. Most hotel carpets consist of a short, hardy pile, but this was long and thick, probably woollen and of an extremely high quality. The swirling black, grey and white pattern that repeated every ten feet or so, was intricate and would have added more to the cost.

Finally, we were shown to a side door that opened out into the alleyway beyond.

Lestrade stood with his arms crossed waiting in impatient anticipation for our arrival. As we stepped into the alley, he unfolded his arms and relaxed slightly. He stepped to his right and unveiled the object of our attention.

Slumped, with his back against the wall was the lonely figure of the victim. His head hung down with his hands folded in his lap and legs jutting straight out from the wall.

He wore a long red velvet frock coat, which was bunched beneath him and soaking up the water from an early morning shower.

Beneath the coat he sported a beige waistcoat, white collarless shirt and a dark brown cravat. His dark brown tweed pants were tucked into knee high leather boots. All his clothing was of exquisite taste and smacked of expense. On first observations, this was a well to do man about town. One that would fit in to the exclusivity of the Ritz seamlessly.

Holmes approached the scene and circled around to the front of the body, carefully avoiding any clues that may lay in the immediate area.

He scanned the ground, bending down from time to time to observe some ephemera. Satisfied that there was nothing of interest he moved in closer to the body.

"Male, Caucasian, approximately thirty to thirty-five years of age," Holmes said.

He stepped back for a moment, scanning the man's entire body.

"Approximately, five foot ten inches in height, about one hundred and seventy pounds. So not overweight, but not overtly athletic," he said.

I piped up with an observation of my own, "There's no hat. The current style for one wearing a frock coat and boots is to accompany it with a top hat, is it not? There is none laying around the immediate area either."

Holmes looked towards me and smiled.

"Very good Watson, very good. What does it tell you?"

"That he either lost it before entering the alleyway or it was taken from him," I replied.

Holmes nodded then reached into his inner coat pocket and extracted his goggles. He placed them over his eyes and turned a small side screw that pushed the lenses away from his face, enabling him to zoom in and magnify some minor details that were invisible to the naked eye. He pulled on a pair of fine kid gloves and for the first time reached in to touch the victim's body.

He gently picked up each of the man's hands, in turn, and examined the palms and especially the fingertips. Murmuring to himself as he did so. He bent down and sniffed the man's palms, which I found a little strange, even for Holmes, but chose to ignore it in the interests of the investigation.

Holmes placed the man's hands back in his lap and turned to Lestrade, addressing the Inspector for the first time since our arrival.

"I assume you have already searched him for identification?"

Lestrade looked affronted.

"I have my orders to leave everything alone and wait for you. I wouldn't want to get Sir Rupert offside now, would I?" Lestrade replied with a heavy dose of sarcasm.

Holmes smiled widely, knowing full well what Lestrade meant.

"Found nothing then?"

Lestrade nodded.

"Nothing at all?" asked Holmes with a hint of surprise.

"Absolutely nothing. Clean as a new bought suit," Lestrade replied.

Holmes murmured to himself.

"Why Holmes?" I asked.

"Because Watson, what we have here is a scene depicting a robbery that has gone a little wrong, resulting in a dead body."

"Yes."

"But if you had just accidentally, or even purposely, killed someone you would take the most obvious things, wallet, watch, maybe keys, and leave quickly. This man has been picked clean, including his hat and possibly glasses or goggles."

He stood and scanned around the area again, then took off his right glove, reached down and felt the collar of the man's frock coat.

"Dry," he said.

"It rained this morning," said Lestrade, "Around seven o'clock."

"Well that gives us our estimated time of death. Sometime after seven o'clock," I said.

Holmes didn't seem convinced.

"Unless," he said.

He hunkered down and pushed his finger into the man's cheek. There was considerable resistance. He returned his attention to the man's hands and prodded the thenar eminence, the fleshy part beneath the thumb, with his finger. The indentation stayed put for quite a while.

"Rigor mortis is quite pronounced," he said.

"Yes. In this weather I would put the time of death closer to four to six hours ago, not two," I said.

"Precisely," said Holmes as he stood up, "I believe this man was killed elsewhere and dumped here. Why? I have no idea and still need more facts to prove my assumption."

He reached into his coat and extracted a strange tool. It was a long wand shaped brass cylinder, with a clear crystal at one end and a small crank handle towards the middle.

Holmes turned the handle which caused the device to emit a whirring noise as some unseen engine within began to turn. As the crystal started to glow with an inner luminescence, Holmes moved it towards the dead man's coat.

The crystal cast a faint blue light over the red material, causing several small specs on the coat to glow white with a slight purple tinge.

Holmes stopped and peered closely at a small spec on the man's coat. He again reached into his coat and pulled out a small pouch of tools. Opening it, he extracted a pair of tweezers then picked the spec out from the fabric of the man's coat. He stared at the item more closely, turning it to gain a better look.

"What have you there, Holmes?" I asked.

"A sliver of glass," he said.

Holmes put the sliver aside, then returned to examine the man, murmuring as he moved the wand across the man's coat, hovering over a bright spot on the left lapel. He opened the man's coat and waved the wand across his vest and shirt. No more spots showed up which must have confused Holmes as he let out a surprised little murmur.

He shifted his attention to the man's legs and moved the wand down his trouser legs. He looked at the man's boots and with the tweezers pulled out another clue. He held it up to the light and adjusted his lenses to magnify the object.

"What have you there, Holmes?" I asked.

"A woollen thread. Carpet. Dark grey. Similar to something we saw not long ago," he said.

"The carpet in the hallway of the Ritz," I said.

Holmes nodded and turned the man's legs out to check the backs as best he could. I noticed a scuff mark on the back of one beautifully polished boot. Another nod of the head told me Holmes considered this to be a clue. I decided to let him continue without distraction.

He pulled back and wound the little device's handle again.

Turning to Lestrade, he said, "Inspector, if you would be so kind, can you tilt the body forward so that I can examine his back?"

126

Lestrade, happy to be useful, leapt at the opportunity and gently tilted the man forward.

Holmes ran his wand across the man's back and let out an exclamation. I moved to a position where I could see his find.

The light now showed several large bright white spots that ran down the man's back from the collar. The spots were ill defined and appeared to be smudges.

"What the Devil?" I asked.

Holmes said, "Blood, Watson, blood. This little device contains an yttrium crystal, which emits ultraviolet light when stimulated by static electricity. The little crank turns a small leather band inside which charges the crystal. Blood stains always show up under ultraviolet light, no matter how well you try to clean them. As we have just seen."

He reached in with the pair of tweezers again and pulled out a small spike of glass.

"And more glass," he said placing it to the side.

He brought his hand up to the man's shirt collar and pulled the cravat away. We all immediately saw a small puncture mark at the base of the man's skull just below his hairline.

"Good Lord," said Lestrade, "That wasn't done by some Johnny on the street, that was done by a professional. It almost looks like an ice-pick or needle wound."

"Very true, Inspector," said Holmes, "Very true."

He stood up and Lestrade returned the body to the wall. I piped up as a small memory came to the fore.

"That wound is very reminiscent of the one we found on Professor Bhargava who was visiting Durham University from Paris two years ago," I said.

Holmes nodded, his face became stern.

"Yes...Yes it is, Watson. We never found the assailant, but my inquiries led me back to the Vishkanya, a league of assassins for hire operating out of India many years ago."

He stared at the body for a moment then up to the brightly lit upper floors of the Ritz hotel.

"I don't wish to jump to conclusions about the assailant, I don't have enough information for that, but I am sure that this man was killed inside the Ritz and was subsequently moved here. I found a small thread probably from the thick carpet in the hallways. Then there are the specs of glass, and the marks on the back of the man's boots lead me to believe that his demise resulted in a large amount of damage to some furniture."

Holmes looked further down the alleyway, away from the blazing lights of Piccadilly. I followed along, leaving a confused Lestrade with the body.

We quickly came to the corner of the hotel and peered around into another darkened alleyway.

"Aha," said Holmes as he spied something sitting near the wall amongst a pile of similar detritus. He moved over to the pile and grabbed hold of a slender cylinder of wood and pulled the frame of a low wooden table from the pile.

He set the frame up on the three remaining legs. The top was missing but appeared to have been glass as there were shards still attached to the frame mountings on each corner.

"What do you make of it, Holmes?" I asked.

"Not a lot, Watson, but if I was to project a story from what we've seen, I would say that our dead man was attacked from behind and stabbed in the neck. He then staggered back, tripped against the edge of this table and fell through the glass top, shattering it and breaking off one of the legs. He was then cleaned up, removed from the hotel room and deposited in the alleyway beyond. The room was thoroughly cleansed, and the broken table placed here amongst the other refuse from the day to day operations of the hotel."

Holmes pulled out his crystal wand and wound the handle once more. He ran the wand around the edges of the table and found another bright spot on some of the glass on one corner.

"Is it the dead man's?" I asked.

Holmes shook his head.

"I don't think so, there were no other wounds on the body. Even the blood stain on the front of his coat wasn't from him. I believe our assailant cut themselves before rummaging around in the man's pockets," he said.

He stood up, put his wand away and brushed his hands together to remove the dust and grime from the table frame.

"In my mind, it does confirm that the man was murdered inside the hotel. The question remains, did the assailant remove him or the hotel staff themselves?"

"Given Sir Rupert's predilection to protect his hotel's reputation, I would say the latter," I said.

Holmes nodded.

"Quite so, Watson."

We turned back towards the corner and the other alleyway when a voice piped up behind us.

"Oi," it said.

We turned and saw a man standing in the shadows a little further down the alleyway. I could just make out his features and realised it was the doorman from the roof. He shuffled his feet and looked around nervously as if expecting to be found out at any moment.

Holmes strode straight up to him.

"Hello Frankie," he said.

"Mr. 'olmes," he returned, tipping his hat slightly, "Sorry I couldn't say anything upstairs. Mr. Croan scares the bejesus out o' me."

"That's fine, Frankie, what would you like to say?" asked Holmes.

Frankie lifted his chin to indicate the adjacent alleyway.

"The body, round the corner, 'e's been 'ere before."

"News travels fast," I said.

"I keeps me nose to the ground, I do. Mr. 'olmes pays me to do it," he retorted.

"Yes, go on. Do you know who the man is?" Holmes asked.

"Nah, but 'e's been here a few times. Comes in an' meets with another gent and the boss, mostly up on the top floor," he said.

"That would be Sir Rupert's office?"

"Yeah, yeah. And then sometimes 'e stays after. Flashes the cash around. Sometimes brings the ladies 'ere. Mostly ladies of the night, if you know wot I mean," he grinned.

Holmes nodded, "Yes, I know what you mean. When did he come this morning?"

"Well that was weird. 'e arrived about four o'clock. I was on duty upstairs, 'e brings in a tall, dark 'aired girl. Beautiful she was. Foreign though, but still beautiful. They booked into a suite and I suppose got down to it. Maid came about seven this morning with breakfast, went in and found 'im dead as a doornail on top of the smashed coffee table. Mr. Croan found out, all 'ell broke loose, and then 'e was dumped downstairs."

"I suppose if I asked anybody else, they would deny everything?"

"Yep, word's gone out. Immediate sacking or worse."

He looked around nervously again.

"I gotta go before it's me," he said.

I quickly butted in, "Can I just ask, you mentioned the other gent, who is that?"

Frankie turned to me, his expression showed that he had no idea who I was.

"It's alright, Frankie, this is Doctor Watson, my associate," Holmes said.

Frankie relaxed, "The other gent is the Scots man, Sir Stannis McDonald."

My mouth dropped open at the mention of that name.

"Thank you, Frankie, you've answered a few questions I had. There'll be something extra in your payment this month," Holmes said.

"Oh, fank you, Mr. 'olmes," he said and vanished through a side door.

"Sir Stannis?" I asked, "Head of the Watt Steam company? What would he be doing here?"

Holmes turned, "It's becoming clearer, Watson, but there are still several pieces missing."

*****

We found Lestrade leaning against a wall, biding his time but becoming frustrated with inaction. He got to his feet as he saw us enter the alleyway.

"Well?" he asked.

Holmes strode up to the corpse again and indicated for both of us to join him. He hunched down and picked up the man's hands again. He turned them over and revealed numerous callouses on the man's fingers and palms.

They were not the hands of a man that the clothes he wore heralded. This man was a tradesman of sorts and a hardworking one at that. I tried to work out how someone in a trade, no matter how hard he toiled, could afford the lifestyle he seemed to be living.

Holmes noticed both Lestrade's and my confusion at the state of the man's palms. He pulled out a small tool and picked out some black matter from beneath the man's fingernails. He held the hands out.

"Smell his hands," he said.

In turn, Lestrade and I leant forward and sniffed at the proffered hand. We both reared back in revulsion at the horrid chemical smell.

"Good Lord," said Lestrade.

"What say you, Watson?" asked Holmes.

"Some sort of oil or spirit-based chemical. It's not paraffin, or alcohol," I said.

"No, it's not," said Holmes as he placed the man's hands down again and stood, "It's a new type of fuel called diesel. It is formed from a fractional distillation of petroleum. The black beneath the man's fingernails is possibly asphalt or alkene, one of the by-products of the process."

"A new fuel?" I asked, "Why would we need a new fuel? Coal is used in everything from cars, airships, heating, manufacturing, electricity. It will never be replaced."

Holmes smiled, "True. We have coal, for now, but what if someone could find an alternative. Cleaner, more efficient, cheaper?"

"The human race would advance even quicker than it has so far?" I said.

"Ever the optimist, Watson, that's one of your traits I do so admire. What about who that discovery might affect?"

I thought for a moment before realising where Holmes was going.

"Good Lord. The coal barons. The steam engine companies," I said.

Holmes smiled widely and nodded.

"Yes. Exactly," he said, "And I think they would pay quite handsomely for any information about the development of such fuel and any engines associated with it."

Lestrade's face was a mass of confusion.

"I have no idea what you two are talking about. Care to fill me in, or should I just take care of the body?" he said.

"I think we will require you for the next chapter in this adventure, Inspector. I believe that there will be a need for the yard's services," he said.

He stared off into the distance for a moment, as if recalling some memory from the great databanks of his mind and finally smiled.

"There is only one place that I know of that would require this type of fuel," he said.

*****

Lestrade had a car parked nearby with two uniformed constables within. He directed one to secure the alleyway and wait for the coroner's men to arrive and remove the body.

The other man, Collins, was to drive us to a destination known by Holmes. He gave the address to the man, who then sparked the vehicle into action.

The ground car was a different beast to the airborne dirigible. Collins fired up the coal furnace below the small boiler, ensuring it was stoked with plenty of the black fuel, and released the steam into the drive train when ready. The car lurched forward with a jolt as the inner turbine reached the required pressure. This form of transport had replaced the simple horse and carriage many years before and Holmes's idea that there was a simpler, ever more efficient system in the winds played through my mind, but I flicked it away with a healthy level of derision.

We took a brief stop at the nearest Police Station in Belgravia where Lestrade exited and strode into the station to organise some assistance for Constable Brown back at the Ritz. He quickly returned, and Collins had us away.

We headed south to the Thames and drove along the sprawling and bustling river, alive with boats and ships belching great gouts of black coal smoke and pure white steam, as they plied their trade along the river and supplied the great city with its needs.

We turned onto the Albert Bridge and crossed over the river. To our left was the expanse of Battersea Park, alive with people and their pet dogs. Children played in the bright sunshine and mothers sat in groups talking animatedly to each other.

I often forgot that the average person does not deal with the morbid and depressing sides of human nature that crop up in the life shared by Holmes and me. The only way that most of these people would learn of a body found in an alleyway, would be to see it appear in a column of the daily paper. Then most would glance at the article and turn the page to seek more light-hearted entertainment.

We entered a highly industrial area made up of large workhouses and warehouses. The area looked decidedly less salubrious than that which we had left in Piccadilly and Belgravia. The people walking the street eyed us both with envy, at the level of dress displayed by Holmes and myself,

134

and with suspicion, as we were in a police vehicle with two officers.

We pulled in through a large set of wrought iron gates, with the sign "British Diesel Company" emblazoned above them. The three wings of the building formed a natural courtyard, and we parked before what was evidently the main entrance.

As we exited the vehicle, a loud droning noise greeted us from above. I looked up and saw a massive airship slowing down above the compound. It stopped in mid-air and hovered. Several men emerged from the nearby warehouse and stood looking up at the ship. A loud clanking sound followed by a whirring noise heralded the descent of the lower half of the aircraft's gondola.

The dirigible was one of the newer types of transport craft. A large zeppelin attached to a split-level gondola, the top half being used for controls and engines, the bottom being purely for cargo.

As I watched, the cargo deck was lowered on thick steel cables attached to winches, supposedly secreted in the upper deck. Within about a minute the lower level reached the ground. It was covered in large cylindrical drums with "North Sea Oil Company" logos plastered on them.

The men unloaded the barrels and rolled them to the bottom of a long flat roller system covered by a large continuous sheet of some strong material. Another man, standing to the side, turned a crank handle at the base of a strange looking mechanical device. The contraption let out a few of what seemed to be mechanical coughs then began to run. It belched out huge plumes of black smoke and a deafening roar. My hands shot to my ears to protect them from the din.

The operator moved to a nearby switch, pulled it forward, and the whole belt began to move with a series of screeches and groans.

The other men started to load the barrels onto the belt and they were ferried off into the bowels of the warehouse.

"Fascinating, isn't it?" Holmes said next to me.

"Loud," I yelled.

"Yes, but the power of that primitive engine is incredible," he said.

I looked incredulously back at the contraption. I then realised this was one of the diesel engines that Holmes had been talking about. I noticed, it was a lot smaller than some of the steam engines I was familiar with. Even smaller than the one in the Police vehicle that brought us here.

"Why do you say primitive?" I asked.

"By the looks, it's one of Rudolf Diesel's early prototypes. Nothing goes to waste it seems."

He glanced up and spied the large smoke stacks above us, plus another smaller chimney which had a constant flame pouring from it.

"Very impressive," he said.

"What is?"

"They have their own refinery for fractional distillation of the petroleum in those barrels we saw. They produce their own diesel fuel here. Small quantities I imagine, just enough to power their prototypes and inventions," he said.

I gaped at the chimneys myself, never imagining that such an operation existed in London.

It was then that several of the workers turned and noticed us watching them. They in turn stopped and stared at us. Some probably suspicious of the two police officers.

Another man stepped out of the warehouse and headed straight for the inactive men.

"Right, you lot, quit your lolly-gagging and get this lot unloaded. We can't afford to have that ship sitting here all day," he said.

They all snapped back to work. The foreman turned his attention to us and walked over, a stern look on his face.

"What do you lot want?" his question directed at Lestrade.

Holmes piped up before Lestrade could begin.

"If I may, my good man. We are looking for someone, and you might be just the person to help us. We think that one of your workers had a slight mishap at the Ritz Hotel last night. The Bar Manager was forced to have him thrown out. But before then he was yelling loudly about how he worked for this company and would have the owner come and buy the hotel. Well you can imagine that Sir Rupert Linklatter was not very impressed when he found out and asked us to come and suggest that the chap stay away from now on."

"Seems a bit strange having the police do that," he said.

"Yes. Well, to be honest, it was either us or Sir Rupert's men."

The foreman's face changed to surprise. He nodded.

"Fair cop. Who was it?"

"We only have a description. Five ten. Brown hair. Dressed like a dandy."

The foreman nodded.

"Bloody Danny Green that would be. Came into some money of late. Big notes himself all the time."

The foreman stood up and yelled at the men unloading the dirigible.

"Oi, any of you lot seen Danny today?"

They all shook their heads. He turned back to Holmes.

"I ain't seen him all day either. He only lives around the corner, 13 Beatty Street. Lives with his Mum, the pillock."

The foreman seemed to think this was the end of the conversation. As luck would have it, the men finished their unloading and the raucous noise of the cargo bay ascending blotted out any hope of immediate conversation.

Holmes waited until the noise abated and the airship began to pull away before pressing the foreman.

"If you would be so kind, I think we should talk to Mrs. Fyord, just to warn her in case Sir Rupert decides to visit unannounced," he said.

The foreman smiled, "It's Miss. Miss Madeline Fyord. She's very particular. But, yeah, follow me, I'll see if she's available."

We headed through the main doors and into a brightly lit reception area. Even though we'd been outside in the sun, the light level within this room was almost disorienting.

The foreman laughed as he saw us shielding our eyes from the bright lights.

"Yeah, it takes a little getting used to," he said, "We generate our own electricity. The Boss likes to show off the capabilities of our engines. You don't get lights this bright with steam turbines."

My eyesight finally adjusted, and I could take in more of the details of the room. It was certainly not typical of the exterior of the buildings. The wood panelling had been painted in a clinical white and lacquered to give it a smooth almost glass like appearance. Polished brass had been used extensively to accentuate the white.

At a desk in the centre of the room sat a young woman who eyed us off suspiciously before replacing the look with a well-practiced but welcoming smile. I looked around and realised the foreman was gone.

"Gentlemen," the receptionist said, "Welcome to the British Diesel Company, can I help you in anyway?"

Lestrade took the lead.

"I'm Inspector Lestrade of Her Majesty's Scotland Yard, we would like to see Miss Fyord, if you please," he said.

"Could I ask on what business?" the receptionist asked, her smile fading slightly.

"It's about one of her employees, a Mister Danny Green," he said.

The receptionist pushed a small switch which lit up. She reached for a black polished handset and turned a crank next to it.

Placing the mouth piece to her lips she said, "Sorry to disturb you Miss, but there are several men from Scotland Yard here to see you."

A small indistinct buzzing came from the earpiece.

The young girl answered, "Yes, it's about Danny Green."

More buzzing and the girl eyed us with a slight tinge of concern on her face. She recovered and indicated the large ornate doors to our left.

"Miss Fyord will see you, please just through those doors."

*****

Holmes opened the door to reveal a lavishly decorated office with a large wooden desk in the centre with brass and leather accents.

I noticed a door to the side closing and saw a hint of a long leather boot with a woman's hand sporting black nail polish drawing it shut. I turned towards Holmes and saw that he was apprised of the situation.

We both turned back to the remarkable woman that sat behind the desk. Miss Fyord was more than beautiful. Artists would vie for the chance to carve her in marble just for the chance to gaze upon her face. She sported long tresses of iridescent blonde hair that fell around her alabaster skin. Her piercing blue eyes gazed out below long black eyelashes.

She stood as Holmes approached, and I could see that she was also tall and slim. She wore long leather pants with knee high boots, and her trim figure was compressed into a tight leather waistcoat over a flowing silk blouse.

She held out one immaculately manicured hand and took Holmes's hand in a firm and lingering handshake.

"I am Madeline Fyord, owner of this little enterprise, and you are?"

"Sherlock Holmes, madam," said Holmes, turning to introduce the rest of us, "My associate Doctor Watson, and this is Inspector Lestrade and Constable Collins of Scotland Yard."

Miss Fyord nodded to each of us in turn then sat down. We looked around for chairs but realised there weren't any. I admired that fact as this presented us in a reverse power game scenario.

"And how can I help you, Mr. Holmes?"

"I'm sorry to say, that we've come about the death of one of your employees. A Mr. Danny Green," he said.

Miss Fyord's expression remained impassive as she seemed to search her memories. Finally, she spoke.

"Green. Yes. Low-level Engineer. Working on the development of a new marine diesel engine prototype. We are hoping to use boats as our first movement into the power unit market," she replied then continued after a pause, "Sad. How did he die?"

"He was murdered. Presumably at the Ritz Hotel, but his body was found in the alleyway next door."

"The Ritz, you say, I must revisit how much I'm paying my engineers. That's not an inexpensive establishment. Well thank you for informing me, I will have my receptionist contact his next of kin and pass on my condolences."

She stood again to bid us goodbye.

"I'm sure you need to rush off to apprehend the villain behind this, so I won't hold you further," she said.

All four us held out places. Miss Fyord looked from face to face. Her stern look melted slightly as she realised we weren't going to leave. She sat down. The atmosphere had turned slightly.

Holmes continued, moving forward so that he towered over the desk and looked down at Miss Fyord.

"Mr. Green, a low-level engineer in your words, had been seen at the Ritz on a number of occasions. He held meetings with Sir Stannis McDonald in the office of Sir Rupert Linklatter."

A smile crossed Miss Fyord's face at the mention of those names.

"You know the gentlemen?" Holmes asked.

"Of course, Sir Stannis is my biggest competitor. The diesel engine we are developing is his biggest threat. We may only be a small company, but we have a mighty product on our hands. As for Sir Rupert, he has the largest controlling interest in the North Sea oil fields. He has been playing us off against British Steam for months. Hedging his bets so to speak."

Her demeanour changed.

"Are you trying to tell me that this Green was selling us out to our competitor?" she asked.

"I cannot say at this point, they may have just been old school friends for all I know," said Holmes, a little too quickly for my like. I recognised it as a tone he took when confronted over a point he could not justify with facts.

"Then what's the problem?" Fyord asked.

"Early this morning, Mr. Green was seen entering the same room as a tall, slender, woman of Indian appearance. The next time he was seen, he was dead in an alleyway with a puncture mark to the back of his neck. The puncture mark is reminiscent of a weapon used by a member of an elite all-female Indian assassin's guild."

Miss Fyord laughed out loud.

"And you think that was me?" she blurted out.

A small grin came to Holmes's face. He shook his head slightly.

"Oh no, madam, I don't think you had anything physically to do with this murder."

He walked across to the door we'd seen close earlier, grabbed the knob and wrenched it open.

Standing inside was a strikingly beautiful Indian woman, almost the same height as Holmes, with a slender, powerfully athletic build. She was dressed in a tight-fitting blue silk blouse, with a black leather bodice and black leather pants. I noticed that there were knife scabbards on the sides of her knee-high boots. I was relieved to find them empty. She also wore a black leather aviator's helmet with thick brass goggles. Her long black hair spilled out of the helmet and cascaded down to her waist.

This was not the look of a simple secretary or office worker. This woman was dressed for business. Bloody business.

"Madam, if you would be so kind, could you join us please," said Holmes.

The Indian woman stood in the small white-tiled room that acted as Miss Fyord's private bathroom. She had a stern expression on her face with her piercing brown eyes trained on Holmes. She looked ready to pounce.

Her demeanour changed when Miss Fyord piped up.

"Parvinder, please do as Mr. Holmes says," she said, "I think we can clear this up quickly."

"As you wish, Ma'am," she said and walked into the office and took an "at ease" stance that would be the staple of any of the armed services.

"Let me introduce Miss Parvinder Singh, my associate and one of my closest friends. I think in future, Parvinder, it may prove prudent to lock the bathroom door," said Miss Fyord.

Holmes blanched a little with embarrassment at the suggestion he'd interrupted the woman. He recovered quickly. Miss Fyord took up the questioning.

"Parvinder, these gentlemen tell me that you were seen at the Ritz Hotel this morning. That you were meeting up with our Mr. Green from the new engine development team," she said.

The Indian woman turned to look at Miss Fyord with a questioning gaze. The blonde-haired woman looked directly in her eyes and nodded slightly. Holmes saw it all as well.

Parvinder turned her gaze forward and nodded.

"Yes. It is true," she said.

"You've been seeing Mr. Green for quite some time now, haven't you, but keeping it quiet, even from me."

Parvinder nodded again and spoke in a deadpan monotone.

"Yes. Daniel and I were in love. We have been together for several months. I think Daniel was going to propose marriage to me this morning. I was very excited," she said.

I almost burst out laughing at the woman's act. It was preposterous. I'm not even sure she knew who the man was, let alone being hopelessly in love with him.

Holmes simply smiled.

"I'm sure young Daniel would have been overjoyed with such a heartfelt response to his forthcoming proposal. Having you kill him probably came as an incredible surprise as well," he said.

Miss Fyord stood up at this suggestion.

"Kill him? Why would she kill him? It's obvious that she loved him."

Holmes turned towards her, his hand on his chin in contemplation of this strange conversation.

"My belief is that you, Miss Fyord, had your associate or should I say your hired assassin here, kill Mr. Green because he was selling your company's secrets to your competitor. You found out and wanted to make sure he died on the premises of one of your enemy's business partners."

"And what proof do you have?"

"For one, we have witnesses that places them both in the same location. We have reason to believe that my suggestion of industrial espionage is true. I will have to approach Sir Stannis to confirm it. He may not be happy, but the truth will come out. And one last piece of evidence would be ..."

He turned and grabbed the Indian woman's right hand and turned it over. She sported a large bandage that covered the palm. Fresh blood had soaked through since the bandage had last been changed.

"The assailant cut herself on a glass topped table, before reaching for Mr. Green's coat and taking whatever information he carried, plus the contents of his pockets."

Holmes turned towards Lestrade.

"Is this enough evidence to at least take Miss Singh here to the station house for further questioning?"

Lestrade nodded in agreement. Suddenly, his eyes grew wide and he thrust a hand inside his coat. He pulled it out holding his pistol and trained it on Miss Singh.

I watched in shock as the tall woman stepped up behind Holmes, wrapped her injured arm around his chest and pulled her left hand out from behind her back.

She held what looked like a small brass pistol in her left hand and pressed the barrel against Holmes's neck. I looked closely and saw the plunger had been withdrawn and was cocked ready to fire.

I copied Lestrade and reached into my own coat and withdrew my pistol. I noticed Collins standing nearby looking a little lost. Constables were only issued with night sticks, not pistols. He drew his truncheon from his belt and held it at the ready.

"Ma'am, you have two guns pointing at you. We only want to ask you more questions to ascertain the truth. Let's not make this any harder than necessary," said Lestrade.

Holmes remained calm and spoke slowly with just enough volume for the Indian woman to hear.

"Hmmm, from the feel of it that would be a Bharat S13 Spring operated needle pistol, developed for the Bengal Infantry and used for close fighting and assassinations. Well that certainly confirms your origins Miss Singh," said Holmes.

The Indian girl remained quiet. Miss Fyord broke the silence.

"What origins? Mr. Holmes?" she asked.

"Miss Singh here is a member of the Vishkanya. A secretive guild of female assassins operating out of India, primarily in the Punjab and Bengal areas," he said.

Miss Fyord laughed out loud.

"Nonsense. Parvinder's family has lived in England for decades. She was born in London and lived around the corner from my Grandfather's house. We have been friends for most of our lives," she said.

"Indeed," said Holmes.

"Is that true, Miss Singh?" I asked.

The woman's face remained impassive. Her hand tightened on the gun as she answered.

"Yes. I have lived in England for all my life. Madeline is my best friend. We went to school and University together. I have worked with her company since I left school," she said in dead monotonic voice.

I could see Holmes wasn't convinced. His face showed a slight tinge of anger at what he thought were obvious lies.

"Then perhaps, Miss Fyord, you could convince Miss Singh to unhand me and accompany the Inspector to the station so that this matter can be laid to rest. If Miss Singh was so in love with Mr. Green, then even a policeman of Inspector Lestrade's experience and expertise could not possibly charge her with Mr. Green's murder."

"Yes," said Miss Fyord standing up, "I think this has gone on long enough."

She raised her voice and directed her next sentence at the Indian woman.

146

"Parvinder, the time has come. You know what to do," she said.

I noticed a flash of confusion and incredulity race across the tall woman's face. She turned to Miss Fyord bowed her head slightly, then turned her face forward. Her face regained its impassive expression again.

"Yes. It will be done," she said.

Parvinder stared off into space and released Holmes who staggered away. He turned back to address the woman just in time to see her bring the needle gun up to her own temple and squeeze the trigger.

The gun let out a stifled ringing noise and what sounded like something punching into meat.

The Indian woman's eyes rolled back into their sockets and she collapsed in an unceremonious heap on the floor. The gun slid away from her and stopped near Holmes.

I looked down at the gun and saw a long brass needle sticking out of the end. It was mottled with red blood.

I looked back at the woman and saw a small puncture in her left temple like the wound on Green's neck. A dribble of blood ran out of the hole and dripped onto the floor.

I couldn't help myself but blurted out, "Good Lord."

Holmes looked at the dead woman then turned to face Miss Fyord. The company owner was calm as if this was an expected occurrence.

Holmes cocked his head and spoke.

"Well, that was unexpected," he said, "Wasn't it, Miss Fyord?"

She turned and looked into Holmes's eyes, her face unmoved.

"Shocking, I would say," she said.

"You don't seem very upset," I said.

Miss Fyord turned to face me, a flash of anger ran across her features.

"My best friend just killed herself, in my office. I will not give you intruders the pleasure of seeing my distress," she said standing up and moving around to the front of her desk.

"Now, if you'll excuse me, I will go home so that I may mourn alone," she finished.

She turned to Lestrade and said, "I assume you will need a statement or something from me. I will remain at home for the next day or two. My receptionist can give you my address."

With that she turned and walked through her office doors and into the reception area before anybody thought of stopping her.

I was flustered. I looked at the retreating figure, then to Holmes and Lestrade.

"What is going on?" I asked keeping my voice from rising to a shrill cry.

Holmes turned from watching Miss Fyord leave, a small sardonic grin on his face.

"What do you mean, Watson?"

"You're letting her go. You said all along that this was a case of espionage. That Green was killed because of what he knew and what he was selling to Sir Stannis," I said.

"Ah, yes, but I don't have any actual evidence. Only conjecture," he answered before turning to Lestrade, "I assume that you are content with the case at hand, Inspector?"

Lestrade looked at the body and then back at Holmes and me. He nodded.

"Sadly, yeah, I agree with Holmes. We've got enough evidence to put this down to a lovers' tiff or something, but not enough to lay any other charges."

He turned to Collins.

"Constable, can you go and organise a coroner's wagon to pick this unfortunate up? There's not much else to investigate at the moment."

"Yes sir, but...?" Collins said.

"I'm sure Mr. Holmes will be continuing the investigation from here on, but as far as the Yard is concerned, it's closed," Lestrade said.

He winked at Holmes, "Isn't that right?"

Holmes nodded.

"Yes. And to allay your fears Watson, I will indeed be looking further afield. There is a lot more to this, and it involves very powerful people, so care is needed at every turn."

He thought for a moment with a finger extended on his chin.

"I may have to consult with Mycroft."

He looked back at the open doorway into the receptionist area and smiled.

"I think, in Miss Madeline Fyord, we have a very intelligent and incredibly shrewd adversary. One that is not above hiring assassins whose code is one of complete loyalty, even unto death. One that is prepared to take on the most powerful men in the country without a drop of fear or doubt, and one that may involve us in many adventures to come. A truly formidable woman," he said.

I stared at the expression on Holmes's face. I shuddered a little as it was one I hadn't seen since we first met a lady that he always referred to as "The Woman", a Miss Irene Adler.

The Hounds of Anuket

by John Linwood Grant

The body lay on the mud-flats, a policeman's cape draped over the head and shoulders. A pale muslin dress, smeared with the slime of the Thames; button-up boots in the latest fashion, filthy from trailing in the mud while the body was dragged from the water. Faroukh stared at the two irregular grooves which marked that journey to the high-tide mark. Surely, they could have lifted her up, carried her?

He squinted against the low morning sun, getting the measure of the two men who had found her. Boatmen, buttoned against the cold, wiping dirt off fingerless mittens and onto their trousers – and from the look of their shabby craft, regulars.

"An hour ago?"

"Aye." The older of the two spat. "Lost more than one fare for 'er. But they sinks, they does, after a while, so we brought her in."

"Very civic and proper." They wanted coin from him, but he wasn't going to pay. "The Crown thanks you."

Gesturing them back, he looked to the police sergeant who stood by the body. His boots were halfway into the clinging mud.

"Any sign of disturbance, Wilkins?"

"No, sir. On my rounds, got asked down here by them fellows. I called it in to the station and thought it best to keep watch."

"You did the right thing, sergeant."

Faroukh bent and lifted the corner of the cape. He would have placed her at eighteen or nineteen years of age. Short dark hair, no doubt stylish before immersion. The brown eyes were open, the face slightly swollen. She must have been beautiful once, but what he saw in that face made him shiver.

Terror.

She must have been in the water less than a day. Gloved hands, with weed tangled around one finger. There was something odd about the gloves, though, an irregular staining. He gently raised the left arm and slid that glove free. Despite immersion, it looked as if there was blood on and between the slim fingers, yet no signs of a wound. He replaced the glove, and let the cape drop. No doubt he should have waited for the doctor.

Wilkins coughed. "Inspector?"

A cab had drawn up on the road, and a small man, black bag in one hand was being helped out by Constable Bale, waiting by the road. The doctor would arrange for the body to be moved; it was time to leave the matter for others and await their reports. There was nothing he could do here, and he had two more calls to which he had to respond - a burglary, and an assault at the fish-market.

The burglary had been a violent one, with a maid badly injured, and his early evening was spent between taverns and shisha lounges. A merchant seaman was the likely perpetrator but finding him would be another matter.

He completed the paperwork on all three cases at the station, passing it to a clerk for it to be coded for the Lovelace terminal. If the 'Lace found correlations, he would know in the morning.

The unnatural death of an Egyptian woman was rare, which was perhaps why it stayed with him through the day. And yet it may well have been nothing more than suicide – she would not be the first from the other half of Empire to find London not a golden-paved wonder, but a dirty, grey-skied monster.

Depressed, he headed for his Hammersmith lodging house. Cheap and cheerless, but better than police barracks. Far in the distance an armoured airship drove through the night sky, heading no doubt for the Greenwich moorings. Its white sides were painted with the proud ensign of the Anglo-Egyptian Empire, proclaiming that all was well throughout the Imperial domains.

Except for one poor woman, at least.

*****

Inspector St John Ahmed Faroukh was not greatly popular with his superior officers in the Hammersmith Division. He had been called many things in London - a mere nuss-Arab, neither one thing nor another; a Gypti mongrel, and a Cairo dog. He didn't mind that one – the lean, tenacious creatures of his birthplace were better adapted to survival than some of the pampered beasts of England.

The lower ranks were friendlier.

"The 'Lace found her, sir," said Morton, one of the terminal clerks. "Reported missing, three days ago. A Miss Dawoud, of Palliser Road. Her father came in yesterday evening and identified her."

"And the doctor's report?"

"Ah." The clerk looked down at his knees. "Out of our hands. It's gone elsewhere."

Faroukh sighed. A connection to a case in another Division, perhaps. "I'd better see the body again, at least."

"That's gone as well, sir."

A flash of annoyance. "Who took it, Morton? Which Division?"

"Home Office, it was, authorised by a Mr Petherton. Sir."

Faroukh strode to the Lovelace room set aside for senior staff. The station's connection was erratic – he suspected that a number of copper cables had been pilfered – but for once the dials on the bulky machine glowed green. He sat down and tapped in a code, then a series of keywords about the case, words which appeared on the tiny, smeared glass screen. Then...

+searching+

Somewhere across the city, a Lovelace Thinking Engine chugged and clicked - or so he imagined. He'd never seen one, only the squat terminals. Eventually a brass slot churned out a strip of paper. The ink was still wet.

+nine zero nine request+

Nine Zero Nine. A matter of national security.

It seemed that this find was no longer his concern. Back at his desk, he could only hope someone was taking care on the dead woman's behalf. He was about to move on to a reported theft when a constable knocked on the half-open door.

"There's a lady here, sir."

Faroukh looked up. His office was little more than a converted storage cupboard.

"Thank you, Bale."

He stood up as the man ushered in a slim, well-dressed woman in her twenties, clearly of Egyptian birth. Her face... he had seen those eyes before, or ones so very like them.

He indicated that she should sit down.

"You are Inspector Faroukh?" Her voice was stiff. "I am Miss Taneta Dawoud. A Sergeant Wilkins tells me that you are investigating my sister's murder, that you found her by the river."

"Your sister? I was called out over the matter of... of a body being found. But it's not my case now."

"Why is that?"

"Miss Dawoud, I'm not in a position to answer—"

"Then who is?" She glared. "My sister was murdered. It was not a suicide, as some suggest."

"You've spoken to other officers?"

"Your superintendent told me to go home and grieve. And then the sergeant kindly gave me your name."

He thrust the papers on his desk aside, placed his elbows on its scratched surface. "Tell me of your sister, Miss Dawoud."

He heard a tale of two young Coptic women, brought up not far from Cairo. Their father, Youssef Dawoud, had taken up a minor role in administration in London, and the family had moved to England to be with him. Their mother had died not long after, of pneumonia. Ese had been the younger, quiet one, Ese the likely bride, and Taneta the girl who refused all suitors the family brought before her.

"I work at the Leighton Collection," she added. "Assisting with their catalogue of Egyptian artefacts, now that many are to be returned to our native soil."

This made little sense. "Is there any reason why your father might be of interest to the Home Office?"

"None. He works with the Foreign Office on unimportant matters. His eyesight is weak – I have seen the documents he deals with, have read some to him. He deals with no secrets."

"Was your sister different in the days before she disappeared?"

"Different? Yes, perhaps. Father spoke of a man who wished to discuss dowry matters. I never saw him; she seemed a little anxious, which I assumed was natural."

Faroukh took up his pen. "The man's name?"

"Abir Mekh. A silk merchant, we were told, trading between London and Port Said."

There had been no warning, and no note, no obvious reason for Ese Dawoud to take her own life.

"I will do my best." He paused and wet his lips. "I am only a junior inspector of police, Miss Dawoud. If I can find out anything, I will let you know."

"Yes. I'm sure you will."

There was neither hope nor confidence in her tone.

*****

The interview with Miss Dawoud bothered him. All families protested that their loved ones could not have committed suicide, but still...

As for the Nine Zero Nine, people were more malleable than the Thinking Engine. Troubled by brown eyes, Faroukh asked questions. No one seemed to place much importance on the Home Office intervention - Petherton was a paper-pusher, by all accounts.

He invented excuses to visit other stations and listened to casual chatter between colleagues. And by chance he encountered a Chiswick sergeant who also had experience with the River Police. In a nearby tavern – a double whisky for the sergeant and a coffee for himself - he heard of another woman's body being recovered from the Thames.

An Egyptian, again.

That had been in July, said the sergeant. An Alexandrian Jew, the eighteen-year-old daughter of a finance clerk. Fully dressed, and although there were no gloves, there were traces of blood or something else rusty red under the fingernails. The officer had noticed because it contrasted with an otherwise fine manicure. The verdict was suicide.

Puzzled, Faroukh quizzed the 'Lace as to Mr Abir Mekh, tapping in codes for a supposed counterfeiting investigation, so that his enquiry would not be connected with drownings. The man had arrived in Britain only the year before, registered as a fabrics merchant, living at an address in West Brompton. No criminal record.

Faroukh requested permission to go and interview Mekh, who lived out of Hammersmith's jurisdiction. This was denied. He asked Superintendent Fisher if he might be party to the findings of any examination of Miss Ese Dawoud's body. This was also denied.

Three days after he had spoken to the Chiswick sergeant, he was called into the superintendent's office, and told that he was not performing his duties as expected. It was an abrupt meeting.

"You'd chase anything but your bounden duties, eh, Faroukh?" said Fisher. "Too good for straightforward policing, are we?"

Pending review of his exact role at Hammersmith, the superintendent said, he would be seconded to F Division the following week, to help with a traffic problem near Paddington.

"Sir, I protest. I—"

"You prefer spending your time on idle speculation, Inspector, rather than following my orders. And I am tired of it. You may see yourself as some kind of fanciful detective – yes, I have heard of your 'outings' hither and thither – but you are not."

*****

As the prospect of Paddington loomed, Faroukh found that his thoughts returned again and again to the expression on Ese Dawoud's face, and the blood under her gloves – he was sure it was blood. Yet he had nothing which he could take to another superior.

It was his habit, when frustrated, to wander the Zoological Gardens at Regent's Park, particularly for the pleasure of the exotic birds and their fine plumage. He barely remembered the Cairo of his youth, though he did recall the dull cry of the vultures as they circled the edges of the city, hoping for a dead dog or a beggar who had given up at last.

He took a seat in the cafe, and sipped at a mint tea. At the far end, three uniformed airmen were amusing the local girls. One of the men was an Egyptian regular, darker and with a hawkish cast to his features, who raised his hand to Faroukh. Abdel Sabahi, a courier pilot out of the small Ravenscourt airfield. They met occasionally for coffee. Faroukh nodded back but was too out of sorts to go over.

His Majesty's airships were the talk of the continent. Trade boomed across the Empire by land, sea and air, London would soon be the most cosmopolitan place on Earth, a meeting place such as the fabled cities of the Silk Roads. Or perhaps a new Byzantium...

He gripped his glass of tea, struck by a sudden memory. What was the significance of that word?

Faroukh walked down to the river. He watched its slow surge, a grey-brown tumble of water specked by pleasure boats and ferry-boats. Slow because of changes which Man had wrought, after the recent construction of the new Molesey Dam, and the flood barriers completed last year – the Tideway Gate on the estuary, and the Kingston Gate to the west of the city.

The Thames, controlled and in service to the Empire, had been called a mighty artery of commerce and success, a symbol of wealth to come. Faroukh saw a great, filthy vein which ran through slums and factories, dragging their waste out to sea – and he saw her face. The large brown eyes, rimmed with kohl, the parted lips and a plea. I was murdered...

He had it.

'Some days, sir, your thoughts are positively Byzantine.' That had been the line. He had heard it from the late Inspector Gregson, Faroukh's mentor for a few short months before the old man's early retirement. A line delivered to a man more skilled than Gregson or Faroukh might ever have hoped to be.

There was one detective in London who might care for a puzzle.

*****

The house was dilapidated, paint peeling from the facade, and the woman who let him into the bare hallway was evidently going the same way, despite her starched apron and neatly-patched dress.

"Good evening. I'm sorry to bother you, but I need to speak with—"

She glanced down the empty street, then closed the door behind them with a creak which must have echoed in her joints.

"Come in, sir. He's in his rooms." She nodded to the stairs. "You'll forgive me if I don't take you up..."

"Of course."

His feet echoed on un-carpeted boards as he made his way up to the landing. One knock, two, on the door.

"Enter."

Faroukh let himself into chaos.

A decent-sized sitting room had been turned into a mad repository of books, papers and apparatus, seemingly without any sense to it. A revolver hung on the wall next to a Persian slipper and the severed wing of a large bird; the table at the window held a telescope, balanced precariously on mouldering volumes, a number of broken teacups and a plaster bust with a hole in its forehead. The air was thick with tobacco smoke.

A lean figure sat in the solitary armchair.

"Mr. Holmes?"

"Inspector Faroukh."

"You know me?"

Holmes smiled. "I keep abreast of developments in the constabulary. In case..." The smile faded. "No matter. Inspector St John Faroukh. Twenty-seven years old, from the Cairo Police, promoted and transferred here as a gesture towards our Egyptian allies. T Division, Hammersmith, under the pedestrian Superintendent Fisher."

"I worked with Inspector Gregson for a short while, sir. He always spoke highly of you – but officially, we are told that you should be left to enjoy your retirement."

The detective inclined his head. "And what else do they say?"

Faroukh hesitated.

"That... that it is no longer appropriate for amateurs to meddle in police affairs; Sherlock Holmes is a figure of the past, a spent force. Great service, invaluable back then, but now – and with your estrangement from Dr. Watson..."

"Indeed. I am in honourable disgrace." A sharp glance took in the younger man. "You have been at the river's edge, Inspector - between Hammersmith and Chelsea, from the mud on your trousers – within the last few hours. A case which is in some way frustrating you, and with Gregson in mind, you decided to consult the pariah, myself. Sit down, tell me of your mystery."

Holmes pointed to the corner, where a pile of books and discarded scarves almost concealed a straight-back chair. Faroukh cleared the chair and drew it up opposite his host.

"Mr Holmes, it may not be a mystery. It may be trivial."

"Pray let me decide if this is trivial or not. Proceed."

Faroukh recounted his recent experiences, including what he knew of the Dawouds. Holmes made no comment until the end.

"I see." Holmes played with an empty pipe. "One or two points of interest there, I concede. Of course, your Chiswick friend may have mistaken silt for blood. Immersion changes the appearance of many substances."

"But why should I be denied further knowledge of the case?"

"It may be politics. With the King's recent marriage, this Anglo-Egyptian Empire of ours is poised either to outshine the other nations of the globe for decades - or to fracture and fail."

"Our new Queen is popular," said Faroukh. "The new Molesey Dam is to be renamed the Queen Sanura Dam in her honour."

"She catches the eye, and is of noble Christian stock, albeit of the Coptic persuasion. Beauty and ceremony appease the people. But the King is not a young man, and there are such politics behind and beyond the Empire that few can predict what will happen in a year or two. Do you remember the explosion in Putney last month?"

"The rupture at the gas storage facility? I understood that—"

"An explosive device. The authorities are concealing an under-swell of activity, from Fenians concerned that success in the East has eclipsed their cause, to Egyptian Nationalists who reject the Khedive's rule." The older man's sunken eyes regarded him. "You are not a Copt, Inspector. A Mohammedan, I assume, by the slight wear in the knees of your uniform trousers?"

"My father is a senior clerk, a Muslim by birth. Do you have some issue with my origins?"

"Not at all. I judge character. A man's church, mosque or temple is his own concern."

"My late mother was English. She took the Faith but raised me to question rather than obey without thought."

"A sound basis for the ideal of policing, but not for the practice of it," said Holmes.

"Would you... advise me, Mr. Holmes? Or should I forget the matter?"

A smoky silence fell for some moments.

"I might advise you not to threaten a still promising career." The inspector made to speak, but Holmes held up one long-fingered hand. "Two bodies, and the blood – if it was blood. I must consider the matter." Holmes laughed.

161

"One last game, perhaps. I shall find you, Inspector, and soon."

Faroukh bowed.

"Thank you, Mr. Holmes."

*****

A late summer smog had settled on the city as Faroukh stood by Paddington Station two days later, arguing with a public works official concerning security and routes for the sleek new steam-trams. Barely a police job at all, except for an obsession of one of the higher-ups that the force should have a role.

Listening to the official drone on, he became aware that a mixed group of *fellahin* and typical local labourers were shouting at their foreman. Faroukh strode over.

"Do we need this?" he snapped.

The foreman, tall and muffled against the cold fog, raised his hands. "Lazy devils, the lot of 'em. Don't matter none where they's from, they want an extra ha'penny an hour to work in this. Says they'll be run down." He spat and grabbed the inspector's arm. "I'm done wiv 'em, see if I ain't!"

And the man stalked off. Faroukh sighed, then felt at his uniform cuff. Something had been thrust under there. He turned away and unfolded a piece of paper.

Follow me. H.

"I will return shortly, Mr Rawlins," Faroukh called out, and hurried down Praed Street after the still visible figure of the foreman. Another minute, and he would lose sight of the man. A turn to the right, down Sale Street, and there he was, beneath a lit gas lamp.

"Mr. Holmes?"

"Inspector." The detective paused, lowering his scarf to reveal an expression which Faroukh could not fathom. Discomfort, doubt? "I have made enquiries – into the Dawouds, your Abir Mekh, and Mr. James Petherton of the Home Office."

"And something is amiss."

"Possibly, possibly. I need you to visit someone, today. I wrote to him with the information you provided, and these new details, but have had no acknowledgement. You are young and clearly intent on justice. Perhaps you can succeed where I cannot."

"Where do you want me to go, sir?"

Holmes passed over a card. "There is a man there who can discover more about the bodies – he may even be able to examine the last victim on our behalf. Inspector Faroukh..." Holmes faltered.

"Yes?"

"You must insist that this is for Miss Dawoud and the others, not for any other purpose. Insist, you understand?"

"I do, but..."

Holmes had gone, into the rolling banks of fog; Faroukh looked at the card.

Dr John Watson, 5a Upper Grosvenor Street.

Mr Rawlins and the Department of Works could wait, thought Faroukh. This may be important, nor was it far from Paddington. An easy stroll.

As he entered the wealthier streets around Grosvenor Square, stately town-houses appeared through the fog. He was soon able to make out the numbers - 5a was a ground floor set of rooms, a brass plaque reading 'John H Watson, MD, FRCGP'.

He rang the bell, and a neatly-dressed young man ushered Faroukh into a reception area, asking his business.

"A police matter," said Faroukh, and showed his identity card.

He was asked to wait. Ten minutes passed, and a stoutly-built older man with a neat grey moustache entered from a door to the rear. He did not look especially pleased.

"John Watson," said the man, extending his hand. Faroukh rose and shook it. "Come into my office." Another large room – cabinets, medical instruments in cases, and an enormous walnut desk. "You have come on behalf of Holmes, I presume."

Faroukh considered this, and what he had heard. The two men, so close once, had fallen out over a case which had ended with one of Watson's friends imprisoned for embezzlement. Holmes had incontrovertible proof, of course, but it was said that Watson had never forgiven the detective. Not for the outcome, but because Holmes had used him, without his knowledge, to gain crucial, confidential information from the guilty party and his wife. They had hardly spoken in over two years, by all accounts.

"Doctor, I come on behalf of a young woman who believes her sister was murdered," said Faroukh, choosing directness. "If you or Mr. Holmes can assist to ease her grief, then I have no recourse but to beg your assistance."

The older man stared, and then smiled, making him seem much younger.

"Direct, by George. Rather taken the wind out of my sails."

"Mr Holmes believes that you can help - on the official side."

Watson paced, favouring one leg. "I have his letter," he admitted. "And I am still retained by the Home Office. I train police doctors, and I advise on confidential matters."

His face grew sad. "My time with Holmes stood me in good stead. I am respected, trusted."

"Then will you see if you can find out more, Doctor Watson? There are two families in mourning. These may be suicides, but nevertheless..."

The older man halted and gave a curt nod. "I will try my best, Inspector. For the sake of the young ladies' families, at least."

*****

There were, by anyone's estimate, thousands of young men and women of Egyptian blood in London. Translators and secretaries were in demand; most menial and clerical jobs here paid better than in Egypt. Businesses from Cairo had set up English and Scottish branches. Cemented by the marriage of Edward and Sanura, Egypt was not a colony, but a partner.

Camel-gunners fired volleys during the Royal wedding celebrations, and Egyptian styles were all the rage. Four Coptic churches and ten new mosques had been built in London within the last year. Had St.John Faroukh been the son of wealthy Alexandrian merchants or related to one of the Khedive's pashas, he would have been in demand in society. As the half-caste only child of a couple who were at best middle class, he was of little importance.

The day after seeing Watson, he called on the Dawouds. If word got back to Superintendent Fisher, then to *Al-Shaitan* with the man.

They were anxious for news, and without mentioning his unsanctioned position on the case, he managed to persuade the father that he should have a few moments alone with Taneta Dawoud.

165

"There are things, sir, that women – sisters - share, delicate matters which might help."

Mr Dawoud, looking tired, consented.

In the small drawing room, she eyed him oddly. Again, he was struck by the resemblance to her sister, and the terrible waste that was Ese's murder.

"You gave me to believe you were not involved in investigating my sister's death."

"I have sought assistance elsewhere, quite unofficially."

She walked the length of the room, moved a vase on the mantelpiece.

"Unofficially. I see." Her huge brown eyes cleared. "Then so must it be. What do you offer?"

"I offer myself, and Mr Sherlock Holmes. We have unearthed a similar case to your sister's, and we seek answers."

"Good. What would you have me do, Inspector Faroukh?"

"Why, I—"

"I will not wait on the sidelines. You must employ me, or I shall seek my own route, and possibly blunder into yours."

She reminded him of his late mother, who had never shirked an argument, even after her conversion to Mohammedism. More than one male friend of his father's had not dared to enter the house.

"Allow me to gather the threads of this, and then..."

"And then," she said firmly.

*****

No one was concerned as to Faroukh's day-to-day activities. Mawson, the Paddington superintendent, was dealing with a series of thefts in the vicinity of the station and was pleased not to have one of his own embroiled in such trivia as tram routes. The inspector therefore had no problem responding to Holmes's request for a meeting, brought to him by a snot-filled gutter boy. In the backroom of a locksmith's shop off the Edgeware Road, he sipped a lukewarm mug of tea whilst marvelling at the presence of Sherlock Holmes and John Watson at the same table.

"There is news," said Holmes.

"I did as asked, Inspector," said Watson. "I spoke to certain friends in the profession, without fuss, of course. I was able to see the initial, handwritten medical notes for both cases."

"And Miss Dawoud?" Faroukh was eager for something substantial.

"Her body is in a Home Office morgue." Watson shook his head. "Shocking business. The young woman had clearly been forcibly drowned. Bruises on arms and shoulders."

"The lungs?" asked Holmes. "What was the condition of those organs?"

"Dashed peculiar, that. If I were pressed, I would say the girls were drowned before they met the river. There was not the particulate matter that you might expect from our murky Thames. I also obtained the police photographs taken of the earlier girl, Rebecca Bensaid. A similar appearance. The fool of a doctor put the bruising down to the body's passage along the river, perhaps impact with jetties or a boat. I shall be having words with the man." Watson pulled a sour face. "The first case was written off as a suicide. As for Miss Dawoud, no connection was made with the case of Miss

Bensaid, but that Petherton chap was mentioned in passing. Mutterings about Fenians, and the body being held in relation to 'other investigations'."

Holmes snorted. "Fenians who claim no credit, make no fuss about their handiwork? No, that will not serve. The other matter I mentioned in my letter, Watson?"

The two were not comfortable, their heads turned so that they never quite looked into each other's eyes.

"There were traces of blood on both hands and feet, but no wounds," said Watson. "Not their blood, I would surmise. And there is something else odd. Their backs retained some faint marks." Watson, seemingly reluctant, took two photographs from inside his jacket and laid them on the table.

Both women were naked above the waist, face down on morgue slabs.

"Symbols – surely Egyptian symbols. Almost washed away." The detective looked to Faroukh.

"It is possible," said the inspector, "But I know next to nothing of such things, Mr. Holmes. The British are more fascinated by our heritage than are most modern Egyptians."

"Just so, just so. Watson, could you ascertain what was used to make the marks?"

"Emulsion or watercolour paint would be my thought," said the doctor. "Nothing permanent – I could make out no more detail than is represented here."

Holmes gave a grim smile. "There is one obvious conclusion."

"I don't understand," said Faroukh.

"Blood on the hands and feet, and now those curious symbols. I believe that these are ritual killings, Inspector. What ritual, and to what purpose, I cannot yet say. Watson, stout fellow, has provided most valuable evidence."

That last was said in an over-eager tone, and Faroukh almost winced at the hurt which lay beneath. He tried to put the emotions in the room to one side.

"What is our next step, Mr. Holmes?"

"James Petherton is the key to progress. I made a few enquiries about the man. He is deeply in debt at his clubs, one of them little more than a gambling den for men above his station."

"You suspect him in league with the killers?"

"Unlikely. I imagine that Petherton has been paid to ensure there is no active investigation, no fuss. All rituals have some purpose. Something is yet to come, gentlemen. Something even darker than these murders."

"Then we confront Petherton?"

"We entice him, Inspector. A note, a telegram, suggesting that he is at risk. That he must come to the 'usual place' as a matter of urgency. And then we ask some quiet questions."

"What if there is no usual place?" asked Faroukh.

"There will be. Anyone involved in clandestine affairs would hardly go to Whitehall or to Petherton's residence. Therefore, he must meet with them – if money has, as I anticipate, changed hands."

Watson looked doubtful. "A rather old trick, Holmes."

"It is one we have used before with success, dear fellow. Why, I remember in the case of..." Holmes hesitated, his face betraying sudden weariness. "Watson, might we put any differences aside, for this young man's sake? For now, at least."

Faroukh saw hope, doubt, so many memories captured in the lines there.

"I suppose… yes, Holmes." Watson stood up and held out his hand. The detective also rose, taking Watson's hand in a firm grip.

"You have achieved one thing at least, Inspector Faroukh," said Holmes, when Watson had left. "The good doctor and I are speaking again."

*****

Holmes was muffled and unrecognisable when Faroukh met him the following evening. They came to together in the shadow of a borrowed hansom cab, close to where James Petherton lived in a moderately well-to-do part of Pimlico.

They watched as the boy Holmes had hired delivered the forged telegram, which was taken in by a maid. Minutes later, a man came out in haste, and spotted the cab. Faroukh, in a heavy outdoor coat with the collar up, tugged his cap further down over his face.

"You there," Petherton called out. "I need to get to West Brompton."

In the glow of the nearby gas lamp, Holmes seemed unsure. "I 'as me nephew with me. 'E's a bit slow, in the 'ead like—"

"That makes no difference to me. Will you take my fare or not?"

"We will, sir. Jonah, mind you don't bother the gennelman."

Faroukh got in the cab, pressing himself against the far side, and Petherton joined him, eyes averted.

"Number 24, Redcliffe Street, off the Square," said Petherton in a loud, harsh voice, only to exclaim when Holmes pushed in next to him.

"We will not be going to see Abir Mekh. I wished only for confirmation of your connection."

"What the Devil!"

"No commotion if you please, Petherton. My colleague has a revolver."

Petherton glowered. "I don't know what your game is, but by God, I am an important figure in Whitehall. The police will have your skins for—"

"Sir Reginald Groves," snapped Holmes. "You have paid him less than half of your debt, and yet even that amounted to almost a thousand pounds."

"I—"

"The Honourable Jack Carrington – a lesser sum, but substantial enough. You have debts you cannot meet, have paid out sums you cannot possibly have earned – not by honest toil." Holmes tore away his muffler. "If you think to bluster, I am Mr Sherlock Holmes. Your last hope is to assist me, or all information I have gathered will be with Special Branch by eight a.m. tomorrow."

Petherton's red face paled, and he began to talk. The tale was not a complicated one. Deeply in debt, the civil servant had been approached outside one of the clubs by an Egyptian merchant and broker named Abir Mekh, two months ago.

"He knew everything, Mr. Holmes. The names you have used, and many more. He offered ruin – or funds with which to meet most of my creditors.

"The condition... the condition was that I should be 'helpful' if needed. Nothing definite at all. I thought it may concern a matter of visas or similar. And then, last week I received a note – I was using my position to delay - only delay, I swear - any investigations into drownings in the Thames, if the victims were of Middle Eastern extraction."

Despite the cold, there was sweat on the man's forehead. "For God's sake, Holmes – a few bloody Gyptis or Lascars, whatever, hardly a great loss. He promised no English lives were at risk."

Faroukh threw off his cap, about to speak, but Holmes held up a hand.

"You are despicable, Petherton," said the detective. "You have lied and obstructed justice. However, I am engaged in seeking a greater quarry. This, then, is why you interfered in the case of Miss Ese Dawoud?"

Petherton assented.

Holmes sat back, taking out a pocketbook and pencil. "You will tell me everything you know about Abir Mekh."

To Faroukh's disappointment, Petherton knew little. He had met Mekh twice at the Redcliffe Street address, once to agree to the deal and receive a down-payment, and a second time to receive a further sum. He had seen two other men with Mekh – both Egyptians, as far as he knew.

"There is a single servant, Mahmed, who I think is Sudanese. He keeps guard over various antiquities – knives, statuettes. Valuable, I assume."

Holmes, writing in his pocketbook, insisted on detailed descriptions of all, including Mekh.

"When should you have seen Abir Mekh next?"

"The third payment is due in four days. After that, Mekh says he will have no more need of me. I am to mark the case of the drowned woman as mistakenly connected with political unrest."

"Take leave of absence immediately. Your fate will be considered when there is time. Health, nerves, any excuse you choose. And do not attempt to speak of this meeting, to Abir Mekh or anyone. If you remember what I once was, consider that some steel remains."

They let the man stagger back to his own house, broken.

The two of them sat there inside the hansom a moment longer.

"What on Allah's name is behind this?" Faroukh clenched his fists in frustration.

"I must have time to think, Inspector. It seems we have perhaps three days, Inspector, until an event of great importance to Abir Mekh."

"If we had access to a Lovelace terminal..."

"As opposed to my failing deductive processes?"

Faroukh flushed. "No, sir, I meant only that the Thinking Engines store much useful information, if the correct keywords are used."

Holmes gave a laugh, almost a cackle. "That is their problem. It is as if one were using a Bradshaw to plan a railway journey, yet one knew neither the point of departure nor the destination. But we shall see, Inspector, we shall see."

*****

Page Two of the morning paper announced a tragic accident in Pimlico. One James Petherton, an official in the Home Office, had suffered a fatal wound whilst cleaning his revolver, some time yesterday evening. To Faroukh, the inference was obvious - Petherton had chosen oblivion to penury or public shame.

He begged two days leave, which was granted without any great interest as to why, and rushed to Baker Street, where he was amazed to find Miss Dawoud in conversation with the great detective.

She looked up. "I am not a patient woman, Inspector," she said. "You mentioned Mr. Holmes, and thus..."

"Do join us, Inspector" said Holmes. "I was about to send for you."

"You have made progress, sir?"

"With Miss Dawoud's assistance. The river is the key. Ritual and the river."

"You mean the Thames?"

"The Thames, yes - and the Nile. Time is of the essence. Petherton's suicide may stir the hornet's nest." Holmes scowled. "It is my fault - I should have foreseen that he might take that road. Ah, well. Miss Dawoud, enlighten the Inspector."

"I have seen those dreadful photographs of Dr. Watson's," she said. "I cannot be certain, but I would say the painted marks were the hieroglyphs for *Shemu*. The mark on Miss Bensaid was that for the first month of *Shemu*, the Season of the Harvest – June, approximately. *Pashons*, as we Copts say."

"Which was when she was found," said Faroukh.

"Yes. And that on... on my poor sister..."

"Was the hieroglyph for the third month of *Shemu*. August, or close enough," said Holmes, in a surprisingly gentle voice. "There will no doubt have been another victim in July. The body may yet be tangled in the river, or have washed down to the estuary and be lost."

Faroukh cast his thoughts back to Egypt. "*Shemu*? Is that the season before the Nile is in full flood?"

"Exactly," said Holmes. "If I am correct, we have here a ritual which requires one victim for each of the four relevant months."

"And the blood on their hands and feet?"

Miss Dawoud saw Holmes's hesitation. "It must be said, sir." She bit at her lip. "Do not spare me, not if it helps find my sister's killer."

"I applaud your courage, Miss Dawoud. The blood will be goat or lamb, I imagine. The young ladies will have been divested of their clothes, 'marked', and drowned, before being dressed again and thrown into the Thames. Let us assume that the sacrifices were important, according to some warped belief, but that unclothed bodies would have drawn too much attention." He looked away. "It is possible that the young women were barely conscious – Watson found evidence of puncture marks."

"*Kuss Ikhtak!*" Faroukh was appalled. He had seen expression on Ese Dawoud's face – she had surely been conscious enough as she faced her own death. "Mr Holmes, this is an abomination!"

"It is. No doubt Mekh made some spurious reason to assess each victim, enough to satisfy himself, and then, most likely they were abducted by his confederates soon after. Bear in mind that these black deeds can only be part of a grander plan. I have obtained a photograph of Mekh, but it seems that we require the use of a Lovelace terminal after all. I assume you know how to use the things? And you understand how the constabulary organise their data?"

"Of course, sir – but my codes have been revoked whilst I have duties at Paddington."

"I myself have never had such codes – but I do know where a suitable terminal may be found. Follow me."

Puzzled, they hurried after the detective and out onto the street. Within minutes they were clattering towards the river in a dilapidated growler.

"Where are we-"

"No questions, please," said Holmes.

They were deposited in a rundown dock area near Southwark Bridge.

"Wait here." Holmes passed a sovereign to the driver.

"Long as you like, sir."

Hazy sunshine outlined once-grand warehouses, between which a deep gloom clung to the detritus of maritime trade – abandoned carts, damaged fish crates and broken spars. Beyond a heap of mouldering sail-cloth, Holmes pointed out a door in the side of one warehouse.

"There."

He stepped forward, Faroukh and the young woman able to do little but follow him. The door was unlocked, the space inside big enough to house a small steamer. Derricks and gantries suggested its previous life as a place of industry. In the far corner there gleamed a lantern, and under the lantern sat a small, grimy man who must have been in his sixties.

"Why Mr. Holmes – and friends! Be welcome in my home." The voice was high-pitched and wavering.

"This is Silas," said Holmes. "Silas – Mr. Faroukh and Miss Dawoud. I was hoping for a moment with your machine."

"Indeed, indeed."

Faroukh thought the man a gnome, watching him hop off a stool and reach at a canvas-shrouded bulk by his side.

"Allah!" The inspector was astonished to see what lay beneath the canvas. "A Lovelace terminal."

Holmes looked pleased. "Silas 'borrowed' it from a decommissioned police station four years ago. It is an old model but is linked to the main banks of so-called Thinking Engines. Sit yourself down."

Seeing no option but the rickety stool, Faroukh took that and placed himself before the small glowing screen.

"No access code needed. And no trace on enquiries can be made from here." Silas wheezed with amusement. "It was made before security had been considered."

The detective and the young woman stood behind him.

"Go ahead, Miss Dawoud," said Holmes.

She reeled off a mixture of terms in Egyptian, and then Holmes added queries pertaining to the flow of the Thames, elevations and various co-ordinates. Familiar with the short-hand that Lovelace terminals used, Faroukh tapped at the ugly board of keys as fast as he could, and then fed the photograph of Mekh – a handsome, clean-shaven man in his forties – into the appropriate slot.

"Half an hour for a full response, I would think," he said at last. "I have never tried a search this large."

"Most of this could be done with books, tables and various monographs." Holmes shrugged. "But might take days. I am able to adapt, you see, Inspector."

The first strips of paper began to emerge from the machine within ten minutes. Holmes grasped each one eagerly, making notes and querying Faroukh or Miss Dawoud from time to time.

"It cannot deduce," he muttered. "It does not understand the questions. Still..."

When the terminal fell silent for a moment, the detective leaned back against it, his eyes closed.

"A young woman will have gone missing around the time of the full moon in July. She will be of Mohammedan stock, from London, and probably of the middle classes. Not so prominent as to garner great attention. Inspector?"

Faroukh tapped the correct keys for a routine missing person search.

"Yes, sir. Alia Al-Rahman. A grocer's daughter, from West Brompton. Nineteen years old."

"The second victim. If we enquire of her father, we will find that someone answering to Abir Mekh's description visited the shop beforehand, or had some social contact, enough to view the girl. Ritual again - maiden girls, sacrifices to bless a dark venture. You concur, Miss Dawoud?"

The young woman was pale. "I have to, Mr. Holmes, however bizarre it seems."

Holmes slammed his fist into the open palm of his other hand. "Damnable. Our friend Abir Mekh seeks to strike at London itself."

The inspector looked to Miss Dawoud, then to the detective.

"I mean no disrespect, but you are surely not considering... the supernatural?"

Holmes sniffed. "My dear Inspector, I hold no truck with such matters. No, the information from Silas's machine leads me to believe that Mr Abir Mekh is also known as Tawfik Abir, an Egyptian Nationalist -but not one with reasoned arguments against the Anglo-Egyptian Empire. He is a fanatic, who set off explosive devices in a Luxor Hotel last year, killing many locals. A most dangerous man.

"Remember the report of statuary and items at Redcliffe Street. Amongst them were figurines of Anuket – Miss Dawoud confirms their identity. Anuket, Goddess of the Nile, to whom people threw precious items as a sacrifice to celebrate the life-giving flood each year.

"Mekh is sacrificing one of each of the 'interloper' faiths as a gesture to the past. A Jew, a Mohammedan, a Copt, do you see? The fourth will be... English – and a Christian, I suggest. A vicar's daughter, charitable worker, a Sunday School teacher. A fine touch, from our opponent's point of view. Pass me the next set of printed slips."

He scrutinised these and consulted a pamphlet he had with him. "Ah, all is clear. Tell me, Inspector – you have been in our city long enough. This has been a year of considerable rain. Why does the Thames not flood London, given the flow from its tributaries and the estuarine pressure when storms rage at sea?"

Faroukh frowned. "It is harnessed, controlled. The Tideway Gate prevents surges from the sea, and the Kingston Gate manages the flow of water from the west—"

"Petherton said four days, and then nothing he did would matter. I have been puzzling over that, and now I have it. Tomorrow night, and into the next day, there will occur what is called a perigean spring tide, possibly the highest of the year." He held up the pamphlet. "And with the heavy rainfall early in the month..."

"The beginning of *Akhet*, the Inundation." The young woman gasped. "If Mekh destroys the Kingston Gate..."

"A bomb!" exclaimed Faroukh.

"Or many bombs." Holmes thrust strips of paper into his pockets. "But damage to the Kingston Gate will not achieve the destruction he wants. There is only one major target whose destruction would affect the core of the city – the Molesey Dam, five miles further upstream."

"Wait, sir." The inspector started tapping at the terminal again. He squinted at the screen. "An Esme Railton, eighteen years of age, is on the Missing Person list. She disappeared early yesterday morning, between errands."

"Her address?"

Faroukh grabbed the paper feeding from the small slot. "The Rectory, St Andrew's, Fulham."

"We have entered the final month of *Shemu*," said Miss Dawoud. "The time of the final sacrifice." She uttered an oath that Faroukh did not know. "That poor girl may already be in the river."

Holmes looked thoughtful. "Possibly not. Mekh is clearly both superstitious and practical at the same time. I

179

would expect him to complete his twisted ritual immediately prior to his key act – or no more than a few hours before." He glanced at a print-out. "Today is Tuesday. The maximum impact would be achieved by breaching the Molesey Dam at around 4 a.m. on Thursday, at the highest predicted point of the tide. A massive discharge of water from the dam would overwhelm the Kingston Gate and meet the tidal waters coming up from the estuary with devastating results. We must save London - but we may also save the girl in the process."

"Why that specific timing, Mr. Holmes?" asked the inspector.

"A new moon at its perigee, its closest to our planet. Such a perigean spring tide only occurs three or four times in a year. Abir Mekh must be aware of this."

"Would he not seek to sabotage the Kingston gate as well, to be certain?" asked Faroukh.

"He will. That is crucial, if the breaching of the dam is to have full effect. Silas, your assistance will not be forgotten."

The odd little man only grinned and began to haul the canvas back over the brass and wood of the Lovelace terminal.

Outside, the growler had waited as promised.

"Who will believe us, sir?" asked Faroukh as they were heading back to Baker Street. "I myself find all this hard to credit."

"I suggest you read the newspapers more often, Inspector." Holmes looked momentarily pleased with himself. "The Tideway Gate was damaged on Friday last, when a merchant vessel hit one of the main support pillars. The captain was said to be drunk. Do you believe, after what we have just discussed, that such an incident was accidental?"

"No, Mr. Holmes. I do not."

"Neither do I. I must talk to Watson. I had influence of old – certain politicians and members of the nobility. If it is not currently expedient for them to acknowledge me in general, they may respond to a direct approach on a matter so grave. One gentleman in particular..." He broke off as the growler arrived at Baker Street.

Once they were in Holmes's rooms, he turned to Faroukh.

"You and I must go to Abir Mekh's place on Redcliffe Street, as a matter of urgency."

"We have nothing concrete with which to challenge him, sir. Not since Petherton took his own life."

"Oh, Mehk will not be at home. He cannot be sure that Petherton did not leave anything connecting the two of them. I expect the servant remains – and if not, we shall find entry by other means. There may be something there which will help our investigation."

Miss Dawoud tilted her head, looking at the detective. "Do you speak Arabic, Mr. Holmes?"

"A little."

She proceeded to release a volley of colloquial Egyptian Arabic which Faroukh could only just follow, a series of low curses on Abir Mekh and his enterprise.

"I speak it fluently,"she concluded. "Better that the inspector and I go there and question the servant, whilst you seek to alert the authorities."

Holmes shook his head. "I have my methods, Miss Dawoud, and—"

"I have a murdered sister, sir," she snapped.

It had been decided.

*****

181

Faroukh met Miss Dawoud in the shadow of a church near Redcliffe Street, just as the clock chimed four p.m. He hardly recognised her at first. She was dressed as a man, in old tweeds, her black hair bundled under a cap and a scarf around her lower face – but the large brown eyes betrayed her..

"My father's discards," she said.

He felt the weight of his police revolver in his pocket, and despite his misgivings, they proceeded to Mekh's house - two Egyptians calling on a matter of importance.

There was no need for 'other means'. The door was opened cautiously by the Sudanese servant.

"Mahmed?" asked Faroukh, gruff. "I have urgent information for *Al-Rayiys*."

The servant hesitated, plucking at his *jellabiyah*.

"The master is not here," he said in Arabic.

"I know that, you fool," replied the inspector in the same tongue. "But we must speak to him. The police have heard his name, and are interested."

"Come inside, quickly."

Mahmed led them into a front room. There, over the mantelpiece, was a statue of Anuket. Faroukh dipped his head to her, and turned to the servant.

"Where is the master now?" He had to guess how much this man might know. "Is he already at the dam?"

The man hesitated. "No. He waits at his house below the river machine. I should tell him you are here."

"I must go there -it is not safe to do this by telephone or message."

Mahmed's eyes narrowed. "What are your names? I do not think—"

An unexpected blur, and the crack of stone against skull. Faroukh gasped. Miss Dawoud stood over the servant's body, the statue of Anuket in her hand.

"He was growing suspicious," she said bluntly.

"And now he can't answer any questions." The inspector bent over the man, who was still breathing. "Not yet, anyway. Miss Dawoud..."

She was already away into another room. "There will be clues, Inspector."

"I hope so," he muttered.

It was clear from a speedy examination that unless the house had been meticulously cleared, this was not the site for any ritual. The cellar held only coal; they found no marks, of struggle, blood or paraphernalia, nothing out of the ordinary apart from three or four figurines of the goddess, some curved knives mounted on a wall, and a few prints of Egyptian temples. Any antiquarian might have such around the house – they proved nothing.

"By the telephone." She called him over. A number was pencilled on the pad of paper which lay by the telephone receiver.

"Nothing for it," said Faroukh. "We must get this man, the number and anything else we can find to Mr. Holmes."

"How?"

He took out his identity papers. "I am still, technically, a Hammersmith police inspector. Until Superintendent Fisher finds out what I have been up to. Stay here, Miss Dawoud, and guard this fellow."

The constable walking his beat through Redcliffe Square was slow in grasping the situation, but at last did his duty. Soon a police wagon had been parked at a discreet distance from Abir Mekh's house. Faroukh and the young woman then 'walked' Mahmed to the vehicle.

"I copied the number," said Miss Dawoud, "And then wiped off the statue and replaced it."

"Good, good." It was disconcerting to find that she seemed more calm than he was. "Baker Street, driver."

The driver of the police wagon looked confused. "Sir, I-"

"Baker Street! This is a matter of national security, man."

Faroukh struggled with the rapidity of events. At their destination, the old lady, Mrs. Hudson, seemed entirely comfortable with the idea of them dragging an unconscious Sudanese up to Holmes's rooms.

"Will you be needing chloroform, sir?" she asked. "If the gentleman awakes?"

"I... no, I think not," said Faroukh. "Thank you."

She smiled. "Mr Holmes will return shortly, I believe. I shall make a pot of tea."

Holmes and Watson arrived within the quarter hour, arguing as they came up the stairs. It was the argument of friends, Faroukh noted, as if the years had rolled back.

"Dammit, Holmes, if you were—"

"I have told you, Watson, we must take them! Mere prevention of this disaster begs another one, one about which we may have no warning."

The two men paused at the sight of the inspector and Miss Dawoud sitting either side of an unconscious man, drinking tea.

"Bravo," said Holmes. "But do you think you might have struck this fellow rather too hard, Inspector?"

"I fear that I struck no one, sir." Faroukh glanced to Miss Dawoud.

"Great Scott!" said Watson.

They explained what they had found in West Brompton and gave Holmes the telephone number.

"A Richmond code. And that mention of the 'river machine', yes. Mekh must have taken a house below the Kingston Gate." Holmes paused, his eyes half-closed. "From there, his victims could be despatched into the Thames. Inspector, if you use your official standing, the exchange should give you the address; I shall consult the street map."

"Did you have any success, sir?" asked Faroukh.

"With Watson's help, yes. The good doctor alerted his Home Office contacts, and I put some stark facts before certain politicians to whom I had been of service some years ago."

"They listened?"

"They were unsure but thought the risk too great to ignore. Royal Engineers and civilian contractors have left for the Tideway Gate, to watch over it and to work through tonight and tomorrow, effecting emergency repairs. They now know how vital it may be that the barrier is restored to its full efficacy."

"And the dam?"

"Munitions experts are on their way to Molesey, with an armed escort. They will check the dam for explosives and watch for further interference. We shall see if they manage not to make themselves too obvious. I worry that Abir Mekh may get wind of their presence and be lost to us."

"What must we do?"

"We go to Richmond, without delay, and hope to come face to face with Mekh himself. I dare not leave this until tomorrow, under the circumstances."

"With the police or Special Branch?"

"And watch them stumble around, struggling to understand what is needed? There is no inspector at the Yard I would trust these days. No, Watson and I have faced worse situations. The three of us, armed—"

The four of us," said Faroukh, and gave Miss Dawoud a weary smile. "I have no wish to be beaten over the head."

Holmes looked displeased but nodded. "As you say." He noticed Watson examining the servant from Redcliffe Street. "I must instruct Mrs. Hudson on caring for this fellow, in case we miss Abir Mekh and need to question him. I assume he will live, Watson?"

"No doubt of that. Should I tie him, Holmes?"

"Best do so. Do you shoot, Miss Dawoud?"

"I have a small pistol in my bag. I am well acquainted with it."

Faroukh took the detective aside. "Mr. Holmes, do you have any sort of flare, or flare gun in your… remarkable collection?"

"I do."

"I may have a use for such, once I have made the necessary calls. I have a friend who may be able to assist - from afar. And there are two good men I could pick up from Hammersmith – reliable and sympathetic. We will need eyes all around the property if Mekh and his men run."

"Very well. But no more than those two." Holmes looked around at his companions. "Let us prepare ourselves."

*****

The expedition to take Abir Mekh consisted of two sturdy carriages – one bearing Holmes, Watson, and Miss Dawoud; the other, Faroukh and his men.

Sergeant and constable appeared unperturbed by the prospect of danger; more obvious in their faces was the excitement of working with the legendary Sherlock Holmes, and a venture which would be in all the papers. To hell with Superintendent Fisher.

"We'll finish them, sir," said young Bale, checking the revolver he'd been given.

Mekh's other house had been easily pinned down - The Willows, End Lane, Richmond. A 'river rental' as Holmes had remarked. "Normally taken for the summer and some light boating. Let us pray that he is there tonight, and the missing girl also."

End Lane was a gloomy, badly metalled track striking out to the north of Richmond. A single street-lamp stood by the closed gates to The Willows, not illuminating as far as the house itself. The place was aptly named. Close to the Thames by stands of willow and alder, it was set alone in poorly tended gardens, the whole surrounded by high iron railings. A lesser, unpopulated track lay behind the house, beyond more trees.

Holmes had the carriages stopped well before they neared the lamp.

"Both drivers have assisted me before. They will hold the road behind us, should Mekh's men try to pass."

He pointed out salient details to the others as they disembarked, checking his map by the light of a bullseye lantern. "Three methods of egress. A smaller gate to the rear, the entrance we face, and the river."

Faroukh's instructions to the policemen were clear – they were to guard the track and let no one escape. When Wilkins and Bale had padded away, the inspector and his three companions moved cautiously along the high railings

187

which surrounded the gardens, clouds obscuring much of the new moon.

From the gates to the front door of the two-storey house stretched a gravel path of some twenty yards; there were lighted windows at The Willows, upstairs and downstairs, and a figure lounging by the portico, smoking.

Nothing could be heard but the lapping of the river, a lone bird trilling to itself, and the drone of an airship passing somewhere nearby, beyond the clouds.

Holmes pointed. "See, by the river - an old boathouse. Miss Dawoud, you would oblige me if you would take up position there, to watch for any escape by water. With Faroukh's men in position, and the road guarded, we have them boxed."

There was a flicker of disagreement on her face, but she assented. Holmes reached into the canvas bag he was carrying and passed Faroukh a massive pair of bolt-cutters.

"If you will effect our entry, Inspector. The gates are observed, and I am too old to be climbing."

In the murk of the night, concealed from the house by alder trees, Faroukh bent to his task, cutting through a railing at ankle and shoulder height. The iron groaned – he paused and cut again.

"Through," he whispered, and the four of them squeezed into the garden unobserved. Miss Dawoud headed for the boathouse, whilst the others crept from one sprawling bush to another, until they were within feet of the side of the building. The guard was still at the portico, clearly watching the front gate. The rear gate, a smaller affair tangled with bindweed, appeared unguarded.

"If we could draw them out – or some of them, at least..." said Watson. "Hardly fancy a siege, what?"

"Wait, and listen," said Holmes. "I believe your own hand will soon need to be played, Inspector. You must judge when." And he slipped away, with only a faint rustle of rhododendrons.

"What does he plan to do, Doctor?" asked Faroukh after a minute or two had passed.

"No idea. Law unto himself, Holmes."

Any further comment was forestalled by an extraordinary sound from the other side of the house - a piercing ululation, the sound of a spirit crying out alone in the darkness. And through the willows glowed an eerie, flickering light, held by a tall, shadowed figure.

The cry resounded again, drawing a gasp from the man on guard. Voices came from within the house, and the front door opened. Two men stood there, one armed with a shotgun.

A third, high ululation shivered the night air, and then a harsh, rasping cry in Arabic:

"Al-Hakam, the Judge, has seen your idolatry!"

The light disappeared and then shone again; the three men from the house advanced on it uncertainly, firearms raised. As they closed on the figure's last known location, between two large trees, they called out angrily, and one of them went further into the bushes.

"As good a time as any," said Faroukh.

Standing clear of the bushes, he raised the flare gun and fired upwards. The shot whistled and then burst above the house, a crimson splatter against the muddy sky. One of Mekh's men turned and fired in the inspector's direction; Faroukh felt a hot pain as the bullet grazed his arm, but Watson fired back, and the man fell.

"Eyes!" cried out Faroukh and put one hand over his face. For a moment, he thought his idea had come to naught...

The grounds of The Willows were illuminated by a harsh white light, blinding Mehr's men, as a huge shape burst through the cloud-cover. The airship piloted by Faroukh's friend Abdel Sabahi was above them all, its great searchlights trained upon the house – Faroukh and Watson, forewarned, leapt forward to the open door, their enemies' shots going wild.

And then they were in, in to a disordered mess with hieroglyphs scratched into the scant furniture, charcoaled on walls, even daubed with paint onto the table in the hallway. The two men rushed from room to room up and down, weapons ready. There was no sign of Abir Mekh.

Holmes darted inside. "Two have fallen, one has run into the road. My fellows will take him. Where is our man?" Then he spotted an open French window at the back, and they heard gunfire by the lane, followed by an Arabic curse and crashing in the bushes somewhat closer.

"The river - his last option!" cried Holmes.

The way to the boathouse was overgrown, but the airship's lights showed all.

"Here, footprints, broken branches," said Faroukh, "Our man came this way."

They pushed through sparse rhododendrons to the near corner of the boat-house and pulled to a sudden halt.

Abir Mekh stood on a decrepit wooden jetty, breathing heavily, arms by his sides. Despite the lines of anxiety on the face, Faroukh could see that this was the man in Holmes's photograph.

The boathouse doors were open, and a small rowing skiff was in the water.

Taneta Dawoud was four paces from Mekh, her gun pointed at his head. "Get in the boat - murderer, defiler." She did not look at her companions. "I shall be revenged for my sister and for the others."

"We will take him," Faroukh called to her. "He will hang, I swear it,"

"Hanging is not the Egyptian way, not of old." Miss Dawoud's voice was ice. "Let him drown like Ese did, if he is so fond of the waters. Let Anuket take her own!"

Holmes pressed close to the inspector, keeping his voice low.

"That old skiff won't bear him for long, Faroukh. Nor, if my watch is correct, will the river suit him soon."

"But if he can swim..."

The woman fired once, into the air. Mekh flinched and eased himself into the small boat. Miss Dawoud's bared teeth glinted like fangs as Abir Mekh struggled with the single oar, trying to push the skiff away from the jetty.

"Allah, the river..." Faroukh stared as a sudden surge hit the boat. The level of the river was rising even as they watched, the currents swirling higher and wilder. Part of the far bank slipped as waves tore at the soft earth, and the jetty shook.

This was not his slow, steady Thames. A rush of wild water tore at the boat, slamming it into the rotting jetty, and the timbers broke, tipping the skiff. Abir Mekh shot a venomous look at the young woman, and tried to leap free, but the painter line was around his ankle. He fell helpless into the water – and he was gone beneath the surge.

Though Watson and Faroukh scanned both banks lest Mekh emerge, there was no sign of him. They stayed until the river lapped the walls of the boathouse, and then it subsided, almost as quickly as it had risen. Miss Dawoud let herself be led away but would not speak.

Watson stood by the house, watching Mekh's surviving confederate. "Did you—"

"He's not escaped," said Faroukh.

Inside The Willows, Miss Dawoud sat silent by the smouldering kitchen fire whilst a more thorough search was conducted. Behind a wall-hanging, Faroukh found a cellar door, and in the cellar was a pale young woman, gagged and bound on a mattress – unconscious, but seemingly unharmed. Beside her, only feet away, lay crates, spools of wire and detonator boxes, surely the tools by which Mekh and his men had meant to carry out their outrage.

Watson took charge of the girl, carrying her upstairs.

"Miss Esme Railton," said Holmes with satisfaction as he watched her settled on a crumbling sofa.

One of the carriage drivers entered. "Got a feller, Mr. Holmes. Bumped 'is 'ead on my lifesaver, but 'e'll talk, in time."

"Good work, Johnson."

Faroukh was tired, and his arm hurt. "I should see to Wilkins and Bale, make sure all is well." He paused. "Strange business, though, Mr. Holmes. A freak current, and a worthless boat."

Holmes tamped his pipe and accepted a box of matches. "Perhaps."

"You don't believe, then, that the Thames took its vengeance tonight?"

"Watson would like the idea. He has a romantic soul." The older man smiled with a humour Faroukh had not seen before.

"Then..."

Holmes drew on the pipe. "We might say that the Thames has its mysteries, as does the great Nile. Or we might rely on the fact that the engines of the Kingston Gate have been struggling against floodwaters for days, and this is the time of the night when, with river traffic light, they open the sluices to relieve the pressure."

"Ah. And your subterfuge to draw them out?"

"Our foes were from Mohammedan roots, despite their later beliefs. A slight adaptation of the muezzin's call from my time in the Sudan, and the lantern to add a certain touch, served well enough, I think. A challenge in English might have caused a stand-off, but such a phenomenon? What could they do but investigate, and save us the danger of forcing our way into the house?"

"I cannot argue, sir," said Faroukh, and went to the hearth. "Miss Dawoud, your sister has been avenged."

Taneta Dawoud lifted her face. Brown eyes, wet with tears. "She is still dead."

He took her hand. "The river brought Ese to us, and she has saved a city. Let us grant her that."

"Inspector, you are... a good man."

"For a Cairo dog, far from home," he said.

And she smiled.

Treasure of the Dragon

By Thomas Fortenberry

It had been a lazy morning spent idly in our rooms in Baker street. It was already approaching mid-day, and so far, all I had accomplished was reading the saga of a Viking named Eric Thorgrimursson. My leisure time ended though when Inspector Lestrade arrived at 221B. Mrs. Hudson ushered him into the study.

The inspector removed his hat and overcoat, unwrapped his scarf, and handed them to our landlady. "Dr. Watson. Mr. Holmes. I apologize for the interruption—"

"Please, Inspector, join us for tea. Mrs. Hudson, if you will put a pot on."

He rubbed his rough hands together. "I will join you for a cup," he shivered as his body began to adjust to the warmth of our room. "There is a wicked chill in the air this morning. Then afterwards, we must leave."

"Must we?"

"I require your help, Mr. Holmes."

A grin broke upon my friend's face. "As presumed upon your arrival. You are not in the habit of socializing. A visit here without cause would be abnormal indeed!"

"Indeed."

"Hence, the tea. Just as one waits for tea to steep, one needs time to extract the details of a story so riveting, I am sure. Sit, sit."

While the inspector settled in a chair, Holmes circled the mantle and gathered some tobacco from the Persian slipper where he stored it. With his back turned and fully displaying the velvet design of his robe, he scratched a match and lit the pipe. Once smoke began to rise, he returned to his seat facing Lestrade. However, he did not speak again until the tea had arrived, so I was forced to make small talk.

After Mrs. Hudson served us and left the room, Holmes asked quite abruptly, "So, tell me of the murder."

Lestrade was familiar enough with his eccentric ways not to be taken aback. "Yes, dive right in. Well, I was called out to Ashbery Hall in the early morning hours, shortly after three, in fact. You might recognize the place already, but it is the home of—"

"Sir Alistair Bergmann," Holmes finished with a puff of smoke.

The name jostled my memory. Alistair Bergmann was a banker with whom we had done business in the past. One of those pompous, somewhat bombastic men, yet capable and driven. Two years previously, Bergmann had helped untangle the finances connected to another fascinating case which I had recorded as, "The Squirrel in the Oaks."

"His wife insisted you knew him. In fact, the wife asked for you specifically, and, to be frank, I am a bit baffled."

"Unsurprising," Holmes offered.

Lestrade settled his cup carefully into his saucer. "Look, this is... See, his wife is insisting she saw something that... well, frankly, if you could see her, you'd know she probably isn't lying. She's frantic. Her eyes completely wild. She has the shakes. A quaver in her voice and then sometimes she just screams out. Absolutely distraught. Now, either she's the greatest actor ever, or she is telling the truth about what

195

she thought she saw. But then that means she is either crazy or probably temporarily snapped due to the stress."

"She may very possibly be, if you are implying in your fumbling way that Alistair Bergmann himself is dead."

"Ah, yes! Sorry. You see the strangeness of this case has got me rattled. Let me start over. Yes, last night Alistair Bergman was murdered."

"At his house, I presume?"

"Correct."

"How?"

"Well, that is the amazing part. He was burned to death."

"Burned?"

"Yes. Damn near incinerated."

I watched Sherlock Holmes eyes brighten and he sat up. "He was burned to death inside the home? Was there a house fire? Anyone else hurt?"

"No. The house is intact. Everyone else is fine. Bergmann was burned outside, in a gazebo on the back lawn."

"I see. No chance of an accidental burning? It was very cold last night. If it is the gazebo I am thinking of, there is a fire pit built into it. He must have had it going last night to be outside."

"Astounding! You have been there, then. Yes, you're absolutely correct. There is a fireplace built right into the centre of it. Nicest set up—or it was. But, not any more. The whole damn thing burned up. All that's left is that chimney and some of the superstructure."

"I see. However, you think it wasn't an accident. He couldn't have fallen asleep, say, and the seat cloths, or clothing, or wood accidentally caught fire by stray sparks?"

196

"Well, that was my original thought. However, the fire was weird. It burned the hell out of the place and even some of the grass around it. Alistair's body is damn near unrecognizable, charred to the bone in spots. So, it was an intense blaze. Plus, there is the wife's testimony. What she claims to have seen."

"And what did she claim to see?"

Inspector Lestrade took a deep breath and then cleared his throat. He took a drink of his tea. His hand trembled. "Now, these are her words, not mine. I questioned and re-questioned her all morning. I haven't gotten any sleep, but I know how to do my job. For hour after hour, though she was very rattled and crying, she's stuck to it straight through without varying a word. She insists she saw a flying dragon burn her husband alive."

"A dragon? As in the mythical creature—as in the story of St. Michael?"

"Yes. A flying dragon. A dragon that breathes fire."

I could see the humiliation burning in Lestrade's face as he stared at Holmes. I knew what it meant for him to say this before Sherlock Holmes of all people. He was a good and serious-minded policeman. I glanced over to see my friend's reaction. I knew instantly by Sherlock Holmes's raised eyebrows we were now involved in the case.

*****

It was a few hours drive out to Ashbury Hall, which lies northwest of London, just past the village of Bordewick. We arrived in early afternoon. Much as I remembered, the manor was quite exquisite in the modern artistic half-timbered style that harkened back to days of yore, with the dark timbers crisscrossing the whitewashed upper story to

197

bold effect. The drive up was picturesque, as the house lay in fields between a wood to the west and a lake to the east.

We were left in a waiting room for almost half an hour before Mrs. Bergmann presented herself. There was the impression of a mountain squeezing through the doorway as she entered. She was wearing a voluminous black dress with a massive hat with long black veils that obscured her entire head and shoulders.

"I see you have... changed clothes, madame," Inspector Lestrade said with frank surprise.

She shuffled over to a couch and sank into it. I could hear sobbing emanating from within the mound of black crape.

After several moments, she whispered, "I bought material from Courtaulds and had a seamstress in London design it last year for the funeral of one of Alistair's associates—Lord Dermott. Last September. Do you remember? It was in the papers and all the talk in the financial community. Lord Dermott was so important and helped legislate in the House. It was vital to be there. This mourning dress was made in honour of Queen Victoria's loss, for the dreadful loss of her dear Prince Albert. Only I never thought I would have to wear it... not a year later... for my own prince, my Alistair. Oh! Oh, Alistair!" Her voice rose into a wail and broke off into wracking sobs again.

After a quivering, sniffle-filled eternity, which lead to uncomfortable shifting on our part and Holmes wandering about the room inspecting knickknacks and pulling down and thumbing through several volumes of books, she quieted.

Holmes seized the moment, whirled and said forcefully, "Mrs. Bergmann! Greetings! I wish that it were under very different circumstances, however, Dr. Watson and I have once more returned to visit your beautiful home.

Inspector Lestrade was gracious enough to seek our counsel and in doing so, outline the horrors of last evening. My deepest condolences. However, time is of the essence and we are here to help. Therefore, if you would not mind lifting your veil, I would like to ask you a few questions concerning the extraordinary events of last night."

Edythe Bergmann complied. She was still the robust middle-aged woman I remembered meeting, yet the toll of the day made her features stark and drawn. The pain of her grief was evident in her red-rimmed eyes and downturned mouth. I took pity on her.

Holmes must have as well, because his questioning was rather more succinct than I expected.

"Mrs. Bergmann, was anything amiss last evening? Was there anything unusual?"

"No, we were enjoying a usual evening."

"Why was he outside? It was a cold night."

"He always sits outside. Every evening."

"So, there was not something personal... such as a disagreement between the two of you? Or a fight with the cook or someone else on staff?"

"No, of course not. He likes to smoke after dinner. I... I dislike the smell, especially if I am reading and getting ready for bed. So, he does not smoke in the house. He always sits out at his gazebo and smokes."

"Indeed! I remember sitting there with him one evening. Hmm. Was there perchance a visitor earlier in the day? Anything different?"

"No. Well, there was a letter that arrived in the afternoon. It seemed to bother him. He did go into his study for a while. I asked about it, but he said it was just work related. Something to do with an old client. He put it aside though so that we could enjoy the day. He never works after

hours, most especially on weekends. That is... was our time."
She put her head down into a black handkerchief. Her
shoulders shook.

"I see. Well, concerning the event itself. The actual
fire. How did you come to witness it if you were inside and
he was out at his gazebo?"

It took a for her moment to collect herself. Her voice
still broke as she answered, "If he has not come back in yet, I
always look out the window at him before I turn in for the
night. I will usually call to him and he will wave up at me.
But, tonight... I mean last night, I—I... I'm sorry...."

Her grief was heart breaking to behold. "It is alright,"
I said. "We understand."

When she recovered, she continued, "Last night when
I looked out, I saw him out at the gazebo. He had the fire
going as usual and was sitting there enjoying his smoke. Just
before I called to him, though, I noticed something out of the
corner of my eye. There was movement. Movement going
towards him."

Holmes stopped his pacing and stared intently at her.
"Movement? From where? Out of the woods?"

"No. It was over the lake. I think I saw it moving
because it blocked some of the moonlight on the water of the
lake."

"So, something was moving across the lake. Like a
boat?"

"No, in the air. I saw something in the air. I couldn't
quite make it out. It was black, and large, and floating
towards him. I must have been stunned because I sat there
looking at it for several minutes, trying to figure out what it
was. I thought it was a cloud or something at first, because it
did have blurry edges, almost like a fog bank. When you see
one like in the early morning. But, anyway, I realized I was

watching it, and it moved swiftly, and I noticed it kind of had more solid shape than a cloud, almost like a long snake."

"I see. And then?"

"Then I did yell out. I called his name. I remember seeing him look back over his shoulder at me, smiling like he always did. He thought I was just calling him to say I was going to bed. But I kept calling his name. I waved my hand and pointed, but he thought I was just waving. So, he waved back at me. He waved at me." She collapsed down again. "Oh, dear Lord! He was waving at me when it attacked!"

It took another ten minutes to get Edythe Bergmann back on track. It was understandable once we knew exactly what she had witnessed.

She crossed herself and continued, "He was waving and it was almost floating above him then and then underneath its body, the mouth of this... this flying thing opened up. Its... mouth on the end just opened like a maw... like some demon out of hell. It was glowing red with flame inside! He must have finally seen it because of the glow. He jerked around in the chair and then stood up. I called his name again. He yelled mine back and then... oh Lord! Then the fire just shot out and engulfed him. It was horrible. The fire just went spraying down all over him and the entire gazebo went up in flames. I—" her voice kept breaking—" I heard him screaming. He tried to run, I think. He took some steps, but then he just fell and didn't move anymore. He just burned. The last thing I remember was seeing the dragon's head and part of the body. I could see the teeth around the mouth and the scales on the skin. It was lit up by the glow of the fire coming out. Then it closed its mouth and the fire vanished. But he was burning. Oh, God, he was still burning on the ground. I know what I saw! It was a dragon! I swear to

God in Heaven! It was a dragon flying in the air and it burned my husband to death!"

She collapsed crying upon the couch, and I moved over to console her. I was concerned in her state that she might suffer an attack. I got her calmed down enough to answer a few more questions from Holmes, but there was nothing more to be gained from her.

Right after that final, horrifying sight of the dragon incinerating her husband, Mrs. Bergmann had fainted or passed out from the overwhelming shock of the moment. The staff, alerted by her screams, had entered the bedroom to find her collapsed by the window and then, naturally, had seen the shocking tableau from the window and learned the fate of Sir Alistair Bergmann.

Holmes decided it was best to leave the house for a while and allow Mrs. Bergmann to recover. He took the opportunity to examine the scene of the attack out back of the manor. Inspector Lestrade followed with one of his men, but at a distance as they discussed something.

We walked down a nice pebbled path to the remains of the gazebo. It was a burned-out ruin, with only a few standing now charred and blackened support beams remaining. Holmes spent quite some time examining the charred wood and blackened floor of the gazebo, and then the ground a few feet away where it was easy to see the outline of the victim in the burned grass.

Holmes took scrapings on blackened material and also samples of the wood and grass and dirt. I placed them inside small bottles I kept in my medical bag for just such purpose. Having worked with him for years, and knowing his inclination towards chemistry, I am always prepared to assist with extra bottles and envelopes.

Holmes then began circling the burned-out gazebo. He walked away towards the woods. I reminded him that Mrs. Bergmann had said the dragon flew in from the lake. He cast a disappointed look at me and then ignored me. He walked along the edge of the woods and then vanished into them for a time.

Inspector Lestrade walked up to me at the burned gazebo. "Where the devil's he off to now?"

"You know Holmes. Thorough, if anything. He is searching for clues, but likes to cover every option."

"Yes, well," the inspector grumbled, "eventually we need to head into Bordewick and get something to eat. I've been at this since last night, you know. Besides, I don't want to bother Mrs. Bergmann. She's very distraught."

I nodded. "She is. I agree. We shouldn't disrupt the household any more than necessary."

Eventually Holmes re-appeared from the treeline and then wandered down to the shore on the lake. After a while of pacing back and forth, he called us over. He pointed out an irregular series of small burned circles.

Lestrade noted, "I haven't looked at these. I didn't come down to the lake."

"Ah! There is a series of such curious marks that seem to run from the gazebo out to the shore of the lake. One presumes into the lake as well, though of course no record would remain." Sherlock looked far out across the waters. "Perhaps the other side as well."

I asked, "What does it mean, Holmes?"

"Dragon venom, Watson," he said with a twinkle in his eye. "The dragon drools!" He brushed his hands and gazed back at the house with an almost jubilant air.

"I do not see what is humorous about this grim situation, Holmes. Her husband was burned to death before her eyes. She is near emotional collapse."

"Exactly so," he said and clasped me on the shoulder. "It wasn't humour, good doctor, but science which brought on a smile. Because in the face of the impossible, hearing a wild tale of a dragon flying through the air and burning people alive, it is good to find concrete proof. We see, indeed, the factual proof that something astounding did happen. She is not insane. She is not lying. She saw something unbelievable. But concrete. Now we must uncover exactly what this concrete fact actually is."

Inspector Lestrade wrinkled his brow. "A dragon? A dragon is what she said. Impossible! It's so screwy. I was hoping you would dispel this foolishness. That is why I came to elicit your aid."

"Indeed, it is. Dragons... pshaw! However, do you believe in magic, Inspector?"

"I—"

"It was rhetorical. There is no such thing as magic."

"Then what do you mean?"

"Obviously, there is a dragon." Holmes then looked out over the lawn at the ruins of the gazebo. "Quite a dangerous creature at that. Therefore, we have no choice. We must find this real dragon."

The inspector was nonplussed by this remark, but I was more familiar with Sherlock Holmes and his rather obtuse way of speaking. When he had an idea, he was like a hound on the scent, and followed it wherever it led. However, for the poor hunters in the party, it was a bit difficult to follow along.

*****

We lunched with Inspector Lestrade in the nearby village during which Holmes spoke of nothing but varieties of pies and methods of their preparation. Afterwards, we returned to Ashbury Hall so that Holmes could ask one further indulgence of the now calmed Mrs. Bergmann.

"I need to search your husband's items, madame. His desk, his papers, his files. They may hold a vital clue."

She nodded her black shrouded head. "I understand. Certainly. It is why I begged the Inspector for your help. I remember what you did for others. I knew that if anyone could help, it would be you. My husband often talked about you, about the conversations he had with you. You impressed him deeply. I realize this situation is... fantastic. But it happened. I am not crazy. I have lost Alistair. You must find his killer."

"I will find the killer, madame. Believe me."

"I trust in you as Alistair did," she said.

"Thank you. If you will lead the way—"

"No. I cannot be here while you look. Mr. Roberts!" she called sharply to her butler. "Please show Mr. Holmes and the Inspector around the house again. But stay out of their way. Thank you. Mr. Holmes, you are free to search everything. I don't care. I just...can't be in there right now. Not in his room. Not with his stuff." Mrs. Bergmann began crying again and walked away, a dark, spectral shape swishing down the hallway.

As we walked down to the library, Holmes asked the butler, "One question, before I search these rooms. When the crisis occurred, when you all discovered Mr. Bergmann burning, and his wife having fainted at the same time, what were you all doing? Attending to her or...?"

"Well, I ran to check on her of course, and Mrs Smith and little Nelly. But, once we knew the—" he cleared his throat "—state of Mr. Bergmann, still burning as he were, I went outside and took the rest of the staff with me. The gazebo was still going and even the furniture and grass somewhat. We all had to help. It took us a while to put the fire out. It was... stubborn."

"Of course. Horrible business. Stubborn, though. It kept burning a bit?"

"Aye, sir. It kept going for a while."

"I see. While you and the men were attending to that, who remained in the house?"

"Just Mrs. Smith and Nelly. Nelly Ginzburg, the young maid. They were attending to Mrs. Bergmann. She was out for a while. I had her checked up on to make sure she hadn't had a stroke. But she was breathing fine. So, I left because of the fire. I thought it was fine to leave her with Mrs. Smith. She used to be a nurse."

"Of course. No, you did fine. In fact, I commend you all, the entire staff, on the way in which you have handled this nightmare. Admirable job! I was merely curious as to who was inside and who was outside. Thank you. Now, shall we search the study?"

It actually did not take much time, due to the fact that Lestrade and his men had thoroughly searched the house just that morning. Sherlock Holmes searched each room briefly, with the Inspector at his side, to whom he would put questions of clarity. He went through everything rapidly and in the end only came away with three items.

Two were physical and one was not.

The first was the letter that had arrived in the post to Alistair Bergmann before his death. It consisted of a single sheet. Emblazoned on it was a Chinese symbol. I did not recognize it.

"Meant nothing to me and the boys," Inspector Lestrade said, scratching his temple. "It's Chinese, but none of us are fluent in that tongue. We were guessing though, that it was maybe something he ordered, or some work-related note from an overseas account, maybe. But we figured there should be some figures with it, if so. Some kind of other paperwork or letters. Not just that... design. We know he handled Far East accounts for the bank. We'll have to find someone who can translate it. Otherwise, I don't know what it is."

"Ah, I appreciate your situation, but let me save you some time," Holmes said. "This ideogram—this symbol—I have seen before. The Tongs use it. It symbolizes a debt, a payment due."

"Tongs!" Inspector Lestrade ejaculated. "You mean the Chinese gangs? Those criminal networks are nothing to be trifled with, Holmes! Are you sure?"

"Quite. I have had my share of... dealings with them over the years. They are indeed a force to be reckoned with. A very serious matter. But perhaps directly relevant to the events at hand."

"How so?"

"Well, it arrived on this tragic day. It made him apprehensive and he retired to the study. In fact..." Holmes said, and at this point he drew out of his pocket the second item which had seized his attention. This was a crumpled piece of paper. He had withdrawn it from a waste basket. Upon it were written the letters GADHAVIBHOJ. Beneath these letters were the numbers 482-483. Both were then scratched through with lines.

"Yes, we saw that. Trash. What of it?"

"Perhaps, but it was very recent. It was in the wastebasket, not emptied, so recent. Furthermore, if you had been paying attention, there were blank papers in the study on the desk."

"Yes." Lestrade's brow wrinkled. "So, he had blank paper on his desk."

"Ah, indeed. But if you turn it into the light, you might see the impression of the letters that were written on the page above it. The fresh sheet at the former time, if you will. Do you remember me inspecting the blank sheet?"

"I do."

"Impressed upon it were the letters GADHAVIBHOJ and those numbers."

Lestrade ribbed his nose. "I see. Good eye. So, the note was written on the sheet above the blank one—"

"And then thrown away subsequently. However, at the time it was the freshest sheet, hence it was written last. Nothing else had been written or other sheets taken since these letters. Probably this is the very last note he wrote on that fateful day. The day when he had retired to his study, worried about this letter, which was inscribed with this ideogram."

"You say it means a debt? The kind a tong might write."

"Yes."

"So, this involves a Tong debt?"

"You begin to apprehend."

"Very well. Something involving a tong debt."

"Is it coincidence that a dragon—the very symbol of Chinese mythology and many a tong—appears magically and burns our victim to death on the day a tong debt notice arrives?"

There was a very long silence. I could see that Lestrade's mind was awhirl.

"I'll be damned," he said after several minutes. "That can't be a coincidence. So, that's it then. Some Far Eastern death cult debt."

"Perhaps. A portion of the story. Though, sadly, as of yet we do not know the beginning or the end of this sorrowful tale."

"Very well," Lestrade said, walking in a circle around. "Very well. I begin to see it now. Somehow the Tong uses a dragon or—err, I mean...."

"I understand it is difficult to wrap our heads around. It baffles the mind does it not? A dragon! It sounds ludicrous. And yet, we have seen the results for ourselves. It is a real thing which burns men alive."

"Dear Lord," Lestrade said rubbing his temples fiercely. "This is maddening. Or madness."

"Ah, you are not mad, Inspector, though you may feel it. I am sorry that you have been awake for a night and a day dealing with this tragedy. It is indeed maddening. But, moment by moment, we are unraveling the knot. Soon we will figure it out."

"I hope so! This is the craziest thing I have ever heard of... OK. What else? You seemed to think this thrown away note important. What about these letters and numbers? Wait!" He snapped his fingers. "A code, I presume. Damn, you are good. OK. A code. I could turn it over to the cryptographic boys. They have some men who work for the government that crack foreign codes all day long. Real bookworm types."

"Indeed, indeed. I know a few of them," Sherlock Holmes laid his finger alongside his nose. "If you will indulge me, Inspector. I might, yet again, save you some time."

209

"How so?"

"It is no code. It is a name. An Indian name. Bhoj Gadhavi. Merely written with surname first. And the numbers are just that. Numbers."

"Wh—" Lestrade growled loudly in an exasperated way. "I'll be damned! Indian you say! Now this is getting even stranger. First Chinese symbols and now Indian names. By God, what does it mean?"

"That question is the key. The key which is, in fact missing."

"What do you mean? What key?"

"What key, indeed! In fact, it is *the* key we are missing! This is the paramount clue." At this point Sherlock Holmes spun on heel and left the room.

Inspector Lestrade looked at me wildly. "What is he doing? Where is going?"

"I do not know. This is how he works."

Momentarily Holmes returned to the study accompanied by the butler.

"One last point of clarification, Mr. Roberts. We have finished our search. I was speaking with Inspector Lestrade and Dr. Watson and something came to our attention. Something missing."

"Yes, sir?" he asked stiffly. I could see the strain of the day was wearing on him as well. With the loss of the head of household and the inconsolable Mrs. Bergmann, I could only imagine the anguish they were all going through.

"Could you please show us where Mr. Bergmann kept his bank keys."

"His bank keys?"

"Yes. He is a banker. His work keys. The keys to the bank in London."

"Yes, of course. Mr. Bergmann always hung them here on this hook." The butler approached the desk and off to the side where there was a hook in the wood. The hook was bare. "Why... I—I don't understand. They are always hanging right here. He hangs them up the moment he enters the house. Always."

"Always? He never accidentally leaves them in his bedroom? Or on a table? The library perhaps?"

"No, sir. He is meticulous. He hangs them here. As a matter of fact, they were hanging here yester—the day he..."

His voice broke. I did not blame him.

"You are positive they were hanging here?"

"Yes sir. I dust every day. I know they were there."

"But you have not had time for dusting, or minor chores, since the accident?"

"No, sir. I have been... quite busy. And then the police were here."

"Of course. Perhaps they have been mislaid in the chaos. If you do happen to run across them, let us know. Thank you, Mr. Roberts."

After he left the room, Lestrade said, "You know they aren't in this house. My men turned it inside out this morning, and then you just went over it again. There isn't a pair of keys in this entire house."

"Exactly," Holmes smiled.

"So, what of it?"

"That is the key to everything."

"The missing keys?"

"The missing keys."

Lestrade stroked his jaw. "So, the missing keys are vital. Someone in this house had to steal them. One of the housemaids... no. No, it must be Roberts. He is the only one

211

that knew where and what those keys are for. So, it must be Roberts."

"No. You truly are a dolt."

"What?"

"Here." Sherlock Holmes handed the crumpled paper and the note with the Chinese ideogram on it to Lestrade. "I laid it all out for you. I suggest you move with alacrity. You see how organized they are. Time is of the essence! Come, Watson."

Inspector Lestrade purpled slightly and sputtered, "What the dickens do you mean? What do these—" he shook the papers in his fist directly in Holmes's face. "—explain? Alacrity? Time? What the—"

"Please, please! Don't spit at us."

Lestrade visibly controlled himself. "Listen, I brought you here to help me. You better explain."

"Explain? I have solved it for you! It is literally in your hands!"

"What is? I have mumbo jumbo from India and a symbol from China. Now you are talking about missing keys."

"Bank keys."

"Yes, I said that…"

The inspector's tirade petered out. He looked dazed for a moment and then blinked several times. "Wait. His bank keys are missing. There is a debtor's note from China. There is a name of an Indian man and a number—a bank box number!"

"Bravo, Inspector."

"Good lord! So, this is international. Foreign monies, perhaps something illicit to do with the Tongs…."

"Perhaps so. He was an international banker. He was given a Tong debt warning. His last act was to write out a name and number. He is now dead. He was killed by a Chinese dragon. One might wonder what treasure a dragon hoards?"

"My God! We need to get to his bank!"

"Indeed, you do! If not too late. Someone else has the bank keys. I do not mean these poor victims in this house. The staff is just as innocent as Mrs. Bergmann. I propose that while the entire house was outside occupied with the death of their master or upstairs dealing with the health of their Lady, someone slipped inside and removed the keys in question. Because, despite the fact that the dragon attacked from the air and was seen coming from the direction over the lake, there are trails in the woods which I followed that lead back to the road. This affords access to the house, though, due to the trees, one could have taken them and not been observed, especially at night."

Lestrade smacked his hands together, accidentally further crumpling the papers. He started marching towards the front door of the house.

"Inspector," Holmes called as he opened the door. "If you wouldn't mind the company, we wouldn't mind the ride back to London. In fact, while we travel, I have some ideas I would suggest."

Lestrade was nodding. "Ideas, huh? I bet you do. You're just full of them."

Mr. Roberts ran up, surprised by the sudden exodus. He held the door open for us.

"Yes, a few suggestions," Holmes said as we retrieved our hats.

We walked to the carriages.

"All right, Holmes. You're just playing with me. What's your biggest idea? Suggest away."

"Perhaps the most important one, you mean. I suggest you bring a lot of men to the bank."

"A lot of men? Why?"

"As large a group of policemen as you can muster. We are talking about the Chinese tongs here. They have a lot of members. Many are trained in exotic fighting arts. Better arm your men."

"Guns! Goodness. In the middle of London?"

"Yes. Better yet, with rifles."

"Rifles!"

"Yes. As a matter of fact, better make it elephant guns. Lots of big game rifles. Make sure you include men with hunting experience."

"What the—? Are you serious?"

"Have you forgotten the dragon, Inspector?"

He was speechless and we rocked along for some moments as the carriage moved up the drive of Ashbury Hall.

Lestrade eventually growled, "I don't know what to think of this dragon business. It seems absurd."

"Absurd it might be, but a very real threat. Just witness what happened to Bergmann. He failed to take it as seriously as he should."

Lestrade nodded and stared out the window a while. "So, we hunt a magical dragon."

"Indeed! However, it is very real. There is no magic. Please, take care to tell your men not to be frightened or distracted by the flaming venom it spouts. A fire-breathing thing can be quite shocking. They must not lose their heads. They must not be intimidated."

"I will tell them to shoot to kill the beast. Stop it before someone else is hurt."

"Exactly. Only with this beast, perhaps because of such apprehension I feel due to the myth of the hydra, I urge you to shoot at the body. Do not aim at its head. Fire upon the main body. It is the only way to surely bring it down. Furthermore, tell them to beware its fire. Do not stand beneath it or you will become victims yourselves. Fire on it, if possible, from a distance. Better yet, from places of height, such as the roof of the bank or surrounding buildings. When battling dragons, you must think like the dragon!

"Now, with that warning, I must turn our attention to ancient Byzantium. We seek the angel's revelation to Porphyrogennotos!"

Lestrade looked quizzically at Holmes. I saw upon his features a worried look of bewilderment and recognized it. I often wore this look as well. It was often hard to follow Holmes or understand where his mind led, though he more often than not he was correct. Often, caught in the frenzy of the moment, his thoughts seemed to bear no relevance to the events at hand. I knew from years of experience they did.

*****

The events which followed were spectacular, to say the least. I am sure you are well aware of the news stories now that the details of the case have been made clear. It was so sensational and also involving those various aforementioned nations, that it made newspapers around the world.

Sherlock Holmes and I stayed at 221B that day. He must have known how dangerous it was to become. He had dismissed our participation at the time as, "I have no desire to fight dragons."

"I thought that was what you did best?" I retorted.

He chuckled, a twinkle in his eye. "Ah, Watson! You poke at me. No, let dragons lie, I say. Why stir them up?

Better a slumbering serpent than one raining fiery venom down upon you. Of course, this one must be slain. It is already riled. The police are well equipped to do such slaying. They have plenty of guns and I have told them exactly where to aim."

I understood his point. However, I still regret not seeing the dramatic events in person. The pictures of the aftermath in all the papers were enough to pique my interest.

Holmes spent the evening reading. He started with a French text. Later I was to realize it was entirely relevant. *Ballon Dirigeable de Henri Giffard* was a detailed examination of the device of the French inventor and an accounting of the first 1852 flight of his airship. Holmes later explained to me the importance of this conceptual model. Then he turned to Greek tales of naval battles against the Persians and the later Byzantine defence of the siege of their city. I was nervous and stayed up late, but eventually gave up watching him turn pages.

When I rose in the morning, though early, I discovered Holmes already up, working with his beakers and retorts.

"Did you sleep?" I knew he often stayed up all night when driven to finish some experiments or obsessed with a project.

He glanced at me. "Enough. Perhaps more than you. You have circles under your eyes, Watson."

"I had a restless night. But I will be fine. Perhaps I need a bite. Care to share some toast?"

"Eh? I suppose. Have Mrs. Hudson start some tea. Actually, I am surprised the Inspector has not arrived."

"Is he expected?"

"After yesterday's battle with a dragon?" he laughed. "I assure you he is eager to share his exploits."

Later when Lestrade showed up he was barely through the frame of the doorway before he blurted out, "How did you know about the dragon, Holmes?"

Holmes walked over to his desk and picked up the French volume he had read last night. He handed it to the inspector. "Logic. We all know that Mrs. Bergmann saw a dragon. Yet they do not exist. As there is no such thing as magic and no such thing as fantastic monsters, only reality remains. Therefore, it had to be a device of some type. I deduced the nature of the flying contraption by the way she said it seemed to float quietly over the lake and yard, not crawling across the ground. It floated, it was silent, and yet seemed shrouded by clouds or fog."

"Excuse me—" I began, confused.

"The damn dragon was a steam-powered dirigible," Inspector Lestrade explained. "The blimp was painted like a dragon. It had a steam engine. The steam clouds came out of its snout, which had the result of enshrouding the body, the blimp itself, in smoke. At night, the disguise would be perfect. During the day we could perceive what it was."

"You might recall, Watson, that years ago during The Great Exhibition that Australian Bland displayed his steam-powered 'Atomic Airship.' It flew around London. It was all the rage at the time."

I sat down in my chair, rather dumbfounded. As usual I was playing catch up with Holmes.

Holmes continued his inquiry. "I assume they attempted an assault on the bank."

"They did. We held them off, but you were correct. There were a lot of those Chinese gang members. They can fight like nothing I've even seen."

"Indeed. They are skilled in the martial arts."

"It was touch and go for a while. Especially when they started with the flame-throwing. Killed several of our men. Horrible way to go."

"I warned you to keep your men well back. The flames came out of the mouth spout, correct?'

"Yes. But they could spray it a lot further. There was some kind of pump in the spout, and that fire sprayed out like oil."

"It was. Greek fire. πῦρ θαλάσσιον *pŷr thalássion.*"

"Come again?"

Holmes waved a hand languidly at his chemical apparatus. "I performed some experiments upon the substances I recovered from the yard of Ashbury Hall. It was a sulphur-rich bitumen. Quicklime, some phosphide. It is, in effect, a petroleum-like resin. Highly flammable and very similar to an ancient super-weapon. It is called "Greek Fire." It was used by the ancient Greeks, among others, to wage naval battles. If you remember your schooling, you probably read about it in your classical studies. Thucydides and other historians recorded it. It was sprayed out of tubes, usually with bellows, from one ship to another. The wood of the ships would catch fire and burn, even upon the sea."

Lestrade snapped his fingers. "Yes. Right. I remember those sea battles."

"And now, like an ancient Greek warrior, you have participated in one of these battles. Only this time the ship floated upon the air."

"I'll be damned." However, Lestrade looked very pleased and sat up straighter.

"So, you successfully brought down a dragon. Congratulations, Inspector."

"Thank you." His face darkened. "It wasn't so pleasant, however. We shot the body until it ruptured, as you urged. But then the entire damned airship went up. It was incredible! The fires that were in the mouth must have ignited the lifting gas or something. It erupted in fires almost like a bomb going off. Engulfed the whole thing. It burned up the skin and the whole airship collapsed down between two buildings, and burned in the street."

"Hydrogen, the usual lifting gas, is indeed quite flammable. I was actually hoping you would puncture the skin and bring it down with a leak of the gas. I was looking forward to studying the craft. Perhaps even flying in it after you had captured it."

"Not going to happen. The whole thing burned up. The only thing left now is a lot of twisted metal beams lying on the cobblestones. That dragon is never flying again."

"A pity."

"A pity you didn't see it. It was something else."

"I had no desire to burned. Besides, there was an off-chance that you would be defeated. Or that they would have beaten you to the bank and robbed it before you could stop them. I had some preparation and research to do to ensure I knew the full nature of the device, its operation, and capabilities, in case we needed to pursue it further."

"Good thinking. But it sure was a sight. No, we got there in time. You were also right about the numbers."

"The bank boxes."

"Correct. Turns out they belonged to an Indian."

"Bhoj Gadhavi."

"Correct. But, he's dead now. It seems he worked decades ago for several of the industrialists and shippers who were involved in that sordid Chinese business—"

"You mean the Opium Wars."

"Yes. From the documents we found, it seems that Gadhavi helped ship the opium from India over to Hong

Kong and other ports. The businessmen all made immense fortunes off this... illicit trade. One box held documents and stocks. The other was filled with gold and jewels which Gadhavi had apparently acquired during that time trading those drugs. An entire box of jewels! I mean emeralds, diamonds, rubies, sapphires...you name it! It was an absolute fortune!"

"The dragon's treasure."

"Absolutely. I have never seen so much wealth in my life. One of my men thought it is worth more than the Crown Jewels themselves. It was staggering to behold."

"I imagine."

"In fact," Inspector Lestrade stood up and patted his coat pocket, "I have something here for you. Word came from on high—I mean truly on high, majestically on high— that you were to receive a token of appreciation for the service you rendered."

Lestrade grinned and reached into a pocket and pulled an item out. Opening his hand revealed a ruby that was the size of a quail egg. It was the largest gem I have ever beheld. It gleamed redly in the light.

"Good Lord!" I gasped.

Holmes raised his eyebrows and actually put his pipe down. "Contain yourself, Watson."

"My God, man, look at it! That ruby is... is—"

"You've been rendered speechless."

"Who wouldn't be?" Lestrade says quietly. He twirled the gemstone which sparkled like a piece of magical, solid flame. He sighed and then dropped it in Holmes's hand. "I've never seen anything like this before."

"None of us have," Sherlock Holmes agreed. He raised the ruby in his fingers. "It is the eye of the dragon!"

Sherlock Holmes and the Clockwork Count

by Benjamin Langley

I'd not heard a knock at the door over the sound of air gushing from the great bellows of Mrs. Hudson's new cooker, so I was taken by surprise when she entered with a letter for Holmes. Her appearance in an iron apron, lightly dusted with flour, held my gaze to such as extent that I neither took in Holmes's reaction to reading the letter, nor saw him stand.

"Watson, I trust you are not otherwise engaged this evening?"

I put down my recently obtained booklet on the latest advancements in steam-powered surgical techniques from the Royal College of Surgeons and realised that it would have to wait. "What do you have in mind?"

"All will be revealed en route." He pulled out his pocket-watch to check the time. "No time to tarry, my dear Watson."

I barely had time to put on my overcoat and grab my walking stick before Holmes opened the door to a crisp October evening. As we ambled down Baker Street, the city illuminated before us—we were following in the footsteps of the lighter of the lamps, and his action lit up otherwise unseen parts of the street. From every grate, blasts of steam hissed, and many a chimney was billowing with smoke. Her Majesty

221

Queen Victoria had boasted of the golden age of discovery and invention that we should be thankful to be living in. Some quack had found himself spending time at Her Majesty's pleasure for interrupting one of her speeches by crying out that it was not so much a golden age, but one of brass and filth. But one cannot stand in the way of progress, and one must be thankful that so much of it is for our benefit. As we reached the edge of a small crowd waiting for the tram, Holmes stopped, looked back along the track, and muttered, "Perfect."

I turned to see the brass beast chugging towards us, carrying its six carriages behind it. London's trams, the envy of the world and the finest fleet in the Empire, were nothing if not reliable, and as the driver applied the brake and sounded the whistle, I couldn't help but check my own pocket-watch to confirm that once again, the service ran on time. Yes, it was a golden age indeed.

Once on board and seated on the plush, velvet cushions, I finally probed Holmes for information on our evening enterprise.

"A client," Holmes said. "He has invited us to see him perform tonight."

"Perform? What, pray tell, is this client performing? Where are we going?" I looked down at my attire. "Am I suitably dressed for the occasion?"

"It will suffice," Holmes said, unable to stop a wry smile from emerging. "Piccadilly is our destination. More precisely, Egyptian Hall."

I pondered for a moment. "Then your client can be only Maskelyne or Cooke." I relaxed into the tram's luxurious seats.

"Once again, Watson, you showcase your value."

I tried not to let the smugness show on my face, but Holmes continued.

"While it is clever of you to suggest Maskelyne and Cooke as my client, given their ongoing residence at Egyptian Hall, you are quite mistaken."

"Then who else could it be?" I asked, incredulous.

"If you were a little more perceptive, my dear Watson, you may have noted that in recent reviews and promotional materials Maskelyne and Cooke have boasted of bringing talents to the stage from all around the country."

Holmes, of course, was right. Their posters had adorned the streets for so long, that I had stopped paying attention to them, and having read one write-up of their albeit impressive sounding illusions, I had no reason to read another.

"Maskelyne and Cooke are hosting our client," Holmes said. "We will watch the performance tonight and meet with him upon its conclusion."

The tram-stop in Piccadilly was only a short walk from Egyptian Hall, which, in recent years has dubbed itself England's Home of Mystery, and while I had never previously visited, I had been assured on many occasions that it was a fine show, and Maskelyne and Cooke were illusionists beyond compare. As we headed towards the southern end of the street, Egyptian Hall came into view, its façade designed to evoke images of Egyptian tombs and adorned with sculptures like those discovered in that antique and distant land. Holmes insisted on paying my five-shilling entrance fee that bought us seats close to the front of the performance and no sooner had we entered Egyptian Hall than the whistle blew to indicate the imminent commencement of the performance.

Throughout Maskelyne and Cooke's part of the show, Holmes watched each illusion intently, nodding knowingly when he figured out the workings of the illusion. I too joined him in this escapade, spotting acts of sleight of hand and misdirection and figuring out most of the tricks (the levitation was very cleverly performed), though some had me stumped.

Once the rapturous applause was subdued by the pleas of Maskelyne, he made an announcement: "Ladies and Gentlemen, I thank you for your warm applause. We have one more illusion to perform for you, an illusion that will leave you astounded, astonished, flabbergasted! But before that, and for one night only, an act the like of which you have never seen before. Performing for the first time in London, it is my great pleasure to introduce an escapologist of extraordinary ability: The Clockwork Count!"

Two burly men wheeled a fabulous contraption onto the stage. A clock at the back of it ticked noisily and a series of cogs turned and parts of the mechanism moved rhythmically. Every few seconds a jet of steam burst from one of the pipes surrounding the machine. Moving in time with the ticking of the clock, jerkily, more like a machine than a man, The Clockwork Count entered, moved to stand in front of the clock, and bowed. His black hair stood on end as if he'd recently received an awful fright.

"Welcome," he cried in a booming voice. "Let me demonstrate my wondrous wheel for you."

The Count pulled a lever, and one of the larger cogs moved in to the centre. To this cog, the Count attached a number of long, wooden poles. He pulled a lever on the other side, and the cog begun to spin, and the blades fell into place. We watched as the blades closed in on the wooden poles. It took no more than two minutes before the end of the first pole was sliced clean off. With each rotation those vicious blades took another slice of the poles. One minute later it had reduced all of the poles to the few inches that remained inside the circumference of the cog.

"Now you have witnessed the power of my machine, I shall place myself at its mercy," The Clockwork Count said without a shred of emotion to show the fear he must surely have been feeling.

From the rear of the hall, a gentleman approached and helped chain The Clockwork Count to the cog. Further chains were wrapped around him, and handcuffs fixed him firmly in place. Volunteers from the audience were called upon to test the chains and confirm that the Count was well and truly stuck.

"Pull the lever," said the Count to one of the volunteers who quickly did as requested.

The Count began to spin on the cog. Jerkily, he moved his body in time to the ever-ticking clock. If the previous exhibition was anything to go by, he had only two minutes to escape before those blades would start to slice away at his limbs. Jets of steam shot out from the machine, drawing my eye.

"Misdirection," whispered Holmes.

I resisted looking away when next a blast of steam escaped and saw the Count's elbow move at an impossible angle. The next time it was his shoulder. It was almost as if he were dislocating his own joints to escape the chains. As the two-minute mark approached, it was clear that his upper body was free, but the ever-circling blade passed only inches from his toes. When it seemed certain that he'd lose them, he somersaulted forward, free of the still spinning machine and the whirling blades to bow down before the rapturous audience.

"Remarkable," I said, leaning in to Holmes to make myself audible over the crowd's noise. "He must be the most double-jointed man I've ever seen." My knowledge of human biology certainly gave me the edge in deducing how this particular escape was accomplished.

"Yes, certainly something unique about those joints," Holmes remarked.

The Clockwork Count's astounding performance somewhat overshadowed the show's grand finale, and Maskelyne and Cooke knew it. While they performed with gusto and received apt praise, one couldn't help but feel that they'd come away with a touch of disappointment about the way that one of their guests has stolen the limelight. I for one couldn't wait for it to be over, knowing that I'd be meeting The Clockwork Count upon its conclusion.

*****

In person, The Clockwork Count moved much more normally than he did onstage–the jerky movements to the ticking of the clock were all part of a stage persona. He was a slight man of average height, his shock of black hair seemingly not part of the stage persona, but an uncontrollable mess that was permanently seeking new heights. Holmes and I were already waiting in a backroom of Egyptian Hall which gave Holmes the opportunity to inspect some of Maskelyne and Cooke's equipment. As Holmes was closely studying the collapsible cage used in the disappearing/reappearing barn owl trick, I approached the Count.

"It's a pleasure to meet you," I said.

He laughed and shook my hand. "Mr. Holmes?"

"No, Watson."

Holmes turned away from the contraption and moved to the Count. "I'm Mr. Holmes, and you, Sir, are not who you claim to be."

The count held up his hands. "Guilty as charged. What do you know?"

"First, you are not a count."

"True. It's a stage name."

"But if you don't yet have a title, you are heir apparent to one."

"Very good, Mr. Holmes. Clifford Kingsley, heir apparent to the title of the Baron of Scarsdale. How did you know?"

"Your manner of address on the letter inviting me here tonight suggested the kind of upbringing one of nobility would have had. One without a title would be unlikely to elect to use 'count' as a stage name. If you already had the status, your profile would be too high to perform to a mid-size audience during the middle of the week."

"I knew you were good, Mr. Holmes, but this is extraordinary."

"Then allow me to continue. You're much less of an escapologist than you are an inventor or engineer as indicated by your calloused hands and the minor cuts and scrapes they bear. These originate from mechanical tinkering, not from constantly squeezing from chains."

"Did you not see my act tonight?"

"I did, and I must say, Kingsley, it was a very impressive performance."

"Thank you. Is there anything else?"

"You fear for your life."

The confidence drained from Kingsley's face. "How... did you know?"

227

"After coming into the room, you have remained close to the door. Several times since entering you've looked back towards it. Both the shadow and the occasional sigh reveal that you have someone waiting nearby for you. That is why you wanted to see me. You want me to find out who wants you dead."

"Mr. Holmes," said Kingsley, his voice no longer strong and confident, panic dripping from every word, "last week, someone tried to poison me. If it weren't for Jack raiding my plate, I'd be dead instead of him."

"Jack?"

"My cocker spaniel. A mere puppy."

"And you think that poison was meant for you?" I interjected.

"There's more."

"Go on," Holmes said, stroking his chin.

"Some of my equipment has been meddled with. Had I have not noticed, I would have received a blast of steam directly to my face."

"You weren't concerned about performing tonight?" I asked.

"I assure you, tonight I was more than safe."

"Mr. Kingsley, you have my attention," Holmes said. "Now, what is it that you would like me to do?"

"Return with me to Sutton Scarsdale. Stay in Sutton Scarsdale Hall. Find the man who wants me dead and stop him."

Holmes turned to me. "Are you available for the next few days, Watson?"

*****

228

Early the next morning, when we arrived at Kingsley's zeppelin, we found him standing upon the boarding platform.

I pulled out my pocket-watch to confirm that we had arrived on time. "I do hope we have not delayed your departure," I said, noting that the crew were making final preparations for take-off.

"Worry not, Watson. This is the time that I asked you to arrive. I had no desire to waste any of yours or Mr. Holmes's precious time waiting for us to load."

Holmes approached Kingsley and shook him by the hand with greater vigour than his usual habit and held the handshake for longer than normal. I could see a dash of unease appearing in the wrinkles around Kingsley's eyes and in the lines forming on his brow, but then Holmes released his grip and looked closely at the platform and the zeppelin. "What's your cargo?"

Kingsley turned to check the cargo doors (an atypical feature of many of the smaller personal airships) but they were firmly closed, and the docking platform retracted.

"Maskelyne and I came to an agreement. In exchange for some of my contraptions, I have taken some of his."

"And I trust it won't weigh the airship down too much?" I asked, wary of boarding a zeppelin too heavily loaded.

"Dr. Watson, I assure you this is one of the finest vessels ever to take to the skies."

I took a step back to take it in. The skin of the airship seemed to be leather: a porous material. The thick rope net that surrounded it would do nothing to keep the air in. The gondola was among the largest I'd seen, and the mahogany and brass finish was certain to add to its weight.

"Is the airship's envelope made from leather?" I asked, as Kingsley pointed us towards the entry ramp.

"I understand your concerns Dr. Watson," Kingsley said. "But I assure you it's quite safe."

Holmes started towards the gondola, and I followed.

"You're concerned that the leather won't hold in the air well enough, and we won't be able to generate enough hydrogen to keep us afloat?"

I nodded in agreement, and he followed behind, urging us to board.

"There is another skin inside–completely air-tight–a thin canvas coated in animal fat. The leather outer-skin is both for show and for the protection of the inner bladder." Again, Kingsley was revelling in the revelation of the technical aspects of his design, and his confidence spread to me as I followed Holmes (who seemed to have no doubt about boarding the vessel whatsoever) onto the ship.

Kingsley led us down to the lowest part of the gondola, a spectacular glass-fronted viewing deck. There were several tables and a bar, suggesting that Clifford Kingsley often entertained on board.

"If you'll excuse me," said Kingsley once he had urged us to sit, "I need to give the crew orders for take-off."

Holmes surveyed the deck. I did the same, though our reasons for doing so were very different. I calculated the weight of all of the tables, while his mind raced through a thousand possibilities, calculating probabilities and testing hypotheses.

"Are you confident that this vessel is safe?" I asked as I felt the rock of the gondola lifting from the platform.

"My dear Watson, there are several factors which give me tremendous comfort here. First, this is the vessel by which Kingsley arrived in London. You saw his equipment for last night's performance. This airship has clearly been used many times with incredibly heavy cargo. Secondly, he is an inventor. This technology would have been tested time and time again before it was put into action. I would imagine that Kingsley can calculate to the ounce the lifting capacity of his creation, which, as you can see, he is clearly proud of." At this point Holmes broke off to point out some of the elaborate decoration around the periphery of the viewing deck. "Thirdly, Kingsley has asked for our help to keep him alive. Therefore, he values his life. I am certain that Kingsley has boarded the vessel which tells me that in his opinion, which is undoubtedly an expert one, this airship could not be safer."

"How can you be so sure that he is an expert in this field?"

"Preparation, Watson. Last night, while you were reading your booklet on surgical techniques, I had a few errands run. By the time you had fallen asleep, I had received a number of pamphlets on the development of airships in the last twenty years. Kingsley has proved himself time and time again in this field and in many others. He is something of a marvel, it seems."

"And could this be why someone wants him dead?"

"There are many possibilities, Watson, more of which will become apparent once we have had a chance to discover his ancestral home in Derbyshire. I shall take advantage of the time on board to catch up with some sleep. You may choose to do likewise."

Sleep, I did not. The view of London from above never gets old. We had taken off from Potter's Field Park in Southwark, so immediately saw views of the Thames. Looking out towards the Docklands you could see the factories with their enormous bellows used to power the suction of water from the river. We passed over the Tower of

London, and soon, the Houses of Parliament came into view. Big Ben, with its newly adorned brass face, rang out to signal that it was already nine o'clock. As we moved further from the city, it was clear that industry was alive in the factory districts, great plumes of smoke pouring from the chimneys of the effervescent factories. Soon England's green and pleasant lands came into view as we left London, and while we were away from industrialisation, agriculture proved itself to be just as teeming with life as farmers worked to harvest the last of their crops.

"Enjoying the view, Watson?"

I turned to see that Clifford Kingsley had returned to join us. "Indeed. May I ask, at what speed are we travelling?" It had seemed that we had left London much quicker than on my last flight.

"We are currently travelling at approximately 50 miles per hour – but the wind is with us."

"That's impressive. Everything about this vessel is impressive."

"I thank you."

"What can we expect to find waiting for us at Sutton Scarsdale?"

"Oh, I assure you the welcome will be a warm one. Father will no doubt air his criticisms about my hobbies. The closer he gets to death the more cantankerous he becomes."

Kingsley must have seen how taken aback I was by the way in which he spoke about his father, Baron Kingsley, as he abruptly brought his tirade to a halt.

"I do apologise. When you meet my father, you will come to understand that we don't have the best of relationships. He abhors my exploits; he calls them ungentlemanly. Both of my brothers are likely to be home. My sister will no doubt remain in the sunroom completing the needlework that has occupied her since mother's passing. My fiancée is also likely to be present."

"And what of servants?"

Both Kingsley and I turned to look at Holmes, whom I had presumed was sleeping soundly.

"Yes, lots of those. The Glossops have been with us for generations. The Bagshaws are a large family in the area, and we have a number of those working for us. There's a rather unpleasant chap that attends to the horses–goes by the name of Thornley. But to be frank, none of them are likely to be the orchestrators of a death plot, even if they have been enlisted."

"I have to say, you don't sound keen to get back home."

"Would you be, if you thought someone wanted you dead? But even before that I've made these forays away from the Hall as frequently as possible. Some nest for life, others fly as soon as they are able."

"But as the heir to the hall and the title, you're surely not expected to fly?"

Kingsley cast his arms wide in an elaborate gesture, causing me to glance at the clouds beside us. "And yet I do, Watson. And yet I do."

We continued our conversation until Sutton Scarsdale Hall came into view. From its position on top of a hill, it dominated the landscape and was surely the finest home in the region. It even had its own hangar for the airship. The crew expertly guided it in and then busily prepared for us to disembark. From the window I spied other airships, much smaller, designed for single riders, the likes of which I'd never seen before. These too were no doubt Clifford's creations.

We were greeted in the hangar by what I could immediately tell was one of Clifford's brothers. He had the same untameable black mane, and matching eyebrows, and while his face didn't bear the confidence of Clifford's, it had a geniality of its own. By their warm embrace, it was evident that Clifford was rather fonder of this brother than he was his father.

"Holmes, Watson," Clifford called to us, "may I introduce you to the baby of the family? This is Walter."

"So, Clifford tells me you're here to look over some of his inventions and give him some guidance on his misdirection?"

"That's quite right," Holmes said, shaking Walter's hand, again holding it for much longer than was his usual practice while I pondered Clifford's own act of misdirection. Was Clifford protecting his brother from the horrific idea of an attempt on his life, or merely keeping a potential suspect from knowing he'd brought in reinforcements? Suddenly I was forced to wonder if the geniality I'd seen was genuine.

"I have to say," Walter said, "Miss Blundell will be awfully glad to have you back."

Clifford smiled and placed a hand on his brother's shoulder and urged him to turn towards the house. "I trust you did a fine job of looking after her."

Walter shook his brother off. "I shall have to see you at the house later. There are a few things I need to attend to in the workshop." He nodded to us and muttered how awfully nice it was to meet us before he hurried away.

We had the opportunity to meet the other male members of the family when we reached the hall. We met James first, Clifford's junior by only eighteen months. If one were to guess, they would surely consider James the elder sibling due to the conservative manner in which he'd tamed his hair, slick against his scalp, and his thick moustache. He looked up from his papers for only long enough to offer us a cursory nod. Clifford greeted him by stating his name. No more. If nothing else, this suggested the warmth with which he greeted Walter was genuine.

Baron Kingsley was in the parlour in a wheelchair quite unlike any I'd previously seen. Behind it was a huge brass tank, and the structure of the chair was far bulkier than those I was used to seeing. Surely something so heavy would be difficult for one as frail as Baron Kingsley to manoeuvre? He quickly proved me wrong by pushing forward a small lever that stuck up from the right arm of the chair, which caused it to creep forward. I could hear the inner-workings of the cogs as it moved.

"Father," Clifford said, taking his father's hand. "How's the chair working out for you?"

Before he could answer a hiss of steam came from the back of the chair, causing the old man's body to stiffen. "Glossop!" he called. He shook his hand free from Clifford's. "The blasted thing is always running dry. You should have made a bigger tank."

"If I'd have done so, Father, it would topple backwards. You'd be stranded like an upended tortoise. We couldn't have that, could we?"

"Glossop!" cried the baron again before turning his attention back to his son. "You shouldn't be wasting your time with such frivolities. It's unbecoming for a man of your stature. You will bring shame upon the family." The baron turned his head to one side, again barking for his servant.

A man entered shortly afterwards carrying a large pitcher of water. I assumed this was Glossop.

"What took you so long?"

235

"Sorry, Sir," said Glossop as he twisted the cap off the tank at the back of the wheelchair and poured in the water.

"Have you any family members that don't already work here?"

"Yes, Sir. My youngest daughter."

"Have her come from now on. She can follow me around and fill my tank."

"Yes, Sir. Thank you, Sir."

Glossop turned to leave the room.

"Don't venture too far away. I'll no doubt need this refilled again shortly."

At this point Holmes stepped forward and shook Baron Kingsley by the hand in his new manner. "A pleasure to see you again, Baron." Holmes urged the Baron to turn away from us, and they were soon engaged in quiet conversation.

"I had no idea that Mr. Holmes and my father were acquainted," Clifford said, turning to me looking for light to be shed upon the situation.

"Before my time, I'm afraid."

"Then may I show you the sunroom? I'm rather proud of my work there."

I responded positively, and while he led me down the hall, he revealed that it was the one room in which his father had allowed him to install any of his inventions, for it was the only room in the house which Baron Kingsley no longer entered.

The sunroom had a warmth that was absent from the rest of the house, and two further people were basking within. Upon hearing our entry, one of the two women rose and approached us.

"Watson, I'd like you to meet my sister, Eleanor."

Eleanor was fortunate not to have inherited the family hair, but she also lacked her brother's geniality and after briefly allowing me to take her hand, she again returned to her seat.

Clifford approached the second chair, which was occupied by the room's other guest. Clifford placed a hand on her shoulder, and she turned, and upon seeing him stood up and took him into an embrace the coldness of which brought a chill to the room.

"This delightful creature," Clifford said, "is my fiancé, Miss Wilhelmina Blundell."

Miss Blundell shook my hand, her grasp firm and looked into me with her piercing eyes. She certainly seemed like a fitting partner for Clifford, though I suspected that their relationship would be equal parts days in the sun and stormy nights. With a quick drop of the shoulders her arms disappeared within the folds of her purple, crushed-velvet mantelet, and she returned to her seat.

"Wilhelmina tends to give me the cold shoulder upon my return from unadvertised jaunts."

"Really, it's not my place to comment..."

"Now, Watson," he said, cutting me off. "Do you know what's significant about this room?"

I took a cursory glance around the room, and then pulled out my pocket watch.

"Exactly. From the position of the room, you'd expect us to have lost the sun by now, am I right?"

"Quite right."

Clifford approached the wall, and turned a crank about a half turn. Sunlight flashed into my eyes and I had to raise my arm to shield myself from blindness.

Sighs rose from the two women in the room, and Clifford cranked the handle back to its original position.

"A series of mirrors give us the sun here all day long."

I nodded. "Remarkable," I muttered.

"That's not all."

Clifford proceeded to show me the wonders of the sunroom. Each lever, pulley, and crank revealed a secret.

"You can have your entire breakfast served in this room without any human interaction outside of these simple operations."

"Oh Clifford, you can be such a frightful bore when we have a guest." Wilhelmina had stood while I was discovering the secrets of the sunroom. "I am going to take some air." She left without a glance back at us. Eleanor, no doubt used to Wilhelmina's ways, continued with her needlework.

"I suppose we really must reunite with Mr. Holmes," Clifford said. "I do apologise if you have found my company tiresome."

"On the contrary," I said. "It's very impressive."

"Alas, a failure. I hoped Father would make use of it. He used to love to breakfast in the sunroom with Mother, but, since her passing…"

As Clifford Kingsley left his words hanging in the air, Holmes entered.

"Ah, we were about to seek you out," Clifford said.

"Your father pointed me in the right direction," Holmes said. His eyes were taking in the room, feasting on all of the little details, no doubt deducing the purpose of each lever and pulley.

"About that," Clifford said, sounding somewhat sterner. "I believe that it was remiss of you not to mention that you were acquainted with my father."

"I apologise if it caused offence. A trivial matter some years ago. It really has no bearing on our current situation."

238

Realising that there were more than us three in the sunroom, Holmes took the trouble of introducing himself to Eleanor, insisting upon greeting her as he had done with her siblings and father – the awkward handshake.

"Now, I believe we should take this discussion elsewhere – to your workshop, may I suggest?"

*****

The day had warmed to some degree to become a pleasant autumn day. My body cried out in jubilation as I took in that sweet and fresh Derbyshire air. One forgets just how thick with smog the streets of London are until one escapes them. Alas, the break was only momentary, as we were soon in the presence of the almighty furnace which was part of Clifford's workshop. It was difficult to ignore the blasts of steam, the rising pistons, and the turning cogs. It was also clear that Clifford wanted to show off some of his contraptions as he started towards a chair with an assortment of locks and brass plates fitted to it, but Holmes urged him to listen.

"Clifford, if your life is in danger, as you claim, and one of the persons in your home wants you dead, then you must listen. You need to go about your daily business as you would have done before. Any changes in your actions could alert the villain that we are on to them. My presence here alone could be enough to stop the wheels of conspiracy from turning.

"Watson, I will need to enlist you to support me in this endeavour."

"Certainly," I said.

"We shall divide our time so that one of us remains always with our client, and one observes the antics of those in

239

the house. If there is no action within five days, we shall have to take another course of action. Mr. Kingsley, is that to your agreement?"

"Yes, though I must insist that some of my workshop is off limits."

I nodded in agreement.

"I am not here to steal your tricks, Mr. Kingsley. Please work on anything you need to freely in my presence. I may even be able to offer you guidance."

"Guidance? I didn't think that you professed yourself an engineer?"

"No, but I see things others refuse to. If you are looking to misdirect, I may be able to make some suggestions."

"Watson, shall I suggest you return to the house, and I shall take the first watch here?"

Having been dismissed, I departed as Holmes made Clifford's workshop his business.

*****

I watched the Kingsleys, their houseguests, and their servants for the next few days without discovering a single thing of interest. Both James and Walter spent time in the house busying themselves in various ways, and they both liked to spend time in the workshop too. It was evident that Walter had more than a little fondness for Miss Blundell, but she treated him with the same distain and cursory comments as she did Clifford upon the occasion of their being reunited days earlier. Despite the clear frostiness between Clifford and James, it was apparent that they had a shared interest in engineering; the difference between them was that James would not exhibit this fondness of ingenuity in public, preferring to portray the character of the respectable gentleman, as if he were the man who would be baron and not Clifford. He even spent time in the workshop when Clifford wasn't present, as did Walter: if either wanted to endanger their brother's life, they could easily tamper with the equipment.

The Baron remained cantankerous as he chugged around the house, with Glossop's poor young daughter constantly topping up his water and running to and fro to make sure her own jug always had plentiful supplies. If I found myself caught in conversation with him, the clocks would slow, and I would be stuck for an eternity. Eleanor was a different kind of tedious, very hard to engage in conversation, and doing little other than her needlework. Miss Blundell was quite the opposite, buzzing around the Hall busily, lounging in no spot for long enough to plant roots. A summer house guest of the Kingsley's, she'd long outstayed her welcome in the Baron's eyes, though she was largely amiable to me and spoke with kindness to the servants. It was her fiancée that she treated with most disdain, and through her cruel barbs I was surprised that Clifford could maintain the smile on his face. In fact, it was Walter that was most annoyed by her quips, perhaps wishing they'd been aimed in his direction instead.

On the fourth morning Holmes came to my door early, long before the rest of the house had woken.

"Would you care to accompany me to the sunroom?" he asked as he stood in the hall in his housecoat and slippers.

"Really Holmes, this is most extraordinary. Is something amiss?"

"Not yet, but I feel it is time to step up our efforts. Come."

In the sunroom, Holmes used the contraption to serve himself coffee. He clearly had no intention of getting any more sleep. I feared that I was likely to suffer the same fate.

"Tell me of James Kinglsey. Does he seem like a nervous man?"

"Not at all. He is sober and resolute: unwavering, I'd say."

Holmes gently stroked his chin, pondering my thoughts. "And Walter?"

"A little more excitable, but I wouldn't call him nervous. I fear he has somewhat fallen for his brother's fiancée."

"Tell me of Eleanor."

"Holmes, she is perpetually at work with needle and thread, but she seems to be making no progress whatsoever. It's almost as if she's emulating Penelope and unpicking it each night."

"Watson, that's it."

"Eleanor?"

"No, Penelope. She unpicked her work each night to delay having to choose a suitor to replace Odysseus, correct?"

"Yes," I agreed. But I did not see how Greek mythology was going to help us here.

"And how did Odysseus safely re-enter his palace?"

"In disguise."

"Exactly."

But Holmes had not brought his face paints and costumes with him, and I could see little benefit from pretending to be anyone else.

"Watson, we are about to move to a new phase in our investigation. I need you to be eagle-eyed today. Watch Clifford carefully and be ready to report back this evening. The outcome of this case is dependent upon you today."

With that, Holmes released me, and I did not see him again until evening. Despite his assurances that we were making progress, I was ready to reveal my frustrations and declare the whole endeavour a waste of time.

"It's all falling into place, Watson," Holmes said, much to my surprise.

"Falling into place? I'm no further ahead than I was when we arrived."

"On the contrary, Watson, I have nearly discovered every last aspect – other than who the culprit is."

"But… how?"

"My dear Watson, it's all there right before your eyes, but one must know where to look, and which lines to read between."

"Care to enlighten me?"

"Alas, Watson, enlightening you would not help me to reach the conclusion. In fact, it could very well jeopardise the plot, though I would very much welcome hearing your findings."

"Finding? Holmes, I assure you that I have no findings. I barely have any observations worth the ink they're written in. And today I got the distinct impression that even Clifford has tired of our presence here. He barely said a word to me all day."

"Again, Watson, in this case I fear you may be mistaken. Tell me about the comings and goings in the sunroom today."

I flipped through the pages in my diary. There really was nothing of consequence to share. "Almost everyone comes and goes in the room. Most often to sit and relax. Only Clifford uses any of the room's ridiculous contraptions, though it seems that both Walter and James have been assisting him with some work in there. Both came in at different times, sometimes with Clifford, sometimes alone."

"And while this work was taking place, was anyone else present?"

"Miss Blundell comes and goes as she pleases. But really Holmes, this cannot be of help to you! Surely our murderer has been put off by our constant observations."

"I'm sorry, Watson, but our presence here has not stopped the wheels from turning. Very soon, Watson, very soon, our villain shall make his move."

"And you feel that you are in a position to stop this?"

"Watson, I've never been surer of anything in my life."

*****

Alas, in the morning we were woken to find that tragedy had struck in the sunroom. Glossop reported that Clifford Kingsley had woken much earlier than his usual hour and had gone into the sunroom. As usual, he had closed the door behind him, and Glossop supposed that he was going through the process of pulling levers and pulleys to have his morning coffee and toast produced by the wonders of the room. But then, there was a scream. Glossop dashed to see if his assistance was required but found the room locked.

"If someone's attacked Mr Kingsley," said Glossop. "Then surely he's still in there with him."

Wilhelmina tugged on the door handle and continued to call out Clifford's name. The fact that no encouragement came from the other side didn't stop her constant appeals. But after several minutes of this rigmarole, she stepped back, and screamed.

Looking at the marble floor by the door it was evident what had triggered this scream: the trickle of blood that ran out from the sunroom.

By this time, the rest of the household had been summoned.

"Walter," said Holmes, "are you aware of any locking mechanism that your brother may have installed in the sunroom?"

Walter could only shrug.

James offered a more helpful answer. "I know that Clifford had placed something by the door that worked on a timer. I helped him carry up some of the materials he needed to do so."

With that Holmes held his head to the wall beside the door. He turned his head to us, demanding silence, and then started to nod on each second. Moments later, there was a metallic crunch. Holmes tried the door, and it swung open. In the middle of the sunroom lay the body of Clifford Kingsley; an open wound on the back of his skull suggested that he'd been struck by a heavy object.

Holmes hurried in and to the body, and then turned towards us. "Stay out of here. It's probable that essential clues will be lost if the crime scene is tampered with." He then picked up the wrist of Clifford Kingsley and felt for a pulse. Seeing the mess that was the back of his head, I knew that attempts to detect any sign of life were futile.

"Watson, I need two things from you. I need you to inform everyone in the house that they must meet in the sunroom in precisely one hour's time. Second, I need your help to remove the body so that we can place it under lock and key for further investigation."

Holmes's calm demeanour in the light of the death of his client surprised me. This was a clear case in which he'd

245

failed to complete the very task he'd been hired to do. Our client lay dead before us, and he was seemingly untouched by such a blow. It certainly sat very heavily on my conscience.

"Would you like me to inspect the body?" I asked, thinking that my own professional take on the cause of death may be of some use.

"Watson, I do not need you to tell me that Clifford's cranium has been caved in. Any troglodyte with the wits to wield a club and cause such injuries could report on the cause of death. No, what I would like you to do is to take hold of the legs."

At the time, I felt that this was part of Holmes's method of dealing with the tragedy and his staunch refusal to let me anywhere near the wound was to stop anyone else from seeing the bloody extent of our failure. Together, we moved the body to a nearby guest bedroom, and Holmes stood guard until Glossop brought a key with which he could lock the room–another method Holmes was using to hide our failure.

The time of the gathering was drawing near. He took me by the arm and spoke in a loud whisper. "Watson, no matter what occurs in the sunroom, I want to assure you of one thing. Clifford was not wrong to report that murder was the intention here."

I avoided rubbing Holmes's nose in the obvious fact that murder had indeed been accomplished.

"Our villain is of a genius that matches his victim's. He has become the Grim Reaper and used his room against him–turned one of his gadgets into the scythe that has struck our client down. We shall not rest until we have this case wrapped up, Watson."

From our position, we could see the members of the household gathering in the sunroom. We started down the hall. The three remaining Kingsley children were gathered in the room, all staring out of the window. Miss Blundell faced the centre of the room, her eyes on the bloodstain. Glossop and a number of the other servants waited outside. After our entry, Baron Kingsley wheeled himself inside, his face stern and solemn.

Holmes leant out of the room and spoke to Glossop, and then closed the door. The click of the door catch was followed by the whirl of a number of cogs from within the wall.

"Ladies and gentlemen," said Holmes. "The mechanism which killed Clifford Kingsley has been reset. None of us are leaving the room until the mystery of his death has been solved."

"You can't keep us locked in here," Baron Kingsley said. He pushed on the lever that controlled his movement, but there was only a crunch of gears. While the baron continued to tut, Holmes beckoned me to his side.

"Thankfully," Holmes said, "my faithful companion here was closely observing poor Clifford over recent days, and he will be able to advise of the repeated actions that he carried out each day – the last of which surely led to his death."

I gulped. While I'd spent a great deal of time with Clifford Kingsley and had indeed observed his actions in the sunroom a number of times, I doubted my ability to accurately recount his exact movements. On many occasions we were deep in conversation while he performed his parade through his contraptions – other than the previous morning where he was distant and non-communicative – and I was loath to give Holmes incorrect information. I did, however, know that he started with coffee, for he liked for it to have cooled slightly by the time he'd had the rest of his breakfast prepared.

"Holmes, he would begin by pulling the handle to your left – the one at hip height."

"And what action does this perform, Watson?"

"It readies the cup."

"Now, as each action is performed, I need complete silence. Baron, this one should present you with no problems."

Fuming, the baron looked up at Holmes. "I will not partake in this nonsense! My son's ridiculous contraptions were the death of him; I never supported his ridiculous endeavours, and I'm not about to acquiesce to your request and partake now."

"So be it," Holmes said. He looked the baron in the eye as he pushed the button. A panel in the wall opened and a cup was revealed. A hidden mechanism nudged the cup into its proper place.

While this had been taking place, Holmes had his hands and one ear against the wall. "Next?" Holmes asked.

"The lever to the right, followed by the pull chain."

"Miss Blundell, would you be so good as to perform the next action?"

Wilhelmina Blundell stepped forward, removing her gloves as she approached the wall. While Holmes listened, she pulled the lever.

The baron flinched as a compartment to the side of the cup opened, and coffee granules tumbled out, falling precisely into the cup.

Without pause, Miss Blundell tugged on the pulley which caused hot water to cascade from above the cup.

A hiss emanated from within the walls and Holmes moved away. "Yes," he said, seemingly talking to himself.

"Something behind the scenes has been engaged. It is only a matter of a few more steps before the trap is armed."

His attention returned to the rest of us. "Miss Blundell, I was rather hoping to allow someone else to perform the next action."

"It's quite alright," she replied. "I'd seen Clifford carry out the process countless times."

"As much as I appreciate that, Miss Blundell, if we are to solve this mystery, we must follow the process step-by-step. Watson, what was next?"

"While the coffee cooled, Clifford would prepare his toast on the other side of the room," I said, leaving out that it was nearer to where Clifford had fallen.

"James, would you be so kind as to carry out the next action?"

The second brother, and new heir to the Sutton Scarsdale estate, moved over to Holmes's side. "What do I... what do I need to do?"

His hesitation and indeed his confusion belied his usual sense of calm. He'd assisted Clifford with some recent changes to the functionality of the sunroom and had even put in place some changes of his own. He knew the process almost as well as Clifford himself.

"Watson?" asked Holmes.

The sun had been pouring into the room all morning, and the mirrors kept the light firmly on us. I was beginning to regret my choice of waistcoat with a particularly heavy shirt. It was too much for Holmes to ask me to recall such trivial details. There were three levers, mere inches apart on the wall. I remember thinking that the order was illogical. "The middle lever," I said.

James looked at the lever. Slowly, he moved his hand towards it. I could see the beads of sweat form, gather together and roll down his forehead. He grabbed the lever and looked up at the ceiling, trying to identify the spot from where an attack could come.

"For Heaven's sake, James, get on with it!" cried Walter. Before James could move, Walter was beside him, holding onto his hand as they pushed the lever down together. We could see the orange light switch on through the eye-level grates. Two slices of bread dropped into place to face the heat.

Holmes nodded his head.

"Walter, as you're already standing, would you be so kind as to perform the next action."

I was about to speak, but Walter replied first. "Mr. Holmes, we must wait for it."

As we all stood looking at the panel in the wall from which the toast would drop, silence descended onto the room. If it were possible to turn up the temperature of the sun, or harness those mirrors to concentrate its power, someone had surely done just that, for the room had become almost unbearable. I could hear the ticking of each second from the pocket-watch I bore, and I thought there must be some kind of malfunction. When I'd watched Clifford, it had surely not taken so long. Finally, a whistle came from the unit, signalling the toast had reached its desired colour.

Holmes nodded, and Walter reached for the next lever.

"Stop!" cried Eleanor.

We all turned to look at her. Did she know something we didn't?

"What is it, Nell?" asked James.

"I can't bear it. That machine killed Clifford. I can't have it kill anyone else."

"And I can't bear to have overdone toast," Walter said. He pulled the lever. A plate swung into place, and the toast dropped onto it, perfectly browned.

Eleanor turned away and faced the window. "I won't look," she said. "This is ridiculous, and I refuse to witness any more of it."

"I agree," said Baron Kingsley. He fiddled with his controls, but the wheelchair only backed him away from our circle, and towards the door.

"It seems," Walter said, "that whatever killed Clifford had nothing to do with the functionality of our little sunroom." He took a bite from the toast. He chewed it for a long time, no doubt finding it dry and unpalatable.

"Butter?" asked Holmes.

"Not for me."

"Watson, did Clifford have butter?"

"Why, yes. That's what the third lever does."

"James, could you do the honours?"

We could all see his nervousness as he stepped forward. Instead of pulling the lever straight down, he crouched, and pulled it from one side, looking up as he did so as if he expected a great weight to drop from the ceiling onto him.

The lever had no obvious function, though I knew quite different, and seemingly Holmes did too. He took the plate, and the toast with it, from Walter and returned it to the side. He then unhooked a thin hose from within the unit and held it over the toast. He reached out and turned a handle. A spray of butter perfectly covered what was left of the two rounds.

Holmes looked at us and frowned. He made an obvious show of looking around the room and then sighed, puffing out his cheeks.

251

"I must apologise," he said before sinking into one of the armchairs. "I was certain that this was the method used in the murder, and now, when I should have been allowing you to grieve, I have put you through this ridiculous pantomime." Holmes rubbed his forehead.

"Well I for one shan't abide it any longer," Baron Kingsley said, manually turning his chair and wheeling to the door.

"Dad, no!" called Walter as his father reached for the door handle.

The next thing I heard was a crash as a concrete block splintered the door, and then swung back on its chain that led to a newly-opened panel in the sunroom's ceiling.

Baron Kingsley, albeit covered in splinters of wood and fragments of concrete, was fine. The trajectory of the block that undoubtedly killed Clifford was above the head of the wheelchair-bound baron.

"Now, Glossop," called Holmes as he stood.

The servant peered through the gaping hole in the door. He tried the door to no success.

Holmes's eyes were already on the block and chain before the strains of cog drew the rest of our eyes that way. We watched the concrete block retreat whence it had come, into the hidden compartment in the ceiling.

"Glossop, have our guests arrived?" called Holmes.

"Yes, Sir. They are waiting in the parlour."

"If you could send them through, we should be free to leave momentarily."

"Our guests?" I asked.

"I took the liberty of asking Glossop to send for the local constabulary. We have two here guilty of attempted murder."

"Attempted murder?" I asked, the memory of Clifford's caved in skull flashing into my mind.

"Yes. James Kingsley's prints are all over it, of course."

"What?" cried James, before loudly protesting his innocence through a series of incomprehensible calls.

"He's quite innocent. The plan was to frame him."

"Holmes, can we get back to the 'attempted' murder?"

"In due course, Watson. Now, our true villains gave themselves away with their actions in the last half hour. The second they entered the room the game was up."

The door opened. Glossop, on the other side, flanked by two police officers, looked to Holmes for instruction.

"Gentlemen, if you'd be so kind as to take Walter Kingsley and Miss Bludell…"

"What?" asked Wilhelmina, bringing her hand to her chest in a show of mock indignation.

"Thank you, Walter, for your lack of protest," Watson said as the police put the two suspects in irons.

"I already knew, Walter. You didn't give yourself away when you cried out to warn your father not to try the door handle."

"Wilhelmina is innocent. Please, this had nothing to do with her." As he spoke his affection for her was plain. Looking to Wilhelmina I saw for the first time that the feeling was mutual.

"Alas, her eyes gave her away," Holmes said. "When the baron went to the door, her eyes went to the ceiling. She knew what was coming, and that makes her an accomplice."

*****

253

Holmes had some details to share with the police officers, and James pushed his father into the sitting room, followed by Eleanor, so that they could indulge in a much-needed brandy to ease their nerves.

Once he'd dispatched the officers and their felons, Holmes urged me into the sunroom.

"But Holmes, how did you know?" I asked as soon as we were out of earshot.

"Elementary! By witnessing the actions of the suspects, it quickly became clear. James's nerves and Eleanor's panic meant they didn't know what to expect. Both Walter and Wilhelmina's confidence in the safety of the contraptions suggested knowledge of the operation of the trap."

"I see. But I still don't understand how it can only be attempted murder...?"

"Perhaps I can explain." Clifford Kingsley stepped into the sunroom.

I dashed over to him and couldn't help but peer around to look at the back of his head. As relieved as I was to find it perfectly intact, I was well and truly perplexed. "But... how?" I asked.

"Would you like to warrant a guess?" asked Holmes.

I considered the scene I had earlier witnessed. I had lifted the body out of the sunroom, with Holmes's help. He had kept me away from the head.

"Was it some kind of false head? Perhaps an over-the-head covering using optical illusion to appear to be caved in?" It was the best I could do, but as soon as I said it, I could see the flaws in the plan, as my viewing angle changed, but the injury did not.

"More than a false head," Clifford said.

Holmes led the way to the guest bedroom where I thought we'd lain Clifford. I couldn't help but stare at the back of Clifford's head all the way there.

Inside, the body remained on the bed.

Was this what Holmes had hinted of when he spoke of disguise? "Well if Clifford's fine, which poor soul has passed in his stead?"

Clifford led me to the head end and allowed me to see what Holmes would not. Indeed, the face was that of Clifford Kingsley. What was inside was quite different. Despite the gore inside, it was evident that there was a series of broken vials inside the copper casing.

"It's a life-sized reproduction," I said, amazed.

"One of which you made the acquaintance with yesterday," Holmes said.

"I did?"

"Clifford has been in hiding in excess of twenty-four hours."

"But that's impossible... for much of the day I was his shadow."

"You shadowed my creation," said Clifford. "My double."

"A working automaton!" Knowing it had never truly had life, I peered more eagerly into the cavity to see its workings.

I felt the skin. Certainly, it was authentic. Was it really human skin, harvested from a corpse? I recalled a passage in the text I had been reading, how skin could be lifted from a body through the use of steam. If that were the process, it would give it the elasticity to allow it to mould to the automaton.

"Holmes knew from the start," Clifford said, pulling me from my wonder-invoked stupor.

"Indeed. Your movements across the stage, the way your limbs moved out of their joints to facilitate escape, the inability to regulate the grip of a handshake: all were indications of an automaton–an impressive creation nonetheless."

"So, the magic show? That wasn't you?" I asked.

Clifford smiled. "Alas, a magician never reveals his secrets."

*****

Clifford Kingsley had us back on the zeppelin by late afternoon, confident that the growing gloom would not cause a problem for his airship. He had much to resolve with his father and siblings, and Holmes was not one to tarry once a case had reached its conclusion.

Once Sutton Scarsdale Hall was out of view, I pondered our return to London and what was still to come in this wondrous golden age of invention and discovery. I thought about its masses of people in its homes, factories and streets each day. I turned to Holmes. "Do you think there are more of them out there?" I asked.

"Automatons? Undoubtedly."

"Doesn't that worry you at all?"

"They can only be as wise as those that control them," Holmes said. "And as such they'll always be fallible."

Maybe the quack that had cried out against Her Majesty and been wrong then; it was not an age of brass and filth, but of brass and fallibility. Strangely, it was that thought which gave me comfort for the journey back to London.

About the Contributors

Brian Belanger is a publisher and editor, but is best known for his freelance illustration and cover design work. His distinctive style can be seen on several MX Publishing covers, including *The Art of Sherlock Holmes* edited by Phil Growick, *The Vatican Cameos* by Richard T. Ryan, *Sherlock Holmes and the Nine-Dragon Sigil* by Tim Symonds, *Sherlock Holmes and A Quantity of Debt* by David Marcum, *Welcome to Undershaw* by Luke Benjamen Kuhns, and many more. Brian is the co-founder of Belanger Books LLC, where he illustrates the popular *MacDougall Twins with Sherlock Holmes* young reader series (#1 bestsellers on Amazon.com UK). A prolific creator, he also designs t-shirts, mugs, stickers, and other merchandise on his personal art site at *www.redbubble.com/people/zhahadun*.

Derrick Belanger is an author and educator most noted for his books and lectures on Sherlock Holmes and Sir Arthur Conan Doyle, as well as his writing for the blogs *I Hear of Sherlock Everywhere* and *Belanger Books Sherlock Holmes and Other Readings Blog*. Both volumes of his two-volume anthology, *A Study in Terror: Sir Arthur Conan Doyle's Revolutionary Stories of Fear and the Supernatural* were #1 best sellers on the Amazon.com U.K. Sherlock Holmes book list, and his *MacDougall Twins with Sherlock Holmes* chapter book, *Attack of the Violet Vampire!* was also a #1 bestselling new release in the U.K. Through his press, Belanger Books, he has released a number of Sherlock Holmes anthologies as well as new editions of August Derleth's original Solar Pons series. Mr. Belanger's academic work has been published in *The Colorado Reading Journal* and *Gifted Child Today*. Find him at *www.belangerbooks.com*.

Minerva Cerridwen is a Belgian writer and pharmacist. Her first novella *The Dragon of Ynys* came out in 2018. She met L.S. Reinholt in 2012 thanks to Sherlock Holmes, and they have been writing together ever since. They are currently editing their first science fiction novel. For the list of Minerva's published short stories and poems, check out her website http://minervacerridwen.wordpress.com/.

Harry DeMaio is a nom de plume of Harry B. DeMaio, successful author of several books on Information Security and Business Networks as well as the ten-volume *Casebooks of Octavius Bear*. A retired business executive, consultant, information security specialist, former pilot, disc jockey and graduate school adjunct professor, he whiles away his time traveling and writing preposterous articles and stories. He has appeared on many radio and TV shows and is an accomplished, frequent public speaker. Former New York City natives, he and his extremely patient and helpful wife, Virginia, and their Bichon Frisé, Woof, live in Cincinnati (and several other parallel universes.) They have two sons, living in Scottsdale, Arizona and Cortlandt Manor, New York, both of whom are quite successful and quite normal, thus putting the lie to the theory that insanity is hereditary. His e-mail is hdemaio@zoomtown.com. You can also find him on Facebook. His website is www.octaviusbearslair.com.

Cara Fox is an English author trying to write her way out of the dark. Inspired by authors such as Mary Shelley, Daphne du Maurier, Bram Stoker and Jules Verne, she favours steampunk, horror and Gothic romance, but you can find her anywhere that stories sink their claws into you and wine flows freely. Her work has been published by Tales To Terrify, Empyreome, Lycan Valley Press, and Horror Addicts, amongst others, and she is working on her debut novel, *The Strange Case of Doctor Magorian.*

Thomas Fortenberry is an American author, editor, reviewer, and educator. Founder of Mind Fire Press and a Pushcart Prize-nominated writer, he has judged many literary contests, including the Georgia Author of the Year Awards and the Robert Penn Warren Prize for Fiction. A huge fan of mysteries, his Sherlock Holmes tales have appeared in *An Improbable Truth: The Paranormal Adventures of Sherlock Holmes, The MX Anthology of New Sherlock Holmes Stories, Vol. VII: Eliminate the Impossible, The MX Anthology of New Sherlock Holmes Stories, Vol. XII: Some Untold Cases, Sherlock Holmes: Adventures Beyond the Canon, Vol. II, and The MX Anthology of New Sherlock Holmes Stories: 2019 Annual.*

John Linwood Grant is a professional writer/editor from Yorkshire, UK, who lives with a pack of lurchers and a beard. Widely published in anthologies and magazines, he writes both contemporary weird fiction and dark period stories, including his 'Tales of the Last Edwardian' series and stories of Sherlock Holmes. His latest novel is *The Assassin's Coin*, from IFD, featuring Mr Edwin Dry, the inexorable Deptford Assassin. He is editor of *Occult Detective Quarterly*, plus anthologies such as *ODQ Presents* and *Hell's Empire*. He can be found on his popular website greydogtales.com, which explores weird fiction and weird art. And lurchers.

Paula Hammond is based in London, but forever dreaming of a castle with its own writing turret in the wilds Wales. To-date she has written over 50 fiction and non-fiction books. Recent published fiction includes Last Words in the best-selling Alternative Truths series and Ghosts and Glory (After the Orange Anthology). When not frantically scribbling, she can be found indulging her passions for film, theatre, sci-fi, and real ale.

Stephen Herczeg is an IT Geek, writer, actor and film maker based in Canberra Australia. He has been writing for over twenty years and has completed a couple of dodgy novels, sixteen feature length screenplays and numerous short stories and scripts. Stephen's scripts, *TITAN, Dark are the Wo*ods, *Control and Death Spores* have found success in the International Horror Hotel, Horror Screenplay and Search for New Blood screenwriting competitions with a win, a couple of runner-up and top ten finishes and a quarter finalist appearance. He has had Sherlock Holmes stories published in *Sherlock Holmes: Adventures in the Realms of H.G. Wells, Sherlock Holmes: Adventures Beyond the Canon* from Belanger Books, and *The MX Book of New Sherlock Holmes stories: Part XI* from MX Publishing. Later this year, Stephen's work will appear in *Beside the Seaside* from OzHorror.Con and *Curses and Cauldrons* by Bloodsongs press.

Paul Hiscock is an author of crime, fantasy and science fiction tales. His short stories have appeared in several anthologies and include a seventeenth century whodunnit and a science fiction western. Paul lives with his family in Kent (England) and spends his days engaged in the far more challenging task of taking care of his two children. He mainly does his writing in coffee shops with members of the local NaNoWriMo group or in the middle of the night when his family has gone to sleep. Consequently, his stories tend to be fuelled by large amounts of black coffee. You can find out more about his writing at www.detectivesanddragons.uk.

Benjamin Langley's previous Sherlock Holmes tales have featured in *Sherlock Holmes: Adventures in the Realms of H.G. Wells* and *Sherlock Holmes: Adventures Beyond the Canon*. His debut novel, *Dead Branches*, a coming of age horror set in the Cambridgeshire Fens, is to be released in the summer of 2019. Benjamin lives, writes and teaches in Cambridgeshire, UK.

Derek Nason lives and writes in New Brunswick, Canada. His short stories can be found in 2017's *Best TransHuman SciFi Anthology* (Gehenna & Hinnom), *Sherlock Holmes: Adventures in the Realms of H.G. Wells Vol. 2* (Belanger Books), and The Nashwaak Review.

Robert Perret is a writer and librarian living on the Palouse in northern Idaho. He has published many Sherlock Holmes stories including tales in the collections *Sherlock Holmes: Before Baker Street* and *Sherlock Holmes: Adventures Beyond the Canon*. He is a member of the John H. Watson Society and Doyle's Rotary Coffin.

L.S. Reinholt lives in Denmark where she teaches languages, math and science at a local school and spends most of her free time writing. Her first published story was "The Durga", a science fiction short story in *Women of the Wild - an anthology*, 2017. She met Minerva Cerridwen in 2012 thanks to Sherlock Holmes, and they have been writing together ever since. They are currently editing their first science fiction novel.

GC Rosenquist was born in Chicago and now resides in Round Lake, IL. He has studied writing and poetry at the College of Lake County in Grayslake, IL and has twelve books previously published, including a collection of Sherlock Holmes stories titled "The Pearl of Death and Other Stories" published by MX Publishing. He has also had a Sherlock Holmes short story published in Sherlock Holmes Mystery Magazine. He has been included in the following Sherlock Holmes anthologies: The MX Book of New Sherlock Holmes Stories Vol 3, 6 and 13; Sherlock Holmes Adventures in the Realms of HG Wells. His love for the mysteries of Sherlock Holmes began as a child when he saw Basil Rathbone in *The Hound of the Baskervilles* and continues to this day with the wonderful modern reinterpretation of Holmes by the amazing Benedict Cumberbatch. Oh, yes, GC Rosenquist is also a huge fan of Sir Arthur Conan Doyle. For more information, go to gcrosenquist.com.

S. Subramanian is a retired professor of Economics who lives and works in the Southern Indian city of Chennai (formerly Madras). His stories have appeared (or are forthcoming) in various publications such as The MX Book of New Sherlock Holmes anthologies; three Belanger Books anthologies; Sherlock Holmes Mystery Magazine; Mystery Weekly Magazine; Mystery Readers Journal; Weirdbook; and Airship 27: Sherlock Holmes, Consulting Detective. He continues to do research in economics, watches cricket on television, and is otherwise generally harmless.

Special Thank You Section

Belanger Books thanks the following people for backing our Kickstarter campaign. Without your generous support, we could not have released this two-volume collection of stories.

- ABF
- Abi Hiscock
- Alessandro Caffari
- Andy Evans
- Anita Thastrom
- Anonymous
- Anthony R. Cardno
- Arran Dickson
- Ava
- B+P-Snegg
- Bradley Walker
- Brian D Lambert
- Brian Koonce
- C. Hardt
- C. W. Piper
- Carol M. Taylor
- Chad Bowden
- CHARLES WARREN
- Chris Basler
- Chris Chastain
- Chris W
- Christopher J MacDonald
- Chuck Cooley
- Conor H. Carton
- Danny Soares
- Dave Dell
- David Rains
- David Tai
- David Wade
- Dean Arashiro
- Deb Werth
- Derek's proud sister
- Douglas I D McLean
- Douglas Vaughan
- Dr. Noreen Pazderski
- Dr. Wolfgang Ditz, Idar-Oberstein, Germany
- DrLight
- Ed Kowalczewski
- Edward Winston Bear
- Erik T Johnson
- Erin Karper
- Fie
- Frank M. Greco
- Gary Phillips
- Genevieve Cogman
- GMarkC
- Granvil the 4th
- H. Baxter
- Harry DeMaio
- Hart D.
- Ida Umphers
- J. Fryer
- Jack Gulick
- Jamas Enright
- James J. Marshall
- Jeff Conner
- Jeff Freer
- Jennifer Osterman
- Jennifer Priester
- Jeremy Frost
- JH
- Jim Jorritsma
- Jim Kosmicki

- Joe Machin
- John Barclay
- John Driscoll
- Josh Patterson
- Kelly Zelnio
- Kevin B. O'Brien
- Krisztina Gaál
- Lark Cunningham
- Lola Gift
- Lora Friedenthal
- Lord Lakenheath
- Louise McCulloch
- Lynn M.
- Margaret Keaveny
- Mark Carter
- Mary M Smith
- Matthew Beckham
- Melissa Aho
- Michael Brosco
- Michael Feir
- Michael J. Schuler
- Michael R. Brown
- Miha Pezelj
- Mike Bundt
- Mrs.Wasden
- N/A
- Nathan Wheat
- Natsutan
- No
- Orren Webber
- Paul Leach
- Per Stalby
- Pete & Christina Bellisle
- Robert L Vaughn
- Robert, Jennifer, Mira and Buddy Perret
- Ron Bachman
- Scarlett Letter
- Scott Maynard
- Scott Uhls
- Scott Vander Molen
- Sean Sherman
- Sharon Nason
- Shaun Osborne
- sherlockholmesbooks.com
- SirLarryMouse
- Stephen Hiscock
- Steven M. Smith
- Thaddeus Tuffentsamer
- Thomas & Emily Hiscock
- Timothy Fisher
- To the Memory of Alan Fulton Barksdale
- Val Hiscock
- Wanda Aasen
- Wiley
- Yes
- Zachary Hicks
- Zean
- Zion Phan

Belanger Books

Printed in Great Britain
by Amazon

51913812R00154